Page 923

w.e.d. wilson

Page 923

ISBN: 978-0-9908060-4-2

TRUTH

Truth is the most valuable
thing in the world. It is so
valuable, that often it is
surrounded by a bodyguard of lies.
Winston Churchill

The man lay in the prone position peering through his riflescope at the couple standing in the living room of their 1950's Midcentury Modern home. Two hundred yards from his mark, he lay just inside the tree line well out of view of the neighboring homes in the secluded Broad View district of Seattle.

Clad in all black tactical clothing, he was almost invisible among the trees and bushes surrounding him. His left hand held firmly to the leg of the bipod attached to the rifle, with his right hand resting against the pistol grip. Devoid of the standard muzzle brake, the rifle was fitted with a suppressor to reduce the noise from the discharge. The scope was attached to a lightweight bolt-action sniper rifle, chambered for the flat shooting and lethal 6.5 Creedmoor round.

Finding his target in the scope, he picked up the range finder, calculating the distance to be 185 yards. He reached up to the scope, carefully amending the elevation, then adjusted the focus and zoomed in on the chest of Danny MacDougal, standing next to his wife, Billie.

Without moving his eye from the scope, he lifted the bolt handle, pulled it to the rear, then moved it forward, chambering one of the rounds. He placed his right hand on the pistol grip, resting his thumb on the safety, and breathed slowly, deeply, readying himself to take the shot.

As he increased pressure to release the safety, completely focused on his target, he didn't hear the figure who had stepped up behind him. The dagger thrust deep into his head from behind, right of the vertebrae at the base of the skull. The man's eyes registered only the briefest moment of surprise before glazing over as his lifeless body slumped forward onto his rifle.

Wearing black clothing with a tactical mask, the figure dragged the blade of the knife across the back of the dead man, wiping the blood from it. Placing the knife in the sheath on his belt, he picked up the Range Finder, placing it in his pocket. He lifted the rifle off the ground, leaning it against the tree. Rolling the body over on his back, he grabbed the arms, lifting the deceased man up in a sitting position. He bent down and lifted the body off the ground, placing it on his shoulder. Picking the rifle up with his left hand, the masked man walked through the thick trees to his vehicle. Opening the back of the van, he rolled the body into the cargo section.

He stepped to the driver's side, opening the door. Sitting down in the seat, he started the vehicle, then pulled away. After driving two blocks, he pulled the cloth mask from his head.

The square jawed man was extremely fit, his face covered with a short scruffy beard. His hair was closely cut, and salt and pepper. The man's large calloused hands displayed the scars of a person who was familiar with conflict. His dark emotionless eyes showed a no-nonsense demeanor, transmitting to anyone looking at him to move away quickly.

Retrieving his cell phone, he punched in the numbers and waited for a response.

"Yes?" the male voice on the other end responded.

"It's done," the man stated.

"Any difficulties?" the voice asked.

"Negative."

"Keep me apprised," the voice replied.

"Yes, sir," he responded, before hanging up.

Lt. Danny MacDougal sat in the renovated office of its former occupant, Phillip Wade. He was in full uniform, with lieutenant's bars on his lapels. He was reviewing cases that Phillip Wade had passed over, or closed that could have possibly been related to the Ballencourt file.

Danny was taking on the task of reviewing old cases, rather than tying his detectives down with extra work. The department was already falling behind due to the loss of four detective positions.

Focused on the files, he heard a knock on his door jamb. He looked up to see Capt. Graves standing in the doorway.

"Do you have a few minutes, Danny?" Graves asked.

"Of course, sir; please come in."

Graves entered the room, closing the door behind him. He sat at one of the two chairs in front of Danny's desk. "Well, it looks like you're buried in work," Graves said, as he looked at the large stack of old cases on Danny's desk.

Danny sat back in the chair rubbing his eyes. "I was just going over the cases that Lt. Wade closed that may have been influenced by his association with Ballencourt."

"Good idea, Danny. We may be cleaning up from that mess for years. Just because Ballencourt's dead doesn't mean we can sit back and relax."

"I agree, Captain."

"You folding into your new position okay?"

Danny sat up in his chair. "Trying to find my groove, Captain. The administrative part of the job is a lot more demanding than I thought it would be. But I'm doing okay."

"Good. I feel better with you at the helm, especially with the workload we have."

"I'll do my best, sir," Danny replied.

Capt. Graves placed his forearms on his knees, lacing his fingers together. "Danny, I've been thinking about the information in the master file. We need to get everyone together to discuss a new direction. Drug and human trafficking are all at record lows up and down the West Coast. You and your team hurt them badly. That lull in trafficking won't last, however; they'll change their tactics and methods.

"I have a few people who could help us. They're old friends who've been in the loop for decades. I don't want to contact them unless everyone is in agreement. I think we need to put together a strategy to move up the ladder. I need your thoughts on growing the team," Graves posited.

"I agree. We've limited our capabilities by keeping the group so small. I don't think we should get too big, however. Keep it at around a dozen."

Graves was nodding his agreement as he responded, "A dozen sounds good at this point. That said, we do need to go after the top echelon. We'll never get ahead of this unless we take out the top players."

"Captain, we discussed 'cutting the head off the snake' before everything went south. After the events surrounding the assaults here and also on Orcas Island, we dropped it. It might be time to revisit that now. What are you thinking?" Danny asked.

"I think we get together for a weekend where we can formulate a plan. A place that's away from the prying eyes of this city," Graves stated.

Danny had a half smile on his face as he responded, "Got just the place. I do think however, that everyone on the team needs to be comfortable with the new prospects. If they're not on board with any of the candidates, we dismiss them. Do you want to vet your acquaintances before the meeting so they can attend?"

"Of course." Graves reached across the desk, pulling Danny's notebook toward him. He wrote down five names on a blank page, along with the agencies/companies they worked for. Sliding the notebook back across the desk, he looked at Danny. "Have everyone dig through their backgrounds. I mean a *deep* dig. I've known them for over thirty years, but that doesn't mean I have full confidence with them for what *we're* doing. I agree with you. If the team's not comfortable with them, they're eliminated from the list," Graves stated.

Danny's eyebrows rose as he looked at the five names, along with their positions. "Talk about juice. These people are pretty impressive, Captain. You must have run in pretty powerful circles over the years," Danny replied.

"I'd have been a part of that circle had I not wanted to come back home to Seattle. We just wanted to move back home to have a normal life," Graves said.

"Normal! How's that working out for you after what we've discovered?"

Graves chuckled before responding. "Out of the frying pan, into the fire. No regrets, you play the hand you're dealt."

"We'll dig into them, Captain," Danny replied.

Graves stood from his seat. "Say hi to Billie for me, Danny."

"I will. Thanks again, Captain."

Graves waved his hand at Danny before leaving the room.

Hidden away from prying eyes, the 12,000 square foot Bar Ten Ranch house sat on over 45,000 acres of prime Texas real estate. Just over a hundred miles southeast of Dallas, the Bar Ten was both secluded and quiet.

Not visible from any public road or highway, the 2003 construction was completed with security in mind. Anyone attempting to get close to the house could be detected from miles away. It was unique from other high security properties around the country in that the primary mode of transportation for the security staff was horses.

The ranch house stood fifty yards from the property's massive barn. Painted in a traditional brick red, the classic looking barn housed all of the riding stock, along with the ranch's two-dozen quad ATV's. The interior of the barn was kept immaculately clean, at the insistence of the property's owner, Gordon Johnson, Governor of Region 6.

Standing in front of the wall of windows in his office/conference room, Johnson was wearing his usual denim jeans, cowboy boots, with a custom-tailored dress shirt. He sipped a glass of Scotch while he waited for the arrival of his guests.

Johnson's family had made their billions in oil, then ultimately transitioned his fortune into the tech industry. He owned one of the largest software companies in the country.

At six foot two inches tall, he was an imposing figure. His salt and pepper hair outlined a tan, rugged face, with a no-nonsense glare. He was both feared and respected by his employees.

As Johnson looked out the window, his Bell 525 Relentless corporate helicopter was making its final approach to the helipad. He watched as the black and gold machine gracefully touched down on the pad.

The six security personnel watched the helicopter from the backs of their horses as the engines shut down. The door on the right side of the Bell opened, allowing the three people to step down the stairs.

The three guests walked from the helipad to the house along a brick path between the corrals. As they reached the house, the Johnson butler opened the double front door to greet them. Johnson waited patiently for the three visitors to be led into his office.

The sprawling ranch house was constructed of dark stained wood, with a large river rock base. The massive peaked roof over the entrance was supported by stone pillars, with a slate entrance walkway. The ranch house was everything you'd expect of a Texas billionaire.

The butler opened the door, stepping into the office. "Mr. Johnson, your guests are here."

"Thank you, Gerald. Please show them in. Make sure their luggage is placed in the bungalows," Johnson replied.

"Yes, sir," Gerald responded.

Senator Harold Gibbs, Governor of Region 2, entered the room, followed by Greta Kline, Governor of Region 9, with Rodney Waterston, Governor of Region 10 behind them. The three people approached Johnson, smiling.

"Did you all have a pleasant flight down?" Johnson asked.

The sixty-year-old white-haired Senator Gibbs smiled at his friend. "Yes, very nice, as always."

Johnson pressed the intercom button on his desk. "Gerald, could we get Scotch for three?"

"Yes, sir."

Johnson motioned for them to have a seat in the conversation area. The room had ten large, red wingback leather chairs, with small side tables next to each chair. Johnson preferred a conversation pit setting rather than the traditional conference table.

Gerald came into the room with a drink tray holding three glasses containing 25-year-old MacCallan Scotch, placing them on the tables next to the guests. He turned toward Johnson. "Will there be anything else, sir?"

"No, that will be all, Gerald. Lock the door as you leave," Johnson replied.

"Very good, sir," Gerald responded as he left the room.

Johnson waited to hear the lock being engaged before he spoke. "Senator Gibbs asked that we all meet here prior to our quarterly meeting to discuss recent events. I'll now turn the meeting over to him. Senator, the floor is yours," Johnson said as he motioned to Gibbs.

"Thanks for coming on such short notice. After speaking with Greta and Rodney, it's obvious we need to do something about our situation on the West Coast. We all have a problem that needs to be addressed," Gibbs stated.

At fifty-eight years old, the thin, statuesque Greta Kline was dressed in her usual business attire, slacks with a suit coat. Her short blonde hair framed an attractive face that gave off the impression she could have been a runway model earlier in life.

With her legs crossed, Kline leaned forward, holding her scotch in both hands. "We're down sixty-five percent from last year, Senator. While the blame for this debacle can be squarely placed at the feet of Governor Waterston's predecessor, I think it prudent we put aside past problems to develop a plan to counter the damage that's been done."

"Which is precisely why I called us together today. Our West Coast operations have been severely damaged, there's no getting around that. Until we can develop a different plan, we need to change our delivery methods, along with a new distribution process.

"I'm being told new legislation is about to be proposed in Congress that will allow us to circumvent existing laws that have held us back regarding our product. That said, we can't wait for one to two years until it's implemented.

"Until then we need a different shipping and distribution point." Gibbs pointed toward Johnson. "Governor Johnson has experienced virtually no interruption of product; we own Texas. I propose we shift our West Coast operations to Galveston. We need to put together a plan that would allow us to change our ports of call to down here," Gibbs stated.

"We haven't been affected that much here in Texas. We could reroute the shipments here, but then we'd be moving product back across the country to deliver it back to you," Johnson said, while pointing to Kline and Waterston.

"If it were just the federal agencies, we could control it, but whoever is doing this is using local law enforcement and news outlets that don't answer to us," Waterston stated.

"Have we been able to identify the people responsible for the interruptions?" Kline asked.

"We have. The plans and files were clandestinely put in the hands of some Seattle Police Department detectives. We lost a lot of upper-level personnel in the Pacific Northwest as a result of that debacle.

"Governor Waterston was brought in to rebuild the infrastructure, a job for which he is uniquely qualified. Even so, it'll still take approximately two years to resume operations," Gibbs advised.

"Why don't we just eliminate the responsible parties?" Kline asked.

"I wish it were that simple. In just a matter of a few months, they've put together a network that has, so far, been undetectable. We haven't established how far the resistance has expanded." Gibbs took another sip of his Scotch. "Oh, we'll find them all eventually, don't worry about that. They've obviously grown their numbers, sharing the file with others they can trust. I have, however, put in place a plan to deal with certain key members of the resistance."

"In the meantime, we're losing a tremendous amount of money, Senator," Waterston stated.

Gibbs leaned forward, irritated. "Look, you're all missing the point here. Profit is not the prime directive. Yes, the money is important, but not the most important. We're here to implement the overall plan, in case you've all forgotten. We answer to the Secretary General, Brussels, and Strasbourg. Our job is to ensure the plans and directives are implemented, not make a buck.

"We've got to put together a plan to ensure the overall directive isn't interrupted. The drugs, weapons, and intellectual property can stall for a while; it's the human trafficking that can't. That's nonnegotiable. Right now, the only place we can bring the human cargo in is here in Texas and the East Coast. We can get some of them through the southern border, but even that's drying up as of late," Gibbs stated.

"Again, Senator, how long do you think it will take to build a new operation on the West Coast?" Greta asked.

"My assessment is two years minimum, Greta. But again, it's the directive we need to keep intact. We've got people in place at the highest levels, and there are still operatives in the system we can use. For now, let's look at keeping product here in Texas. We need to address trafficking."

"What if we could do both?" Johnson stated.

"How so?" Gibbs asked.

"We have a ten-thousand-foot runway just a ways down the road. We go 'old school'. The field is still in great shape, even though the place has been inactive for ten years. We lay out a flight plan for off-hours flights in and out of remote fields. There's old abandoned civilian and military airfields all over California. We could fly the human product from here to, say, the old George Air Force Base, for instance, then truck them into the city. No one is going to question flights within the country. We can generate cargo manifests, even create an entire shell business around it," Johnson stated.

"Where are we going to get the planes?" Kline asked.

"I can lay my hands on eight C-130 Hercules aircraft right now. They're the L-100, the civilian version of the military's C-130. There's a transport company in Dallas that's fallen on hard times. We get our pilots for the flights, then lease the aircraft from them. They'll jump at the chance to stay solvent," Johnson stated.

Gibbs was in deep thought as he stroked his eyebrows with his right hand. "What kind of a business are you thinking about creating as a cover?"

"Beef. It's a perfect cover for selling from Texas. We have old freezer containers sitting in Dallas we can paint up and stamp a company logo on the side. The air cargo company doesn't even need to know about it. We drop the containers off at the prescribed time, they transport everything in one neat package," Johnson mused.

"It just might work temporarily until we can get back up and running. We already have the infrastructure set up in Galveston; we just change the delivery point from Dallas to here. It won't be a permanent solution, but it could work for the short term until we're back on line," Gibbs stated.

Waterston leaned forward in his chair. "You know, this just might work for us. There's a lot of old secluded runways around the outskirts of Seattle. Or maybe even Yakima. We already have the transport companies in place.

None of this is in any file we have, so the opposition wouldn't know about it. We even have our own pilots. This could work."

Greta Kline smiled as she responded. "The whole state of California is littered with secluded and abandoned runways. It's not ideal, but it *can* be a temporary fix to our problem. Like Rodney said, the opposition doesn't possess this information."

"It could work. Let's discuss it further and put a plan together first thing in the morning so we can present it to all the governors at the quarterly meeting. Put your thinking caps on so we can discuss it further tomorrow morning. In the meantime, Gordon, can we get something for dinner? I haven't eaten since breakfast," Gibbs asked.

"Dinner will be in an hour. The chef has prepared a barbeque for us that's guaranteed to satisfy. Your luggage is in your bungalows in case you want to freshen up first."

The four governors downed the remaining scotch in their glasses as they moved to the door of the office. Smiling, they patted each other on the backs as their moods switched from business to leisure.

2

Danny was locking his office to leave when he heard the text message alert sound on his cell phone. He placed the keys in his pocket, then pulled the phone from his coat.

He looked to see it was from one of his detectives, Larry Colton. *Lieutenant, meet me in the Broad View District at the park just off 116th Street by the Environmental Learning Center. Important!*

Danny's brow furrowed as he realized the area he was being summoned to was by his house. He put on his hat and coat, hurrying to his car.

Danny parked the dark brown Ford Crown Victoria on 116th Street next to the park. Fall was in full bloom in Seattle as light rain came down from the gray sky above. Danny always welcomed the rainy season, as it brought a fresh and clean aroma to the city.

Looking to the edge of the tree line in the park, he saw Detective Larry Colton waving his arms. Danny acknowledged him by raising his right hand as he walked toward the detective. As he approached, Danny noted the former Marine was devoid of his usual cordial demeanor.

Sensing the seriousness of Colton's summons, Danny got right to the point. "What's up, Larry?"

"Lieutenant, we got a call from a woman walking her dog through the park this morning. The dog alerted, pulling her over to a spot in the trees." Larry motioned for Danny to follow him. As they got just inside the tree line, Colton pointed to the ground.

Danny looked down to see a large area covered in blood that had partially soaked into the ground but was clearly identifiable. "Has the area been processed?"

"Yes, sir. It's not blood from an animal. It's human. The lab's already finished with it. The blood came back as type O positive. Ron said there's brain matter throughout. There's no splatters around anywhere, so we can assume the victim was stabbed."

"How many people have been on the scene?" Danny asked.

"We eliminated the woman's shoe prints. There's only two other prints here," Colton replied.

"Not much to go on, Larry," Danny stated.

"Lieutenant, sorry to be hypersensitive, but this is too coincidental. There hasn't been a homicide in this neighborhood in over twenty years. It just doesn't smell right. I can't help but notice how direct the line of sight is to your house," Colton mused.

Danny had also noticed it, but was trying to combat the knot slowly forming in the pit of his stomach. He thought of Billie being alone in the house and forced a smile as he looked at the detective. Danny put his hand on Colton's shoulder, trying to sound casual. "I understand, Larry, but let's not jump to conclusions. This could be anything from a drug deal gone bad to a gang-related killing. The thing that makes me suspect this is professional is we can assume the killer carried off his victim."

"If this was drugs or gangs, they would have left the body to send a message," Colton stated.

"Agreed." Danny rubbed his chin before responding. "Let's keep this close to the vest until we have more information. Keep me posted on this one," Danny directed.

He placed his right hand on Colton's shoulder. "Have a look around the neighborhood, Larry. Let's see if we can find his transportation and ask if anyone saw anything. We might get lucky." Danny patted Larry on the back. "Good job, Larry. Get a report on my desk as soon as you get everything together, will you?"

"Can do, Lieutenant."

"I'll get patrol to keep an eye on the neighborhood and the surrounding area," Danny said as he turned to leave.

"Are you going to tell Billie about this, Lieutenant?"

Danny turned his head to the side as he was walking away. "You're kidding, right? If I don't tell her, I'd be praying I was the victim."

Danny entered the house from the back door into the mudroom. He took off his uniform hat, placing it on the wall hook, along with his slicker. "Hey, baby, I'm home," he said loudly as he turned to enter the kitchen.

"I'm right here," Billie said as she stood at the stove.

Danny scratched Buster on the head as he passed the top of the refrigerator where the cat was lying. He came up behind Billie, reaching his arms around her waist. He kissed her on the cheek as he hugged her tightly from behind. "My wife is making dinner. This is cool."

"Hey, don't get excited. It's just spaghetti, the only dish I can cook."

Danny took the wooden spoon from her hand, placing it on the counter. He turned her around while holding her in his arms. As she faced him, she placed her arms around his neck. "A man in uniform. MacDougal, you sure know how to pique my interest," she said before kissing him on the lips.

Danny looked his wife in the eyes. "Has anyone told you yet today how much you're loved?"

"Nope. Feeling pretty neglected in fact."

"Well, I do, more than you could ever know. I love you, Mrs. MacDougal."

Billie kissed Danny hard on the lips as she hugged him tightly. "Get out of that uniform and into some sweats. I need you wearing something I can rip off quickly after dinner."

Danny snapped to attention, saluting Billie. "Yes, ma'am. The lieutenant is available to comply with your orders, post haste," he said as he turned around, walking to the bedroom.

Taking off his uniform, Danny raised his voice as he spoke to Billie back in the kitchen. "The captain wants to bring some of his old government and military buddies into the circle."

Billie responded, "Do you think that's wise, Danny? I have to admit, it makes me a little nervous to bring in unknown individuals, especially this late in the game."

"I told him I'd run it past all of the team—that we'd only consider it after they had been vetted completely. He agreed."

"Who are they?" Billie asked.

"Every one of them packs a lot of juice. There are generals, admirals, deputy directors from CIA, the National Reconnaissance Office, and the COO of Apex Industries."

"Danny, that list of people could just as easily be some of the people we're up against," Billie mused.

Danny's voice lowered as he came into the kitchen. "I know. Graves said he trusts each of them implicitly. He's had a history with every one of them for over thirty years. He insists that all of us dig deep into their backgrounds, just to be sure," Danny replied as he pulled a bottle of water from the fridge.

As Danny turned one of the kitchen chairs around to face Billie, he sat down, opening the water. He took a long drink from the bottle as he looked at Billie. "So, what do you think?"

Billie set the wooden spoon on the counter, then turned the stove burner off. She stepped over to Danny, closing his legs with her hands. She straddled him, sitting in his lap facing him. "What I think, Lieutenant, is that we wait for dinner until we both go in and mess up the bed," she said, kissing him.

Danny set the bottle of water on the kitchen table. He turned back toward Billie, placing his open hand on her cheek. "We need to talk about something before that," he said with concern.

"Oh, what's wrong?" Billie responded with a frown.

"Nothing, hopefully," he said as he stood, holding Billie's hand. He led her into the living room, stopping in front of the window. "About a half hour ago, I met Colton at the edge of the park, right over there," he said while pointing to the far edge of the green zone.

"There was a possible homicide last night back in the trees. One of the residents' dog alerted on a spot back in the trees as she was walking him. The woman called the police after seeing a large pool of blood on the ground. Larry responded, calling me to meet him there."

"What happened?" Billie questioned.

"We don't know yet. No body, just a pool of blood. The lab checked it, and there was brain matter in the blood, with no blood splatters showing. Larry thinks someone shoved a knife into someone else's head. It's conjecture, but it makes sense at this point," Danny said.

Billie's eyes narrowed as she rushed to the side of the window, quickly closing the drapes. "Do you think this is related to the file? Are they still after us, Danny? I mean, this is just too coincidental. This is a safe neighborhood, Danny, that's why we chose it," Billie said nervously.

Danny led her back into the kitchen. "Sweetie, I'm sorry to bring this up, but we promised we would keep nothing from each other, always being honest." He held both her hands as he talked to her. "Look, there's not enough information yet to raise the alarm. This could have been drugs, gang-related. Let's not get wrapped around the axle over something that may not be related to us or the file."

"I checked this neighborhood out before we moved here. The last homicide that happened here was twenty-three years ago, and that was a wife who shot her abusive husband. Now, we move here, and a random killing just *happens* to occur three months after we get here. Danny, I'm a detective. I get paid to be suspicious," Billie responded.

"Honey, nothing is going to happen to you. I—"

Billie slapped Danny on the shoulder, interrupting him. "Stop it, Danny! I'm not worried about me; it's you I'm worried about!" Billie sat in the chair, looking at the floor. Her voice was softer as tears fell down her face. "I'm not stupid, Danny. When I got shot, it was because Buster knocked you to the side. The bullet hit me, but you were the target." She looked back up at Danny. "I can't lose you, Danny. For the first time in my life I'm happy. I'm finally and completely in love. I can't lose you."

Danny got down on his knees in front of Billie, holding her hands. "Sweetie, nothing is going to happen to me, or you; it can't.

Billie looked at Danny with a smirk. "And exactly how do you plan on stopping that from happening? What crystal ball do you possess that tells you nothing is going to happen? You don't know that."

"I know that nothing is going to happen to me because we just started on this fifty-year journey together. Nothing is going to stop that," Danny stated emphatically.

Billie wrinkled her lips before responding, "Only Scottish wisdom could come up with such mindless drivel as that."

"And only German wisdom would dare to question a Scotsman," Danny said as he squeezed her hand with a smile.

"Danny, stop clowning around This is serious."

"Billie, I didn't just fall off the turnip truck. I know who the target was. I've had a boat load of guilt over what happened. It tears me apart every day, and I do mean every day! I *never* want to go through seeing you in a hospital bed again, not knowing if you're going to pull through or not. I can't do that again.

"Before you, I didn't care if I died. For me, at *that* time of my life, it would have been merciful had I died. All that changed the day I fell in love with you. I want to spend the next forty or fifty years holding you, loving you. I won't ever do anything to interrupt or damage what we have."

Tears fell down Billie's cheeks as she looked at Danny.

"Billie, we made the decision *together* to keep fighting and remain with the PD. We could have pulled our retirement funds, started a restaurant, or opened up a gym. There's any number of things we could have done to make a living. We chose to continue to fight the evil that has fallen on this country.

"The thought of losing you terrifies me, but I can't think of myself. This is way bigger than the two of us. I can only promise that I'll do everything in my power to keep you safe."

Danny pointed toward the front of the house. "I told Larry to start regular patrols around the neighborhood. Nothing is going to happen to you, I promise."

Billie kissed Danny as she held onto him tightly. "How'd you get so tough, Lieutenant?"

"I married a tough woman," he responded with a smile.

After looking in Danny's eyes for a long time, Billie responded, "Okay, for now I trust that you and God will take care of it."

"And we will," Danny said.

"Besides, you're probably right. He can't take you yet. You haven't finished reading me my favorite book."

Danny's head snapped back as his eyes opened wide. "You heard me reading to you?"

"Oh, Danny, you ninny, I heard everything you said to me while I was unconscious. My body just wouldn't let me respond."

"Everything?" he said with shock.

"Yup. I even felt you stroke my hair, kiss me, and put the ring on my finger."

"Okay then, what did I say to you when I put the ring on your finger?" he said with a snicker.

Billie moved her face close to Danny. "You said 'I'll love you forever, Billie. I want to kiss and hug you for the rest of my life and see that you're happy every day we're together. I love you, Billie Hardesty, please come back to me' right?" Billie said with a grin.

Danny's mouth and eyes were wide open. "Well, I'll be dipped."

"So, I guess you meant it, 'cause I've been happy every day we've been together?" Billie stated.

"I meant every word of it," he said before kissing her.

"Okay, wait here," she said as she left the kitchen.

Danny smiled as he looked at the ring finger on his left hand. "I'm the luckiest guy on the planet, Billie." As he smiled, he heard Billie's voice at the edge of the kitchen.

"Hey, Lieutenant, I need some help here," Billie announced.

Danny turned to see Billie dressed in the black evening gown she had worn to the gala at Ballencourt Towers. Her hair was draped around her face, while she wore the high-heeled strappy dress sandals. He slowly stood with a huge smile. "And just how can I help you, miss?"

"I'm having a hard time figuring out how to get this dress off," she said with a coy smile.

"Then you came to the right guy, ma'am. More than happy to help a damsel in distress."

Danny scooped Billie up in his arms, kissing her passionately. "You'll never know how much I love you, baby," he said while carrying her off to the bedroom.

She smiled back at Danny. "Yes, I do, Danny. I knew a long time ago," she said while kissing him.

3

As the four governors sat at the twelve-foot dining table of the Johnson ranch house, they waited for the morning meal to be served as Senator Gibbs prepared to speak. The kitchen staff was delivering breakfast as Gerald, the Johnsons' butler, poured coffee into the governors' cups. The four people remained silent as the food was delivered, waiting for the staff to leave.

Once the food had been placed, Gerald stepped next to Johnson. "Mr. Johnson, we'll leave the room now. If you need anything else, please ring for me."

"I will. Thank you, Gerald." Johnson waited for the staff to move into the kitchen. Once the doors were closed, he turned to the four people. "Enjoy," he said while motioning to the food on the table.

Taking a bite, Gibbs wiped his mouth with the napkin before speaking. "Gordon, did you come up with anything further last night?"

"I did. If all governors approve, I believe we can be back up and running on the West Coast within the next month, maybe sooner. I made a few calls last night regarding the eight aircraft in Dallas. Initial conversations indicate we can get all eight aircraft. The C-130 isn't the optimum aircraft for what we want to do, but we can get them for thirty percent less than a smaller cargo plane.

"With the initial investment, maintenance costs, fuel, fees, and other related costs, I calculate we're looking at forty million in overall costs over a three-year period—tops. That number is pocket change. If it takes longer than three years to put a new system in place, we can always renegotiate a lease extension."

"And what about infrastructure? What are the costs or concerns about using the existing airfield here?" Gibbs asked.

"It's been abandoned for eight, maybe ten years, Senator. The State of Texas leased the land it was built on to an aircraft manufacturer that went belly up. I haven't looked into it yet, but all we need to do is throw a hundred thousand dollars at Congressman Atwill, who represents that district. He'd be happy to let us have it for as long as we need it.

"We spend a few hundred thousand renovating the hangar, out-buildings, and the runway, then we're up and running. I can have the old refrigerated cargo containers delivered to the airfield in a hot minute. We paint them up, put a logo on them, then we're in business," Johnson responded.

"Won't we be putting the cargo at a greater risk by putting them in the containers for so long?" Greta Kline asked.

"They would be inside for less time than they are on the ships. That said, we lose ten percent—tops," Gibbs stated.

Governor Johnson raised the index finger of his right hand. "If I can interject, Senator."

"Of course, Gordon," Gibbs responded.

"Thank you. For shipments to Texas, the human cargo is loaded on the container ships at the port of origin, then kept in the cargo hold. They're placed into the containers just before arriving in port here in Texas. The containers they're in are the first containers removed from the ship, then immediately loaded onto container trucks. The containers are driven to Dallas, where they're unloaded at the designated warehouses. The cargo is, at most, locked in the containers for ten hours.

"Flying the cargo to West Coast airfields from here keeps them in the containers for no more than four hours. We're still under the window of losing ten percent or less. That's an acceptable loss ratio," Johnson concluded.

"How large are the containers you're planning to use for air transport from here?" Gibbs asked.

"They're custom-built containers, eight by ten by six feet tall. The C-130 can carry six pallets, one container per pallet. That's four for the human cargo, with two containing other product. At ten per container, we can get forty delivered every trip, plus the other product," Johnson stated.

Greta Kline nodded in agreement. "That's approaching the numbers we previously had." She smiled as she responded. "This could work, Senator."

Senator Gibbs was running his thumb and index finger over his right eyebrow as he replied, "Gordon, have you taken security into consideration?"

"Of course. We can convert one of the out buildings at the airfield to house one hundred fifty people. We keep a small contingent of the security staff on site to cover the cargo until we can get them on a flight. The property is fenced off, so unauthorized access would be almost nonexistent. The security at the ports here is already in place and more than adequate, so no need to change or alter that.

"What we do need to discuss is security at the receiving airfields, once we determine which fields are viable," Johnson stated.

"I'll get my staff on it as soon as I get back to Palm Springs," Kline stated.

"I'll do likewise," Waterston replied.

"Okay then, we all have our work set out for us." Gibbs looked at Governor Gordon Johnson. "Gordon, I need to catch a flight out tonight. Would it be possible for your pilot to get me to the Dallas Airport by three?" Gibbs asked.

"Of course. I'll have the pilot ready and waiting for you." Johnson stood, pushing his chair back with the back of his legs. "I've arranged an afternoon horseback tour of the ranch for you," he said while looking at Kline and Waterston. "We can finish the ride with a round of trap shooting."

"Excellent," Waterston and Kline responded in unison.

Sitting under the covered sidewalk patio of the Café Milano on Prospect St. NW was a distinguished sixty-five-year-old gentleman drinking a latte. August Marchand stood out from the other Georgetown, Washington DC patrons because of his three-piece tweed suit. He looked quite European as he sat formally in the high back chair sipping his drink.

His white hair, dark brown eyes, perfectly groomed moustache, and impeccable clothing implied he had discriminating taste, with the wealth to accommodate. He took a sip of his Latte, softly dabbing his lips with the linen napkin.

He smiled at the waitress after she placed the plate of salmon on the table in front of him. As he draped the napkin over his right leg, the phone in his coat pocket rang.

Lifting the phone to his ear, he spoke with a distinguished French accent. "Yes?"

"Sir, we haven't confirmed that the package you requested was delivered in Seattle."

"Was the courier delayed?"

"He hasn't responded to inquiries, sir. Should we contract with another carrier?"

"Not at this time. Let's wait another day to see if the delivery was delayed. Contact me if there's any change."

"Very well, sir."

Placing the phone back into his coat pocket, Auguste began eating his salmon. The café was sparsely occupied, as the noon meal had concluded two hours earlier. As he continued to eat, he read from the folded <u>Washington Post</u> paper lying next to his plate.

A man stopped next to Auguste's table, clasping his hands together in front of him. Marchand looked up from the paper, gesturing with his left hand for the man to sit.

The short, muscular man was dressed in cargo pants with a wool sweater. A short scruffy beard outlined his weathered, suntanned face. He sat at the table across from Marchand.

Marchand wiped his mouth with the napkin, then placed it back on his lap. "We may have a problem. The package wasn't delivered in Seattle."

Replying with a British accent, the man responded. "Do you need me to follow up with it, sir?"

Marchand reached into his waistcoat pocket, retrieving a pack of Dunhill cigarettes. He glanced around the café, looking to see if anyone was watching them. He set the cigarettes on the table, sliding them across to the man.

"Mr. Claiborne, this is the next package. You need to deliver it within four days. The address and profile are there. If you're needed in Seattle, dispatch will contact you with the details of the last package." Marchand said while pointing to the cigarette pack."

He picked up the pack of cigarettes and placed them into his sweater pocket, buttoning the top of the pocket. "Yes, sir. Any further instructions, sir?"

"None," Marchand responded as he returned to eating his meal.

Hugh Claiborne stood and left the café without any further conversation.

Danny entered Capt. Graves' office, stopping in front of Lisa Morton's desk. "Is the captain in, Lisa?"

"He is. Just a minute, Lieutenant," Lisa Morton replied as she lifted the telephone receiver to her mouth. "Captain, Lt. MacDougal is here to see you. Very well, I'll send him in." She looked up at Danny with a smile. "He can see you, Lieutenant."

Danny opened the door, stepping inside the office. "Can I have a few minutes, Captain?"

"Of course, Danny, have a seat. What's up?"

"Are we still on for tonight?"

"Your house, seven pm. Is everyone else coming?"

"Yes, sir, we have confirmation for everyone." Danny leaned forward in his seat. "Captain, I want to thank you for authorizing the coverage around my house."

"Not a problem. We'll keep it in place for as long as necessary. Has Larry come up with any additional information about the homicide?"

"We have the DNA, blood type, and boot prints. Not much else. We may never know who the individual was," Danny replied.

"Okay, it is what it is. Have you started looking into the names I gave you?"

"We have. Billie, Larry, Rick, and I are digging into them. It'll take a while, but if there's anything in their background that's sketchy, we'll find it."

"With your permission, I want to get some additional input from one other person, if that's okay with you?" Danny asked.

"Who are you thinking about?"

"Reverend Winters," Danny responded.

"Okay by me, Danny. This is your case. We may all be in this together, but you're the point man. If you want to use Winters, be my guest."

"He was Delta Force, Captain. He has personal knowledge regarding a lot of people. Not only that, but his contacts are too numerous to count. He's already up to speed on the file. I read him into it three months ago. I trust him implicitly."

"Danny, you don't need to justify anything to me. I trust your judgment. The only thing I ask, is that you not put my neck in a noose with the Chief," Graves responded.

Danny stood up from the chair. "Captain, your neck can't be put in the chief's noose, there's no more room. My neck has been in there a lot longer than yours ever could."

Graves smiled as he responded. "See you at seven, Danny."

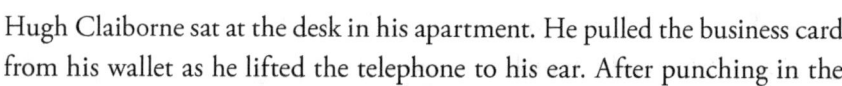

Hugh Claiborne sat at the desk in his apartment. He pulled the business card from his wallet as he lifted the telephone to his ear. After punching in the number, he leaned back in the chair.

The call was answered on the other end of the phone. "Landon Automotive Rentals, how may I help you?"

"Mr. Landon, this is Judd Black. I need a rental car for two days, beginning on the twenty-third at noon," Claiborne stated.

"And where will you be picking the vehicle up from, Mr. Black?"

"San Diego, California."

"What sized vehicle would you like, sir?"

"Full-sized sedan."

"And what options will you need with the vehicle?"

"Option eight, please," Claiborne responded.

"Very well, Mr. Black. There will be a Cadillac STS waiting for you at Lindbergh Field at the usual pickup location. Will there be anything further I can help you with, sir?"

"There may be. Could you please have a vehicle ready should I need it at Sea-Tac Airport in Seattle for the same time period or shortly after?"

"And what options would you like for the Sea-Tac vehicle, sir?"

"Fully loaded, with Special Options 4 available. Will that be a problem, Mr. Landon?"

"Not at all, Mr. Black. Please call at least two hours before you land. The car will be ready for you at the usual pickup location. Is this to be billed to your corporate account?"

"It is. Thank you, Mr. Landon," Claiborne said before hanging up.

4

The MacDougal house was a large midcentury modern home from the early 1960's with a newer five-stall garage at the rear of the property, detached from the house. The three-bedroom two-bath home had a fully finished basement, which currently occupied Billie MacDougal's gym equipment.

The home underwent a full remodel in 2005 by the current owner, who turned it into a rental property in 2010. Danny and Billie had decided to rent a home, rather than buy one, especially in light of the escalating home prices in the Seattle area. The two newlyweds were putting all their efforts into the property on Orcas Island for their retirement. Until that time, they wanted to enjoy a full-sized home rather than apartment life in the more expensive downtown Seattle market.

The MacDougal house had volunteered to be the permanent meeting place for the small group of people doing battle with the forces surrounding the Mortenson file. Danny and Billie's home was the only place where the group could meet without risking exposure of the file's contents to outside family members.

Billie was busy doing some last-minute cleaning as Danny stood at the stove preparing appetizers. The house was filling with the smell of cooking shrimp, stuffed mushrooms, and Danny's signature Rosemary Focaccia bread.

As he pulled the Focaccia from the oven, Billie bent over, smelling the bread. "Danny, if you don't stop cooking like this, I'm going to weigh a thousand pounds by the time I'm forty."

Danny kissed her on the cheek. "Anyone who runs on the treadmill for an hour a day could never *possibly* be overweight."

Billie slapped Danny on the bottom. "Okay, you've been warned."

As the two were laughing, the front doorbell rang. Billie walked to the door, looking through the window at the top. She smiled as she opened the door to see Capt. Graves, Rick Barker, Larry Colton, and Reverend Winters standing outside.

She smiled broadly at the group as they entered the home.

Once inside, each shook Billie's hand, greeting her with a smile.

"Danny's in the kitchen, you guys. There's wine on the table, with beer, water, and soda in the fridge. Help yourself," Billie stated.

As the team members entered the kitchen, Danny greeted them while taking the appetizers to the dining room table. "Help yourself, you guys," he announced.

After delivering all the appetizers, Danny wiped his hands with a towel, then draped it over his right shoulder. After cracking open a bottle of water, he addressed the group, "Let's move into the dining room."

As they were seating themselves, Danny opened the meeting. "First order of business, we'd like to welcome Reverend Winters into the fold. His qualifications need no introduction. He, and he alone, is the reason Rick, Larry, and I are even here tonight. Thank you, Gary."

"Thank you for the honor. However I can help," Winters stated.

"First off, with the exception of Gary, everyone knows of the incident in the park across from our house. We don't know the particulars surrounding it. It may be something, may be nothing. That said, keep your heads on a swivel.

Larry, after the meeting is over, could you fill Gary in?"

"Sure thing, boss," Larry responded.

"Capt. Graves needs to bring us up to speed on any updates regarding our progress on the file. Captain?" Danny said as he motioned to Graves.

Graves wiped his mouth before speaking. "All indications from the crime statistics coming into the department is you guys hurt them bad," Graves replied. "Trafficking is down all along the West Coast. That, of course, won't last. My guess is they're formulating new plans as we speak.

"The common wisdom is that it will take them at least two years to formulate a new plan with the needed infrastructure. The up side is we know all the names of the responsible parties. The downside is we won't know the new shipping and receiving methods they'll use. So, we need to continue to monitor the principal parties. Billie, has anything come out of the feds that can help?"

"Nothing so far. After the operation, they're being very guarded regarding their cooperation with us. I'm forming relationships with a few people, but that may take a little longer," Billie stated.

"Okay, we'll just have to be patient," Graves stated.

"Which brings us to the elephant in the room," Danny announced. "We've reached a point where we're overstretched, outgunned, even outclassed. The captain has given us some names of people he trusts. These are people who are working *in*, or who've *been in* the system, but not a *part of* the system." Danny handed Reverend Winters a three by five card with the names on it.

"Larry, have any of you discovered anything about the five names?" Danny asked.

"No, not yet," Larry responded.

"Me either," Rick replied.

"I still have some contacts that can help. I'll put out inquiries in the morning," Winters stated.

"Billie and I have been looking into them, but nothing so far. Once we've vetted them, we need to all get together to brief them. We chose a place to meet; it's Billie's parent's hotel up in Leavenworth. They have a semi-secure conference room, an excellent restaurant, along with nice rooms. Billie checked with her parents, and they said they'd be happy to provide it for us. No charge for the rooms, but we need to tip *very* well," Danny said with a smile.

"Mom and Dad said it's the perfect time, as the next two months are the down times of the year, until Oktoberfest comes. After Thanksgiving, there are no vacancies until spring. I told them we'd need ten rooms. They said all they need is 48 hours' notice," Billie advised.

"Once you guys give me the notice about the names, I'll get them out here," Graves stated.

"Captain, are these people going to be able to come out here with such short notice?" Barker asked.

"I have the magic words, Rick. Trust me, they won't be able to resist. They'll be here," Grave stated.

Billie leaned forward in her seat. "We also need to recruit someone with unique computer skills. I mean we need an ultimate hacker. Alice Ransom at the IT Department is very good, also trustable, but I don't think it prudent to put a 52-year-old grandmother in jeopardy."

"I agree, Billie. She's good, but that's non-negotiable," Graves stated.

Winters picked up one of the stuffed mushrooms before he responded. "Got just the guy," he said as he popped the mushroom into his mouth.

"Can he be trusted, Gary?" Danny asked.

"He's perfect for you guys, and beyond reproach for our purposes. He'll need a bit of cleaning up, though. We just got him back from rehab," Winters stated.

Danny winced as he heard the information. "Boy, I don't know about that, Gary. Are you sure he can be trusted?"

"He was one of the men at Fort Lewis in my old unit, Danny. He came into the unit about seven years after I retired. I know his commanding officer, who was impressed with him. He fell on hard times and turned to alcohol. He's clean now, and ready to get back into society." Winters leaned in toward Danny. "He had a security clearance, at or above Top Secret. He can hack into any system in the world. He's a Christian who needs a second chance, Danny."

"Where's he staying?" Graves asked.

"He's at the mission for now, helping out," Winters replied.

"Tell you what, Gary, we'll come by and talk to him. If he checks out and we both sign off on him, I'm sure I can get him a position somewhere," Graves stated.

"Fair enough," Winters replied.

"Okay, now for the big issue," Danny said as he put his forearms on the table, lacing his fingers together. "Once we get additional personnel onboard, we need to step it up a notch. Billie, the captain and I have been looking at the file. We want to go after the mid-level people," Danny stated.

"Who are you thinking about, Danny?" Larry asked.

"The Deep State is being sustained by dirty politicians, Hollywood, the corrupt media, and corporate cronies giving cover to the higher echelon. We don't have the apparatus in place yet to go after the Regional governors, but we can take out the mid-level bureaucrats," Danny stated.

"And how, may I ask, do you plan to take out half of Washington DC?" Winters asked sarcastically, with a smirk.

"Captain?" Danny said as he motioned his open hand toward Graves.

"The file gives us everything we need to know," Graves said as he sat upright. "The Deep State controls half of the politicians in Washington through blackmail. The file contains everything those bastards are into. A lot of them are pedophiles, perverts, thieves, and traitors. We tell them to leave office or we'll expose their actions publicly," Graves responded.

"You know a lot of them won't leave, right? They'll call our bluff," Rick mused.

"It's understood that we'll have to expose some of them. We pick the most egregious ones, bombard the press and the Internet with proof of their actions, including videos. It won't take long until the rest of them grow some brain cells and leave," Danny stated.

"Man, that's risky, Danny. You're dealing with people's livelihoods. Of greater concern, you're dealing with their power. Power is a much greater aphrodisiac than money. They'll come after you hammer and tong," Winters warned.

"We've thought about it at great length, Gary. That's one of the reasons Billie wants to get a computer whiz kid on board. If we hit them hard, and clandestinely, they won't have time to react," Danny said.

"And all this is in the file?" Winters asked.

"You didn't get that far down in the file when you read it. They're all involved, Democrats, Republicans, Independents, the whole lot of them. They're taking bribes in the form of campaign contributions from pharmaceutical companies, defense contractors, foreign governments, banks, drug cartels, even from hostile despots around the world.

"There are videos in the file of them in compromising positions. They're blackmailing the powerbrokers into submission. These videos include them molesting children, sexually assaulting both women and men, taking obscene amounts of money to sell out their country. These vermin need to go down," Danny said with a sneer.

"We all need to go over this with a fine-toothed comb. Look for anything that could go wrong. Come up with a good plan, one that has the best chance of success with contingencies should it go wrong," Graves responded.

"Danny, I'm on board, you know that, but this would have to be planned down to the smallest detail. Absolutely no chance for failure," Winters warned.

"Understood. That's why you're in charge of putting the plan together." Danny winked as he placed a stuffed mushroom into his mouth.

"Why doesn't that surprise me?" Winters said with a smirk.

Danny smiled at his friend as he leaned to the side of his seat. "It's your fault. You were trained too well in the Army. Besides, your plan at the cabin on Orcas Island was brilliant."

Winters' lips curled up at the corner. "I just may take up drinking again after tonight."

Hugh Claiborne parked the Cadillac STS in the parking stall in front of the Executive Terminal at Lindberg Field. He exited the vehicle, pulling his overnight bag from the passenger seat. As he closed the door, he handed the keys to the older gentleman waiting for the car.

With an emotionless face, the gentleman addressed Claiborne. "Was the vehicle to your satisfaction, Mr. Black?"

"Yes, completely," he responded.

"And the options you requested, were they satisfactory?"

Claiborne responded as he lifted the cell phone from his pocket. "Yes, everything was in fine order. The options are in the boot, only slightly used."

The older man lifted the clipboard, holding it out toward Claiborne. "Very well, sir. If you'll sign here, we'll get you on your way."

Claiborne signed the name J. Black to the form, then handed it back to the man.

"If you'd like to have a seat in the waiting area, the shuttle will take you back to the main terminal, sir."

Claiborne nodded toward the man, then stepped to the waiting area while dialing the number.

As he sat on the bench, the call was answered. "Yes?" Auguste Marchand responded.

"The package was delivered, sir."

"Were there any additional deliveries made?" Marchand asked.

"No, sir, only the one package needed to be delivered."

"Very well. You can proceed to Seattle for the other delivery," Marchand stated.

"Yes, sir. I'll get the next flight out," Claiborne said as he terminated the call.

He immediately dialed the second number. "Landon Automotive Rental," the voice announced.

"Yes, Mr. Landon, this is Judd Black calling. It appears I *will* need that rental we discussed for Seattle. I'm catching the next available flight out of San Diego."

"Very well, Mr. Black. The vehicle you ordered will be waiting for you at the usual place. Thank you for choosing Landon Automotive Rentals."

Claiborne disconnected the call, placing the phone back into his pocket.

Senator Gibbs walked to the Johnson ranch's helicopter, as one of the flight crew carried his bags. The helicopter was running up as he approached the ramp.

After placing the senator's bags on the aircraft, the crewmember turned toward Gibbs, speaking loudly over the engine noise. "You're all loaded, sir. Have a nice flight."

Gibbs nodded toward the man as he stepped up the stairs into the cabin. The helicopter's cargo door was closed, muffling out the majority of the engine noise. After buckling himself in, Gibbs pulled the cell phone from his pocket.

Auguste Marchand answered the call. "Yes?"

"Was your package delivered?" Senator Gibbs asked.

"Not yet. We've sent another courier for the delivery," Marchand stated.

"Is there a problem?"

"We haven't determined that. We have not yet spoken to the courier," Marchand replied.

"I was given to understand that your couriers always made deliveries on time. Was I misinformed?"

"Not at all. I'll let you know the minute the new delivery is made," Marchand stated.

Gibbs terminated the call, placing the phone into his pocket. He looked out the window as the helicopter slowly lifted off the helipad.

Gibbs' lips pursed as the helicopter flew North, gaining altitude. "Most unfortunate," he said in a low voice as the aircraft turned toward Dallas.

5

Danny and Capt. Graves entered the Rescue Mission wearing civilian clothes. The hall was almost empty as they tried to see Reverend Winters.

Danny looked to the rear of the hall, seeing Winters in the kitchen. Both men walked back to the rear of the hall to meet him.

As Winters turned around, he held up his right hand. "Hold on, I'll get Walt. Have a seat, guys," he said as he went into the office area.

Rhonna Collins approached Danny and Capt. Graves with two bottles of water. She placed them on the table next to the men while smiling at them. "Can I get something else for you guys?"

Danny smiled at his friend. "Not for me, Rhonna."

"No thanks, Rhonna," Graves replied.

"Good to see you both," Rhonna said, before turning to walk away.

Danny looked up to see Reverend Winters bringing a man into the main hall. He tried not to frown as the men walked toward them. The man appeared to be in his early to mid-thirties, with long hair tied into a ponytail. His clothes were something a homeless person would be wearing, but clearly, they had been washed and ironed. His pants had splattered paint on them but were clean and pressed.

He was wearing an old tattered pair of Converse tennis shoes that were ragged and torn. He had an old Army shirt on, with all the nametag, rank, and insignias removed. It was washed and ironed as well. The man's hair was clean, but in dire need of being cut.

As they got closer, Danny noticed his eyes. They were brown and clear, telling him he'd been sober for quite some time. The whites of his eyes were clear and shiny as well. Danny had relief as he saw a sober man approaching him.

Danny and Graves stood as the two men stopped in front of them. "Gentlemen, this is Walter Killian," Winters stated.

Danny reached out, shaking the man's hand. "Danny MacDougal," Danny said, as he shook Walter's hand.

Graves greeted the young man. "Michael Graves. Nice to meet you."

"Please, have a seat," Winters said, motioning to the chairs around the table.

Walter Killian sat in the chair in typical military fashion. He was sitting at attention without his back touching the backrest, as he looked both Danny and Graves directly in their eyes.

Danny leaned forward in his seat. "Mr. Killian, did Reverend Winters tell you what we need from you?"

He turned his head toward Danny. "Yes, sir. He told me you need an IT specialist. He additionally said it's a sensitive position, requiring the utmost confidentiality. And sir, please call me Walter or Walt."

"Fair enough, Walt. This position goes far beyond confidentiality. If this information ever gets out, people will die. I can't stress that enough," Danny stated.

Graves nodded while looking at Walter. "Walter, I second my colleague's concerns as to how dangerous this is. Any breach of security could cost you your life, as well as the lives of your team members."

Walter turned toward Graves with a cold and determined look. "Sir, I *have* been dead. I spent the last five years dying every day. I should have died so many times, but God had a different path for me." He looked back and forth between Danny and Graves. "Gentlemen, I realize I may not look like much, and my past would scare anyone, but I'm ready to serve. I want to get back into the fight, sir. If you select me, I can promise that I will not disappoint you, even if it means to the point that it costs me my life."

Danny looked at Winters. "Gary, could we have a minute, please?"

"Of course," Winters said as he stood. "Walt and I will get some coffee."

As Winters and Walt walked back to the kitchen, Danny turned toward Graves. "What do you think, Captain?"

"I wish he had a little more time of sobriety under his belt. That said, I think the risk is worth it. By all appearances, he's clear, focused, and in control. What do you think?"

"I agree with your assessment. Winters vouches for his computer skills. The fact that Gary is comfortable with him is enough for me. The reverend wouldn't put him forth without complete confidence. He knows how important this is. Do you have a position you can put him in?" Danny asked.

"I'll talk with Alice in IT. If he's as good as Gary says he is, she could use him. Until we can get him onboard, maybe we can get him in the Custodial Department. At least that'll get him some income until Alice gets him in."

Danny stood while raising his hand toward Winters. The two men walked back to the table. As they sat down, Danny looked at Walt. "Walt, we'd like to have you with us. Capt. Graves believes he can get you a position in IT at the department. Until that happens, would you mind working in the janitorial department? It wouldn't be that long, just until we can get you in IT."

A smile formed on Walt's lips. "That would be fine, sir. I won't disappoint you," he responded.

"Very good. Gary, can he stay here at the mission until we can get him a place to live?" Danny asked.

"Of course," Winters replied.

Danny reached into his back pocket, retrieving his wallet. He extracted a hundred-dollar bill, handing it to Walt. "This is for some new clothes and a haircut. I'll pick you up tomorrow morning and we'll get started."

Graves stood, shaking Walt's hand. "Welcome aboard, Mr. Killian."

As the two men turned to leave, Winters looked at Danny. "Thanks, Danny," he said with a head nod.

Winters addressed Walt as they walked back to the kitchen. "There you go, son. You got your second chance."

"Thank you, Sergeant Major, I won't let you down," Walt replied.

"I'm counting on that," Winters stated. "Also, from this point on, Mr. MacDougal's and Mr. Graves' first names are lieutenant and captain, understood?"

"Yes, sir," Walt replied.

"One last thing, Staff Sgt. Killian. This is to be handled as a team operation. We work together, all the time, every time. Now that you're a Christian, God's name may be tattooed on your forehead, but your rear end belongs to me, clear?"

"Crystal, Sergeant Major," Walt responded.

Winters snapped his head toward Walt. "Oorah."

With the sky under full cloud cover, the Broadview District neighborhood was pitch black and silent at two in the morning. Not even the wildlife was active.

Moving through the trees, the lone figure dressed in black tactical clothing quietly made his way toward the MacDougal house. Wearing a backpack, the figure slowly and quietly opened the driveway gate.

Once inside the yard, the man knelt on the left side of Danny MacDougal's unmarked police vehicle, while carefully removing his backpack. He reached inside, extracting a device. As he bent down to reach under the vehicle, a figure appeared from behind. A knee to the center of his back knocked the man to the ground. A pair of gloved hands grabbed his head, snapping it to the left forcefully, breaking his neck.

The figure returned the device to the backpack and lifted the body onto his shoulder, walking back to the gate. After quietly leaving the property, he walked through the trees to his van.

Once at his vehicle, the man opened the rear door, laying the body inside. He removed the backpack from the body, tearing off the facemask. After pulling the dead man's identification, he closed the rear cargo door.

Once inside, the man started the vehicle, driving away from the site. He removed his own facemask as he pulled into a parking lot a mile from the house. The square-jawed man ran his hand through his salt and pepper hair, then rubbed his scruffy beard, relieving the itching effect of the mask. He opened the backpack, looking at the device, then focused his attention to the dead man's wallet.

Keeping the device in his lap, he lifted the cell phone from his front shirt pocket. Punching in the number, he waited for a response.

"Yes?" the male voice responded.

"He was intercepted, sir."

"Any problems?"

"No, sir. I had to wait for him an extra day, though. He was delayed for some reason."

"Do you have an ID on him?" the voice asked.

"His Virginia driver's license shows the name Hugh Claiborne."

"Are you familiar with him?" the voice asked.

"No, sir, but he was with the Special Air Service. The tattoo on his right forearm says *Who Dares Wins*. That's their credo."

"Okay, he'll be easy enough to chase down. Anything else?"

"They're getting bolder, sir. He was going to place a device on the car containing two pounds of Semtex."

"That's enough to level the house along *with* the car," the voice responded.

"Correct. They want him bad, sir. After a failed second attempt, they'll come after him with a team."

"Agreed. I'll get more people out to you as soon as I can. Do you have personnel you'd prefer to work with?"

"Yes, sir. I'll text you eight names as soon as we're done. Do you want me to get rid of the car?"

"Not necessary this time. Remove the contents and leave it where it's parked. Let the police deal with it. I'll be in touch."

"Very well, sir," the man said as he terminated the call.

Detective Rick Barker parked his unmarked police vehicle on Arroyo Beach Place SW, next to a police cruiser and the Medical Examiner's van. He exited the vehicle, walking down the sidewalk between two of the homes. He looked out toward Arroyo Beach to see a uniformed officer taking a statement from one of the residents.

He nodded to the officer as he walked past him. Barker continued to walk down to the water's edge to see the M.E. standing over the body of a woman.

"What do we have, Ron?"

Yamashita spoke while still looking at the body. "Female, looks to be in her mid-fifties, Hispanic," he responded.

"How long's she been dead?" Rick asked as he knelt next to the body.

"Best guess, three months."

"Any signs of trauma?"

"Post death, yes. Bruises all appear to have happened after she expired. The only thing I can see that may have happened before death, is a needle mark on the side of the neck. I'll know more after the autopsy."

Rick looked at the woman's legs. There were lesions around the ankles. "Looks like she was bound around the ankles." He looked at her arms. "No lesions around the wrists. Maybe the ankles were tied to some kind of a weight, then thrown into the water. Any identification on the body?"

"No, nothing," Yamashita responded.

Rick put on his latex gloves. "Well, better get to work," he said as he began examining the scene.

anny entered Capt. Graves' office with Walter Killian in tow. "We're here, sir," Danny announced.

Capt. Graves looked up from his desk, trying to fight off the shock of seeing Walter cleaned up with a haircut. His eyes opened wide as he spoke. "Well, you clean up pretty nice, Mr. Killian."

Walter had his hair cut short with a clean-shaven face. He was wearing new cargo pants with hiking boots. A new wool shirt was under his lightweight raincoat. "Thank you, sir. It's nice to feel normal again."

"Have a seat," Graves said as he turned around to retrieve a laptop computer from the table behind him. As he set the computer on his desk, he slid it across to Walt. "A little test, Walt, if you don't mind. Could you try to break into the Seattle Police Department's classified personnel files for me?"

Walter turned the computer on and began typing furiously after the computer booted. Danny and Graves looked at each other with half smiles, waiting for Walt to finish.

Graves looked at Walt. "It may be a little difficult, we pride ourselves on a secure—"

Walt interrupted Graves as he slid the computer back across the desk to him. "There you are, sir," Walt said without emotion.

Graves looked at the screen to see the open personnel files of the department. He turned the computer around to show Danny. They were both surprised as they stared at Walt.

"I'm sorry it took so long, sir. I've been out of practice for a while," Walt stated.

Danny's eyes opened wide as he responded. "That's quite alright, Walt," he said as his right eyebrow rose.

"I can compromise another more difficult site for you if you'd like, sir?" Walt stated.

Graves held up his hand toward Walt. "No, no, that'll be fine." He smiled as he looked at Danny. "Better tell Alice to beef up the security for IT."

Graves depressed his intercom button. "Lisa, could you tell Mitch we're ready for him?"

"Right away," Lisa responded.

Graves turned toward Walt. "We secured a position for you on the janitorial crew until Alice can make room for you in IT. We're all going to meet at Lt. MacDougal's house tonight. Can you ensure Walt gets to your house at seven, Danny?"

"Of course, Captain," Danny responded.

"Lt. MacDougal will provide you with a new laptop with the file loaded on it. Please review it before tonight's get-together. Because of the size, you won't be able to get through it all, but try hard to at least get through the first five hundred pages. The bulk of the generic information is in those first pages," Graves stated.

Graves' intercom sounded. "Sir, Mitch is here."

"Thank you, send him in," Graves said.

Mitch Collier, Building Maintenance Manager for the City of Seattle, entered Graves' office. The sixty-year-old man was slight of build, wearing Levi's, with a blue city work shirt. He stopped next to Danny and Walt. "Captain, how can I help you?"

"Mitch, this is Walter Killian, the man I spoke to you about."

Mitch turned toward Walt. "Nice to meet you, Walt."

Walter stood with a smile. "Nice to meet you, sir," he said as he gave Mitch a firm handshake, looking him directly in the eyes.

Graves looked at Mitch. "Do you have a place to park Walt until we can get him on with IT?" Graves asked.

"We don't have any more custodial positions available, but we do have a position in the maintenance department." Mitch turned to Walt. "Do you have any mechanical experience, Walt?" Mitch asked.

"Yes, sir. My first job in the Army was working on M1 Abrams Tanks, sir."

Mitch's head snapped back. "Well then, looks like you got a job, Walt. Did you do a background investigation on Mr. Killian, Captain?"

Graves picked up the envelope on his desk, handing it to Mitch. "It's all here, Mitch. Came back clean as a whistle."

As Mitch took the envelope from Graves, he looked at Walt. "Can you be ready to get started Monday morning, Walt?"

"I sure can, sir."

"Good, meet me here in the lobby at seven am Monday morning. We'll go down to personnel and get you sorted out," Mitch said.

Walt reached out to shake Mitch's hand. "Thank you very much, sir."

"You're welcome." Mitch turned to Graves. "Do you need anything else, Captain?"

"No, nothing. Thank you for your help, Mitch," Graves responded.

The three men waited for Mitch to leave the room before speaking. As the door closed, Graves looked at Walt. "Until we can get you into IT, you're going to be spending a lot of time between maintenance and working with us. Can you handle the extra hours?"

"Not a problem, sir." Walt looked at Danny and Graves. "I want to thank you both very much. This means a lot to me. I promise I won't let you down."

Graves stood, shaking Walt's hand. "Counting on it. Welcome aboard, Mr. Killian."

Danny stood as he addressed the captain. "We'll see you tonight, sir."

Graves nodded as he returned to the work on his desk.

Danny looked at Walt as they were walking to the lobby. "You worked on Abrams tanks?"

43

"Yes, sir, for my first two years in the Army."

"You're a surprise a minute, Walt. Can I give you a lift back to the mission?"

"No thank you, Lieutenant. I need to walk off some of this belly fat I've acquired over the past few years," he replied.

"Reverend Winters has your laptop. Make sure it's secure every time after you use it. Detective Rick Barker will pick you and Reverend Winters up at six-thirty tonight," Danny stated.

"Yes, sir." Walt held out eleven dollars toward Danny. "Here's the change from your money, sir."

"Keep it, Walt. It's going to be a while before you start getting a paycheck. If you need more money, just let me know."

"Thank you, sir. See you tonight," Walt said as they stepped away from each other.

Danny was shaking his head as he walked to his car. "Never been sir'd that much in my whole life," he said while shaking his head.

Auguste Marchand sat in the leather chair in the living room of his Georgetown townhouse reading the New York Times as Brahms played in the background.

As was his daily routine, he was dressed in a suit and tie, with a cup of tea on the table next to him. As the cell phone rang, he folded the paper together answering the call.

"Yes?" he said.

"Mr. Green, this is Daniel from Landon Automotive Rental."

"Mr. Landon, how may I help you?"

"Sir, your rental car hasn't returned to our facility. Has Mr. Black been sent to another delivery location?"

"Not that I'm aware of, Mr. Landon. What vehicle did Mr. Black request?"

"A full-sized sedan, fully loaded, with Special Options 4. Additionally, Mr. Green, have you heard anything regarding our other rental vehicle? It still remains outstanding."

"Not at this time. I'll get back with you as soon as I have more information."

"Thank you, Mr. Green," Landon said as the call was terminated.

Marchand punched in another number on the phone. He leaned back in the chair as the call was answered.

"Yes?" the voice responded.

"It appears as though another courier has entered our delivery routes. Our delivery to Seattle has been interrupted for the second time. We need to meet as soon as possible to discuss a more aggressive posture," Marchand stated.

"Very well. Tomorrow at two pm at the usual place."

"Two pm," Marchand said as he terminated the call.

Danny opened the double door of the garage as the flatbed tow truck slowly backed down the driveway. He stood to the left of the truck, motioning to the driver with his hands in the air.

Ten feet from the garage door, Danny gave the driver the stop signal. The airbrakes hissed as the vehicle stopped. The woman stepped down from the driver's side, and began tilting the bed up to load the vehicle.

Once the bed was extended, the driver walked toward Danny. "Is it ready to go, Danny?"

"Yeah, Sharon. The engine and transmission are out. If you give me a hand, we can push it up to the edge of the bed."

As the driver entered the garage, her head snapped back. "Danny, what the hell did you do to my dream car?" she shouted as she looked at the 1969 Camaro Z28.

"Never give your keys to a parking valet, Sharon," Danny responded with a smirk.

"Man, Brent's gonna be pissed. Does he know how bad the damage is?"

"I told him over the phone. He said he'd give me a call once he gets it at the shop."

The two people entered the garage and started pushing the Camaro out of the enclosure. They stopped the car at the back of the bed.

"It looks even worse in the light Danny!" she shouted.

"I know, don't rub it in. Let's just get it loaded."

Sharon pulled the cable out and hooked it onto the frame at the front of the car. The winch whined as it pulled the Camaro up the ramp. After it was in the center, Sharon began lowering the flatbed.

As Danny was wiping his hands with a shop rag, Winters, Larry, and Walt walked through the driveway gate.

Excited, Walt hurried to the side of the tow truck. "Wow, a 1969 Z28! Yours?" Walt said excitedly.

"Yeah," Danny said with sadness in his voice.

"Gee, what happened to it? It looks like it went through an airstrike," Walt said.

"It did," Danny replied as he winked at Winters.

Sharon stepped next to Danny. "It's all tied down, Danny. I'll have Brent call you when I get it to the shop."

"Thanks, Sharon."

As the tow truck drove down the driveway, Danny walked back into the garage with Winters, Walt, and Larry following.

"Is this the engine and transmission for the Camaro?" Walt asked with wide eyes.

"Yup. Hopefully it will be again if the body shop can put it back together," Danny responded.

"What kind of horsepower?" Walt asked.

"Four-fifty."

Walt stood up tall as he looked at the two other cars in the garage. "You sure have a nice 56 T-bird here."

"It belongs to the wife," Danny responded.

"And a 1967 Volkswagen Beetle! Lt. MacDougal, I'm impressed."

"The bug has been in storage for ten years. It's just another of my projects that'll probably be on the back burner till I retire. It doesn't run."

"If you need any help working on it, I'd be happy to help," Walt stated.

"Sure. I just don't have the time anymore," Danny said as he threw the shop rag onto the bench.

"Come on, you guys, we better get inside before Billie skins me alive," Danny announced.

Danny closed and locked the garage door, then walked to the house with the three other men. Billie was setting out the boxes of pizza on the dining room table.

"The delivery man was just here," she said as Danny stopped next to her, giving her a kiss.

"Honey, this is Walter Killian," Danny said as he turned toward Walt.

Billie reached out, shaking Walt's hand. "Nice to meet you, Walt."

"Very nice to meet you, ma'am," Walt responded. "You really have a nice Thunderbird, Mrs. MacDougal."

"Thank you. It was a wedding gift to Danny and me. So, I gather you're a car guy?" she stated.

"Yes, ma'am, always loved old cars," Walt responded.

"Well, you and my husband should really get along then," she said, chuckling.

As they were talking, the doorbell rang. Billie went to the door to see Capt. Graves and Rick Barker through the window. She greeted them as they entered the home.

"Just in time, you guys. The pizza was just dropped off," Billie stated.

As Graves stopped in front of Billie, he shook her hand. "How's our Government Liaison Officer?"

"Doing good, Captain," she said with a smile.

Danny was at the sink washing up. He spoke loudly as he rinsed his hands. "Everybody dig in." Setting the towel on the butcher block, Danny stepped to the table, sitting down with the others.

Billie passed the paper plates around the table as everyone grabbed some pizza.

"Okay, hope you don't mind eating while we talk," Danny said as he placed the pizza slice on his plate. "First order of business, this is Walter Killian, our new IT specialist."

Walter dipped his head to everyone at the table.

"Walt will be working in city maintenance until we get him into the PD's Computer Department with Alice." Danny turned toward Walt. "Did you get a chance to read the file, Walt?"

With an emotionless face, Walt responded. "Yes, sir. I got about two thirds of the way through. I'll finish the rest of it tomorrow," Walt responded.

"Don't burn yourself out," Danny said as he looked at Walt.

"Next order of business. Have we all vetted the names Capt. Graves gave us?"

"I looked at them. I couldn't find anything in the records," Rick stated.

"Same for me. Nothing shows up," Larry Colton announced.

"Danny and I both dug deep. We couldn't find anything either," Billie stated.

"I did a check with *my* people. Doctor Glenn Packer was a member of the Council on Foreign Relations. As I don't trust those guys as far as I can throw this house, I want to dig deeper," Winters stated.

"I'm aware of that, Gary. He left the council just before he retired. He found out they didn't have the country's best interest at heart. That said, I encourage you to dig deeper," Graves responded.

"Okay, better to be safe than sorry," Danny responded.

Everyone nodded in agreement.

"Captain, unless there are concerns from anyone, you can proceed with the notifications of the five people. Packer can attend, but only after Gary digs deeper," Danny stated.

"Understood. Once Billie gives me dates for the hotel, I'll contact them," Graves responded.

"Very good. Now, we need to put together a plan for the elimination of midlevel players. Walt, we need your input for delivering the data to the key players. Can it be done without detection?" Danny asked.

"Yes, sir. The problematic way is to snail mail it to them. That has its own set of risks, however. Getting into the wrong hands, mail delivery, office staff opening it before it gets to the intended party are just a few of the problems. In my opinion, that won't work for us. I can send it to their personal accounts that are password protected, insuring they're in all probability the only ones opening it."

"Okay, electronically is the method then. You can get into their personal accounts without being detected?" Danny asked.

"Yes, sir, not a problem. I can also tell when and where they're watching it. I can even get video if you'd like," Walt stated.

"Okay, we flood them all with the information in the file. We hit them all at once. The ones who don't respond, we put it out into the media. Since there's video and photographic evidence in the file as well, they can see there's no way out but to resign, find other employment, or leave the country," Danny said with a sneer.

"Each of us need to draft the best way to present it to them. We can finalize the plan once we're up at the hotel and get the input from our new members."

Winters wiped his mouth with the napkin before speaking. "Danny, the crap is going to hit the fan if you go through with this. They're onto you, which means Billie is also at risk. I think that once we put the data out, you and Billie need to leave for a while. I just married you two. I don't want to officiate at your funerals a few months after the wedding ceremony," Winters stated emphatically with a frown.

"Danny, Gary's right. The only way you'll get me to buy off on this is if you guys take a leave of absence once we send the letters out. The incident here at your neighborhood may have been nothing, but we need to be careful," Graves stated.

Danny leaned forward, glancing around at his colleagues. "When Billie and I first discovered the file, we brought Arnie and Chuck on board. We asked them before and after they read the file if they wanted to go forward, because it was dangerous for both them, and their families. Arnie said 'I'm not going to sit back in safety while others suffer. It's the job we signed up for.'

"Arnie died a few days later fulfilling that oath. Chuck wasn't comfortable going forward with it because of his family, but said 'If my partner's on board, I am too.' Chuck is now disabled in a wheelchair, and his partner's dead.

"Every one of you has taken that same oath, either in the military or for the City of Seattle—some of you for both. Billie and I had a decision to make while we were on our honeymoon. We were given an incredible opportunity by Capt. Graves to continue this journey. We decided to accept that offer, no matter the consequences. I'm terrified of possibly losing my wife, but that decision is not mine to make; it's God's, and hers. It's my duty to support her in that decision. If I cower in a corner after their sacrifice, I couldn't live with myself.

"If I've learned anything from Reverend Winters over these past months, it's that none of us dies one second before, or one second after we're supposed to. God's in control."

Sitting next to Danny, Billie smiled as she squeezed his hand.

The people at the table remained quiet after Danny spoke. They merely looked at the two of them with half smiles.

"Okay then, let's dig in," Danny said while taking another slice of pizza.

Auguste Marchand walked on the gravel path past the National Air and Space Museum on the Washington DC Mall. The crowds on the mall were smaller now that the fall months had arrived. Joggers, along with a small number of visitors and locals were on the paths enjoying the cooler weather. The coming fall season was evident in the changing leaves of the trees.

Dressed in a brown tweed suit, a light overcoat with a brown Homburg hat, Marchand strolled slowly down the mall. He touched the tip of his walking cane on the gravel path lightly as he walked, scanning the path in front of him.

Coming up to him from his left side, a man dressed in a suit with a top-coat began walking next to him. The two men avoided looking at each other, keeping their focus ahead.

"Your meeting, your agenda," Peter Cornell stated.

"It appears we've been compromised. Someone has intercepted our operations twice now," Marchand stated.

"Seattle?" Cornell asked.

"Yes, same target."

"Do you know the circumstances surrounding the interceptions?" Cornell asked.

"Only that the vehicles weren't returned," Marchand stated.

"Looks as though the request to do this quickly with a message wasn't the best approach. Do we know the protections surrounding the target?" Cornell asked.

"Minimal. We chose evenings as the best time to avoid detection," Marchand stated.

"I'll look at internal operations before we proceed. Compromise may be the issue," Cornell said.

"We'll wait for your instructions before proceeding," Marchand stated.

Cornell moved away as Marchand continued walking down the mall.

Danny and Billie entered Sean's Irish Pub through the back door. The pub was being readied for the noon meal and had not opened yet.

An excited Marilyn Cooper smiled broadly as she saw her best friends enter her kitchen. She hurried next to them, hugging Danny and Billie tightly.

Danny smiled broadly at Marilyn. "Good to see you, Mom."

"It's so good to see you guys too. Come on, Sean's in the bar setting up the hors d'oeuvres."

As the three people rounded the corner, they saw Sean setting up the tables. "Man I miss being here for your lunches," Danny said as he smiled at his friend.

Sean turned to see Danny and Billie. He hugged them both, tightly. "We've missed you guys."

"We've missed you too," Billie said while kissing Sean on the cheek.

"Can we take a few minutes of your time?" Danny said while shaking Sean's hand.

"Of course. Have a seat at the bar while I finish setting up," Sean replied.

"First of all, we'd like to have you guys over to the house for dinner on Sunday. Can you make it?" Billie asked.

"Of course, what time?" Marilyn asked.

"Seven. Is that good?" Danny asked.

"We'll be there," Sean responded. "Can I get you guys something to drink?" Sean asked.

"No, we're fine," Billie replied.

"Can we bring anything?" Marilyn asked.

"Just an appetite," Danny answered. "Melissa Mortenson and Reverend Winters will be there too. We want to thank you guys for all you did for us," Billie stated.

"That'll be fun. Count us in," Marilyn said.

"We have a favor to ask of you if you can?" Danny said.

"Anything, just name it," Sean replied.

"We have a new employee in the department. He's a former military man who needs a place to live. If you can, could you rent the old apartment to him if it's available?" Danny asked.

"It's been empty since you left, Danny. We were going to use it for overflow storage for the restaurant, but that was just for a few things. That wouldn't be a problem." Sean stated.

"He was in the Army for ten years, then ran into some personal troubles. He's one of Reverend Winters' volunteers at the mission. He had an issue with alcohol, Sean. He's clean now, but you need to know his past. Are you sure it would be okay?" Danny stated with a tilted head and raised eyebrows.

"Danny, if you and Winters vouch for him, I'm sure he'll be okay. Besides, if you guys hired him on, I'm confident he passed your muster," Sean stated.

"Thanks, Sean, I really appreciate this," Danny said while shaking Sean's hand. "His name's Walter Killian."

"Tell him he can move in any time he's ready. Marilyn and I will keep the rent at the same rate we had when you were here," Sean said while taking the apartment's key off his ring.

Billie hugged Sean, then kissed him on the cheek. "Thank you," she said as she took the key.

"I only have one condition, Danny," Marilyn stated.

"What's that?" he replied.

"You come into the kitchen and give me the recipe for your potato salad?" Marilyn asked.

Danny grabbed Marilyn's hand, leading her into the kitchen. "Come on, I'll show you now," Danny said while chuckling.

Gordon Johnson exited his black Mercedes Benz G 550 into the warm afternoon sun. He reached across the driver's seat, grabbing his brown felt cowboy hat. After placing his sunglasses and hat on, he walked to the entrance of the hangar.

The airfield, along with the buildings, were built in the 1990s, and were abandoned in 2010. The white metal buildings were dirty, neglected, and turned into rodent magnets. The white buildings were trimmed in blue and looked as though they were built on a budget, without permanence in mind. It was difficult to tell the property was fenced off, as the nine-foot chain-link surrounding the facility was almost completely obscured by tumble weeds.

Johnson stopped next to a man wearing a yellow vest with a white hardhat on his head. "What's the verdict, Lee?"

Lee Craddock turned to address his employer. "We did an inspection of all the buildings, Mr. Johnson. Mostly they're just dirty. Some minor structural issues that can be dealt with quickly.

"The warehouse needs some attention in the rafters, but that's easy to take care of. The metal roofing is loose in some spots, but again, easy to repair," Craddock said while pointing to the warehouse next to the hangar.

"Wiring, plumbing, what about that?" Johnson asked.

"Haven't made it that far yet. I'll have an assessment for you by tonight. I focused on the structural issues first."

"What about the runway?" Johnson asked.

"Rolly's out there now looking at it, sir. I gave it a quick look when we first got here. There's some crumbling, for sure. We won't have a complete picture until we put the sweeper to it. Worst case, we can seal it to stop any further deterioration," Craddock stated.

"It doesn't need to be pretty, Lee, just functional. Good power, working bathrooms, hi-speed Internet, along with a completely secure warehouse. Reseal the runway if you think it needs it. We're going to be landing C-130s on it, so make it safe," Johnson stated. "What do you think our worst-case scenario is?"

"Time—two weeks tops, probably sooner. Cost—two fifty at the very most," Craddock speculated.

"Okay, that works. Try to keep it at or under the two-fifty mark. Make the hangar your first priority. I've got containers coming in the first of next week to be refitted, so we'll need the floorspace.

"Yes, sir. I'll get the crew on that first."

Johnson patted Craddock on the shoulder as he turned to walk away. "Thanks, Lee."

Auguste Marchand awoke to the ringing of his cell phone on the nightstand. He reached over, turning on the lamp, revealing the time on the clock as two-thirty am. Swinging his legs out of bed, he placed his feet on the cold wooden floor. Dressed in his pajamas, he slid his feet into slippers as he picked up the phone.

"Yes?" he answered.

Senator Gibbs responded, "Do we have any word on our cancelled deliveries?"

After turning on the bedroom light, and putting his robe on, Marchand slowly walked from the room into the hall. "Not as of yet. We're waiting for further information before we proceed."

"So, you haven't dispatched another courier?"

"No, we're not able to determine the severity of the threat," Marchand replied.

"Need I remind you there is a time factor to this delivery?"

"Always with you people there are time factors. It'll be delivered, but not before it's determined to be viable," Marchand stated as he entered the living room.

"So then you've made no progress on why the deliveries were interrupted?"

Turning on the floor lamp next to the couch, Marchand saw two sets of tactical clothing sitting on the cushion of the sofa. Both sets had boots, wallets, hats, and pistols placed on top of the clothes. "It appears we *are* making progress after all," he stated as he terminated the call, continuing to stare at the equipment of his two men.

Danny looked into the eyes of William Barnes as he placed the tip of the dagger against Barnes' knee. "Who do you work for?" he shouted.

"I'm an independent contractor, I work alone. I—" He was interrupted as Danny shoved the dagger deep into Barnes' knee.

Barnes' ear-piercing screams echoed off the walls of the warehouse as he writhed in pain.

Danny shot up in bed as sweat poured down his forehead. His actions of three months ago flooded his mind as his eyes were closed tightly. He was breathing heavily as he rubbed his face. Now fully awake, he reached over, grabbing his t-shirt off the nightstand.

Pulling on the garment, he walked quietly from the bedroom into the kitchen. Opening the refrigerator, he grabbed a bottle of water, quickly removing the cap. He drank deeply as he stepped into the living room.

Collapsing into an overstuffed chair, he finished the remainder of the water. Danny stared out the window as he attempted to control the trembling in his body.

As he looked out the front window, Billie wrapped her arms around his shoulders from behind. "More bad dreams?" she asked.

"Yeah," Danny replied as he turned his head, kissing her hand softly.

Billie came around in front of him, bending down on her knees. Laying her arms on his legs, she looked at Danny with concern, "Wanna talk about it?" she asked softly.

"Nah, it'll be okay," he said while continuing to look out the window. "Just residual crap from the Ballencourt case."

"It might help to talk about it," Billie said while patting him on the leg.

Danny placed his hands on Billie's arms as he gave a half smile toward her. "It'll pass, baby."

Billie stood while still holding his hands. "Come to bed, honey. Let me hold my husband while we try to get some sleep," she said tenderly.

"I never pass up an offer to get my hands on you," he said with a smile as he wrapped his arm around her waist from the side while walking to the bedroom.

Danny and Billie sat at the dining table with their guests, Sean and Marilyn Cooper, Melissa Mortenson, and Reverend Winters. The group of people were almost done with their meal as they chatted and laughed with their hosts.

"Danny, I could get used to you cooking for me," Melissa stated.

"I agree. Cornish game hens, wow. What a treat," Winters responded.

"No one misses his cooking more than us," Marilyn replied.

"Flattery will get you guys anything you want," Danny said with a grin.

With the guests finishing their meal, Billie excused herself from the table. "I'll be right back," she said as she walked to the bedroom.

Billie came back into the dining room carrying three wrapped gift boxes. She handed their guests a present. "We wanted to thank you all for everything you've done for Danny and me. You'll never know how much you guys mean to us," Billie said with a big smile.

As they opened the boxes, each person smiled broadly. "A Geneva Bible printed in 1884. Wow, thank you guys very much. I don't know what to say," Winters stated.

Melissa Mortensen held the wine bottle carefully in her hands. "How in the world did you guys know I've been looking for one of these? They're extremely hard to find," she said with surprise.

"Danny contacted your wine broker in California. Stephan said you'd been looking for one," Billie stated.

"A 1986 Mouton Rothschild. These are almost impossible to find," Melissa said with glee.

Billie smiled. "I'm glad you like it," she responded.

Marilyn Cooper got up from her seat, hugging Billie tightly. "A new set of All-Clad Chef's pots and pans for the restaurant! This is too much, you guys," Marilyn said tearfully.

"I got tired of seeing you guys cooking with the same equipment I used to use when I worked for you. And since I knew you'd never get new ones, we decided to force you into the twenty-first century. Just take the receipt down to the kitchen store on fifth and they'll deliver it to the pub," Danny said with a smile.

Billie looked around the table at their guests. "You are all more than friends you're family. We're unbelievably grateful to have you in our lives. We love you."

Danny stood, speaking as he turned to go to the kitchen. "I hope you all saved room for dessert?"

As they were responding to Danny, the front doorbell rang. "I'll get it," Billie announced as she got up from the table.

The smile Billie had changed to a look of concern as she opened the door, seeing Tanya Blaine standing in front of her. "Tanya, so nice to see you," Billie responded.

"Billie, I'm sorry to just drop by without calling. I wanted to speak to you and Danny if I could," Tanya asked.

"Of course, please come in, Tanya."

Tanya's eyes narrowed as her brow furrowed. "No, you have company. I shouldn't have come. I'm sorry."

Billie motioned toward Danny as she stood at the door. "Danny's coming. Please wait."

As Danny approached the door, Billie moved to the side, revealing Tanya Blaine, Danny's deceased ex-partner's wife. His lips pursed as he stopped next to Billie. "Tanya, it's good to see you. Please come in."

"No, I can't stay. Danny, I just wanted to come by and see you guys. First of all, I wanted to congratulate you on your wedding. I'm very happy for you, and I know Mark would have been as well.

"I'm so glad you came through your injury okay, Billie. I really am. Last, I wanted to say how sorry I am for unloading on you, Danny. I've been in a bad place for three years now. I guess it all just came bubbling to the surface. I had no business taking it out on you. I just wanted to say how sorry I am."

"Tanya, you don't need to apologize for— "

Tanya interrupted him. "No, no, no, I do need to apologize. Mark loved you like a brother, Danny, I know you loved him. Please forgive me for taking out my pain on you three months ago. His death wasn't your fault, Danny. Mark violated procedure. There's no other reason he died than that. This wasn't your fault," Tanya said as tears formed in her eyes.

Danny reached out, hugging Tanya. "I miss him very much. I wish he were still here."

Tanya wiped her face with her hands as she looked at Danny and Billie. "Please, you guys, come by the house some time. The boys miss you, Danny."

"We will," Danny responded.

As she began to cry again, Tanya looked at Danny. "Thank you for everything," she said as she turned to walk away.

Danny and Billie held hands as they watched Tanya get into her car. They both smiled at her as she waved back at them.

They closed the front door, walking back to the dining room, holding each other.

Winters looked at Danny. "Is everything okay?"

"Just when I thought this evening couldn't get any better—it did," he said while squeezing Billie's hand as they sat at the table.

A light rain fell as Billie walked to the Federal Building for her ten-a.m. meeting with the US Customs Agency. The sidewalks were full as she negotiated her way around the foot traffic. Wearing her lightweight raincoat with the hood pulled up over her head, her peripheral vision was impaired.

As she walked past a store front, Billie looked at the forty-five degree angle front window of a storefront to see a man walking fifty feet behind her. The man was looking directly at her as he negotiated his way around slower walking people. He was wearing denim pants with tennis shoes and a dark blue hoodie.

She shifted her focus to the car windows on her right to watch the man. His eyes continued to be locked on her as he maintained the fifty-foot distance.

Billie looked ahead to see an alley entrance on her left. She ducked in front of a group of people, turning left down the alley. She pulled the hood back on her shoulders as she walked faster toward the rear of the building.

She ducked back behind the building to her left as she pulled the weapon from her holster. Billie held the pistol at a forty-five degree angle in front of her as she waited for the man to come around the corner.

As he turned to walk down the alley, another man grabbed his head from behind, jamming a sharp-tipped pen into his neck. As the hooded man collapsed onto the pavement, the square jawed man placed the sharp-tipped pen in his pocket, then walked out of the alley and down the sidewalk.

Billie slowly moved away from the back of the building, continuing to look toward the alley. As the entire alley came into view, she saw the hooded man lying on the pavement twenty feet from the alley entrance.

She quickly moved toward the man with the pistol at her side. Once she reached him, she placed the index and middle fingers of her left hand on his carotid artery. After failing to get a pulse, she holstered her weapon, rolling him over, beginning to perform CPR. As she began compressions, Billie shouted toward the people on the sidewalk, "Somebody call 911!"

The square jawed man lifted a cellphone from his pocket as he continued to walk down the sidewalk. Dialing the number, he waited for an answer.

"Yes?" the male voice responded.

"Sir, we may have additional players here."

"Why? What's going on?"

"There was just an attempt on the woman," he stated.

"Is she okay?" the male voice asked.

"Yes, sir. The subject following her made some rookie mistakes. She picked up on it and ducked down an alley."

"Was he taken care of?"

"Yes. The threat was eliminated."

After a momentary silence, the male voice responded, "The additional assets will arrive your location this afternoon—coordinate with same. Increased vigilance is in order. Were you compromised?"

"Negative. But she'll now know she's a target. I didn't have time to clean the subject."

"Okay, it is what it is. I'll put out inquiries and see if we can identify the additional threat. Put together an airtight response in case it's needed," the voice responded.

"Yes, sir," he said as the call was terminated.

In full uniform, Danny entered the morgue. He saw Billie standing next to Ron Yamashita as they looked at a body lying on the metal examination table.

He mouthed the words to Billie, You okay?

Billie responded with a nod.

"So, what do we have here, Ron?"

"One Alex Rodriguez, twenty-nine-year-old Hispanic male. Billie has his personal data and belongings to be placed into evidence," Yamashita stated.

"Cause of death?" Danny asked.

"Haven't got that far yet, but looks like a heart attack, based on the blood draw. Billie found a syringe on him. I checked, and it contains Succinylcholine, also called 'Succs'."

"And what is it?" Danny asked.

"Anesthesiologists use it to relax muscles. If it's administered in a high enough dose, it can stop the heart. He was carrying enough in the syringe to stop a horse."

Danny's jaw set as he looked at Billie. "Could that also be what caused his heart attack, assuming that's what he died from?"

"If you look right here on his neck, you'll see a needle mark. This is just a guess, Danny, but it looks as though someone did him in before he could use the syringe—course, that's just my guess. I'll know more once the autopsy's done."

"You've got everything to place into evidence?" Danny asked Billie.

"Yeah, over there," she said while pointing to another table.

"Okay, let's get this down to the station. Ron, let me know as soon as you know more," Danny stated.

"Will do," Yamashita said as he turned back toward the body.

Danny and Billie walked out of the morgue into the hallway carrying the evidence bags. As the door closed, Danny turned toward Billie. "What happened?"

"I was on my way to a meeting in the Federal Building. I caught a glimpse of that guy following me. I kept looking at him through car and shop windows as I walked. His eyes were locked on me the whole time.

"I ducked down an alley, then moved back against the rear of a building, waiting to see if he would follow me. I waited, then slowly moved back out into the alley, where I saw him lying on the ground.

"I performed CPR, but he was gone. The paramedics arrived and transported him here," Billie stated.

As they exited the building, Danny looked at Billie. "Can you come down to the office now so we can go over this?" he asked.

"Sure. This blew all my meetings for the day," she said as she entered the car.

As Danny closed the car door, he looked at Billie. "You sure you're okay?"

Billie looked back at Danny with a frown. "Danny, stop being overly protective of me! I'm a big girl, I can handle myself," she said angrily.

Danny looked at the mirrors as he pulled out into traffic. "Sgt. MacDougal, you're my wife first and foremost. I'll always be protective of you. That said, you're also part of the Seattle Police Department, and as your superior officer, there are protocols I'm required to follow.

After an attempt on an officer's life, a shooting, a death in the officer's family, or anything else that could be considered a traumatic event, I need to find out if you need assistance or professional help. So, the question remains— are you okay?" Danny said with a professional tone.

"Yes, I'm fine," Billie responded curtly.

Danny knew Billie was upset about the incident and only lashing out because of what had happened. He chose to give her the space she needed.

The white Ford van pulled up at the Executive Terminal of the Seattle-Tacoma Airport. The square-jawed man exited the driver's door, walking to the opposite side of the vehicle.

After opening the rear luggage door, then the side cargo door, he waited for his passengers to come out of the terminal.

Seven men and one woman exited the building, walking to the van. They acknowledged the driver with half smiles. After putting their bags in the rear, they entered the van.

The driver reached over to the passenger's seat, retrieving eight legal-sized envelopes. He held them over his shoulder as he drove away. "These are the principals we're covering. Everything you need is in there; addresses, photographs, routines, etcetera.

"There are six people in the files, although it's a high probability they'll be adding more members to their team in the near future.

"There have already been three attempts on the primary principals, Danny and Billie MacDougal. The last attempt was on Mrs. MacDougal," Brad Carver explained.

"Single or multiple players?" Monica Meyer asked.

"Single. The first two were at night. The third one was in daylight on a busy downtown sidewalk. The third one had skill levels that weren't that of the first two. It's being looked into. The next time they try, they'll bring in two or three members, so keep alert.

"Your cars are at the hotel. The room keys are in the packets, along with all the adjoining rooms. I'm staying there as well, so we can all be available to each other. If there's anything you need, let me know immediately. We'll get together at 1900 hours.

"I'll need one of you with me for the MacDougals. The rest of you can team up on the remaining principals. I'll need one of you to be roving for rapid response. As I've worked many times with each of you, I trust you to select who you want to be teamed up with. We meet every night at midnight. Everyone exchange cell phone data. No mistakes on this one, understood?" Carver stated.

The entire team acknowledged in the affirmative as the van pulled up in front of the Hilton hotel.

Danny sat at the dining table as he looked over the data from Billie's encounter earlier. Wearing workout clothes and flip-flops, Danny sipped at his coffee while poring over the file.

Billie came into the room, sitting across from him. Without looking up, Danny addressed her. "NCIC doesn't have this guy. Have we checked anywhere else?"

"I ran a complete check on him. I even went back to the Ballencourt Security files, along with Red Rock Security. I couldn't find anything. He did have an Army tattoo on his right forearm. Other than that—zip," she stated.

"Maybe we get Winters, or Walt to take a look at it. I checked the address on his Washington State driver's license. It's the old Hancock Hotel downtown. They don't show him as living there. So far, this guy's a ghost," Danny mused.

"Did you get a look at his skin?" Billie asked.

"Not really. Why?" Danny said as he looked up at Billie.

"His skin had a gray tone to it, and the whites of his eyes looked cloudy. I'd bet the autopsy comes back with drugs in his system."

Danny sat back in his chair as his lips pursed. "Why would anyone use a deadbeat for a hit?" he mused.

"Someone desperate maybe?" Billie responded.

"This guy made a lot of mistakes while he was following you. A professional wouldn't lock their eyes on the target. This *does* scream desperation," Danny posited.

As they were talking, the doorbell rang. Danny got up, walking to the front door.

He was greeted by one of the Seattle PD technicians. "Lieutenant, I'm all done here. The cameras are up and running. You have full coverage around the house with a sixty-day digital backup," Stuart Grinnell stated.

"Great. Thanks, Stu," Danny said as he shook the man's hand.

He came back into the house and sat back down at the table. "Well, we're covered. A mouse comes on the property, we'll be alerted."

Billie looked at Danny with relief. "That makes me feel better." Billie lowered her head as she continued to look at him. "Danny, I'm really sorry for lashing out at you earlier. That whole thing freaked me out. I'm sorry I took it out on you," she said as she reached across the table holding Danny's hand.

Danny set the pen down on the table looking at her. "Honey, apology quite unnecessary. I forgave you the second you said it. It scared you, just like it would have scared anyone, including me. Don't even think about it," he said with a tender smile.

Billie squeezed his hand as she responded, "That's why I love you. You keep me grounded. You know, this was our first argument," she said as Danny looked at her.

"I know. May they all be so easily resolved," he said as he winked at her.

"Well, they will be, so long as you listen to me," she said with a wry smile.

Danny leaned back in his seat with a stern look. "But since I'm your husband and the head of this house, you need to do what I say."

Billie threw her head back and laughed loudly. "Oh, Danny, you're so funny. You make me laugh."

"Not too convincing, huh?" he said as he leaned across and kissed her.

"No, you weren't. But keep on trying," she replied as she put her arms around his neck.

As Auguste Marchand closed the book he was reading, his cell phone rang. His lips pursed as he saw the number. "Yes?" he answered.

"Have you dispatched another courier yet?" Senator Gibbs asked.

"No; as I've said before, it has not yet been determined to be viable," he replied.

"You need to dispatch someone to take care of this. It's imperative this package be delivered. Do you understand me?" Gibbs demanded.

"I shall review your request again. Possibly things have changed that will allow us to proceed for another delivery."

"I'll raise this issue with your employer. Possibly they will be able to persuade you of the importance of the situation," Gibbs threatened.

"I look forward to communicating with them. Have a nice evening, Senator," Marchand said as he terminated the call.

Gordon Johnson exited the warehouse at the airfield. He looked up to the skyline to see the sun going down below the horizon. The temperature was already starting to drop as he walked toward the hangar. He lifted the cowboy hat off his head wiping his brow with his right forearm.

"It sure was a hot one today, Mr. Johnson," Lee Craddock stated as he stood at the entrance to the hangar.

"Yeah, there's only two seasons in Texas. Hot and Hell's front porch," Johnson replied. "I see you got all of the runway and taxi areas sealed."

"Yes, sir. After the sweeper was done, it wasn't as bad as we thought," Lee stated. "Is the warehouse okay, sir?"

"Yeah, clean, functional, and secure. Should work out okay, Lee. You guys busted butt," Johnson said.

"We only had minor issues, Mr. Johnson. The hangar will be done by tomorrow night. Few more wiring problems, some work on the plumbing, then we'll be done with it. It was all still in pretty good shape."

"How much capital did you go through?" Johnson asked.

"Right now, we're at two-hundred ten. Way under budget."

"Very good. When your guys are done, give each of them a five-hundred-dollar bonus. You all worked hard," Johnson stated.

"Thank you, sir, the guys will appreciate it," Lee responded.

Johnson entered the hangar through the main aircraft doors. He could see the two hundred freezer containers placed on the concrete floor against the walls. "How long to paint the containers, Lee?"

"Not long. We'll get an assembly line going. Blast 'em, paint 'em, then put the stencil on. One day's hard work. Do you want us to go through the refrigeration units on them?"

Johnson swept his hand to the side. "Nah, they were serviced in Dallas before they were shipped down here. No worries, Lee."

As the two men were talking, they heard a high-pitched roar coming in from the north. They walked to the front of the hangar to see one of their C-130s approaching the runway. The all-white plane was lacking any distinguishing marks, other than the required tail numbers.

Johnson rolled his wrist over, looking at his watch. "Five minutes early."

The C-130's wheels barked on the runway as it touched down. The aircraft's turboprops reversed, bringing it to a halt just across from the hangar.

They both watched as the plane taxied to the tarmac in front of the hangar. As the aircraft stopped, the pilot waived toward the men. He shut the engines down as the stairway was being lowered down from the side.

Wearing cowboy boots, Levi's, and a short-sleeved t-shirt, the pilot removed his aviator's sunglasses as he stopped in front of the men.

"What do you think, Jerry?" Johnson asked.

"They're fine, sir. We had to change out an engine on one of them, but the rest are in excellent condition. The last of the annuals were done three months ago, so we're good to go," Jerry Harper stated.

"As they come in, put the stencils on the tail. We'll paint over them when the lease is up. We're gonna have a couple of weeks of downtime before the first shipments leave, so get in your relaxation now before the real work starts.

"When you're done here at the airfield, get the ranch hands working on the Grove when you can. We only have a few weeks before the festivities start. I want everything working perfectly," Johnson ordered.

"Will do, sir," Craddock stated.

"Make sure everyone gets to the bar-B-Que this Sunday. Don't want anyone missing out," Johnson said as he turned to leave.

Lee and Jerry slapped each other on the backs as they both walked to the hangar. "It's Miller time," Jerry said to his friend as they entered into the building.

Brad Carver opened his hotel room door to see the eight team members standing in the hall. Without saying anything, he motioned for them to enter. As the last person came into the room, Carver threw the deadbolt into the locked position.

Carver's room was the largest of the eight team members rooms, with a living area and kitchen. The members all sat on chairs, the sofa, and kitchen stools as they waited for instructions from their team leader.

He handed out eight by ten envelopes to everyone. "I want all of your personal data in the envelopes—wallets, cellphones, anything that can be traced back to who you are. No pictures of friends or family."

He passed around additional envelopes containing each of the team's new phones, driver's licenses, and identification in them. "There's your cover documents with your new identities. New cellphones, with each of the team member's numbers already loaded on them.

"Last, here's the number you call if you're arrested or questioned," he said as he passed around the small piece of paper. "Memorize it, then destroy it."

One of the members looked up from his folder. "This is a lot of precaution for a protective detail, boss. What's up?"

Carver nodded at Jason Wardly and replied, "Jason—and I want all of you to listen up as well. One screw-up, one misstep, or one hiccup, and everyone in this room could be dead. I hand selected each of you for two reasons. First, we've all worked together over the years on many difficult missions. I trust each of you implicitly. The second reason you were chosen from the others is because none of you are married and don't have children.

"There is, or should be, no reason for anything to be used against you. I can't tell you who's behind all of this or even who we're working for. That said, this is the most dangerous mission you've ever been on. It's imperative that the principals in this case are protected no matter what—even with your own life if necessary. Does everyone understand?" Carver asked.

All of the team members nodded in agreement. "Okay, now is the time if any of you want to back out. Just say the word and you can leave. It won't be held against you or sway my feelings for using you in the future, but I need to know if you have reservations," Carver ordered.

"I'm in," Jason stated.

"Me too," Bernard "Red" Caron responded.

"Ah hell, you know I'm in," Bobby Higgins replied.

"We're all in, boss. Otherwise, we wouldn't be here. Just tell us what needs to be done," Bob Walgren stated.

"You know I'm in," Monica Meyer stated. I only have one thing to ask. Who's the asshole who decided to give me the cover name of Trudi?" she said as she looked at her packet.

They all laughed as Carver silenced them. "That would be me," he responded.

Carver held his hand up. "Okay, I assume you all paired yourselves up. Who's gonna be with me?" he said as he looked around the room. Monica Meyer raised her hand.

"Okay, who's the odd man out?" Carver asked.

Bobby Higgins raised his hand. "Okay, Bobby, yours is the most important. You need to be ready to respond to any of the others in a millisecond."

Higgins nodded in acknowledgement.

"The latest Intel shows our subjects are going up to Leavenworth this weekend. It's a small tourist town in the Cascades, about a hundred and forty miles east of here. They'll be staying at Billie MacDougal's parents' hotel, along with some other invited guests. We don't have their names yet, but that information

71

should be here by the time we get up there. I'll make reservations at another hotel for us. We all need to be there except team four and Higgins. I need you guys down here, keeping an eye on the team members, their houses, and their families.

"The assumption is they're bringing in more people as team members. I'll let you know as soon as I find out more information. Each team is assigned their subjects. Let's get to it, people," Carver said as the groups broke up.

10

L t. Danny MacDougal stopped under the porch of the Mortenson house. After pulling the hood of his raincoat off his head, he rang the doorbell.

Melissa Mortenson opened the door with a big smile to greet Danny. "Come on in, Danny. Thanks for coming," she said as she took Danny's coat.

"Happy to do so, Melissa. You sounded concerned," Danny responded.

"Well, it may be nothing, but I thought I would ask you about it. Please, come in."

After sitting down, he crossed his legs. "How can I help?"

"I'm a little worried. Just about three months ago I got an email from Rosie saying she had to go back to Mexico City to be with family for an emergency. She said she was thinking about retiring and staying there."

"Had she talked to you about retiring before?" Danny asked.

Melissa leaned forward. "We had talked about it, but she wanted to work until she was at least sixty. I told her she could stay as long as she wanted."

"She was in her early fifties, wasn't she?"

"Fifty-two to be exact," Melissa responded.

"Was the pull to her family that strong?" Danny asked.

"She used to send money to help out her mother and sister. After she became a US citizen, she told them when she retired, she wouldn't be able to send money anymore, as she wouldn't be able to afford it. She was saving for her retirement in Florida."

"Did she have any children?" Danny asked.

"Yes, two boys. That's where I started to get worried. She only took three trips back to Mexico after getting her citizenship, and would only stay for about a week at a time in the winter. She didn't like going back there. She wanted to move to Florida to live with her sons," Melissa said with a furrowed brow.

"Did she say she was going to get back with you in the email?"

"No. That's why I'm worried. She would always keep in touch with us. I wasn't too concerned until her oldest son emailed me yesterday asking if I had heard from his mother."

"Has she left in a hurry before?" Danny asked.

"No, first time she's done that. I wasn't too worried until I got the email from Roberto."

"What about personal property? Did she leave anything behind that she would have normally taken with her?"

"Yeah, one thing she always took with her. We got her a portable DVD player for her last birthday. She'd watch old movies in her spare time. It's still in the pantry where she kept it."

"Was she on social media?"

"Yes, she had a Facebook account. I looked on it after I got Roberto's email. She hasn't posted anything since she left," Melissa responded.

Danny handed her his business card. "Could you please forward her emails to me? Also, her Facebook page?"

"Of course," she replied.

"Was she married or was there a man in the picture?"

"No, her husband abandoned her and the boys when they were just toddlers. Rosie never talked about him other than to say he left," Melissa said.

"Is there anything else you can think of? Something out of place, something unusual? Anything at all?" Danny queried her.

Melissa looked to her side. "Maybe. I found a button on the floor by the front door," she replied.

"Do you still have it?"

Melissa spoke as she stood. "I put it in the junk drawer. I thought maybe it fell off someone's coat or sweater," she responded as she stepped toward the kitchen.

After she retrieved it from the drawer, she walked back over to Danny. "Here it is," she said as she handed him the button.

Danny looked at the large button as he rolled it over. There were remnants of the thread still left on it. "This is a military button, Melissa," he announced.

"What makes you think that?"

It's OD in color and shaped like all the buttons they use."

"OD?" Melissa said curiously.

"Olive Drab. It's a military color. Where did you find it?"

Melissa walked to the front door, pointing to the baseboard. "It was right there next to the baseboard, behind the floor vent."

Danny bent down, looking closely at the area. "Melissa, where did Rosie usually enter the house?"

"Right here at the front door."

Danny slowly ran his right hand, palm down, over the carpet around the area by the vent and front door. After removing the vent register, he pulled his pocket flashlight out, shining it down into the duct. He reached down with his fingers, removing a small half-moon shaped object from inside.

"Did you find anything?" Melissa asked.

"Yeah, a small piece of plastic. Probably nothing, but I'll have the guys at the lab look at it. Do you have a couple of sandwich bags I can have?"

Yes, I'll get them for you," Melissa said as she walked to the kitchen.

Danny stood as he looked at the button and the small half-moon object. He didn't want to alarm Melissa, but he was positive the object was a piece of a fingernail.

Melissa handed him the sandwich bags. "Here you go."

Danny placed the objects into the bags, then put them into his shirt pocket. "Did you vacuum the area around here?" he asked.

"Yes, that's how I saw the button. It was hard to see because of the color of the carpet. Pure luck I saw it," she responded.

"You didn't empty the vacuum, did you?" Danny asked.

"Yes, every time I use it."

"Has your garbage been picked up since you threw it out?"

"Oh, yeah, that happened weeks ago," Melissa stated.

"Okay. Well, I'll take these down to the lab and get them analyzed. I'll let you know if we find anything out, Melissa."

"I appreciate it Danny. Sorry to bother you with this. Guess I'm getting a little paranoid in my old age," she replied.

"Nah, you're just observant. I need to get going, Melissa. I'm meeting Billie for lunch," he stated.

Melissa handed him his raincoat as she responded, "And thanks again for the wonderful dinner. It was a very special evening, Danny," she said as she hugged him.

"Any time. Like Billie said, you're family. We'll do it again soon."

Danny opened the door, stepping outside. He lifted the hood up over his head as he spoke. "Thank you. I'll take a deep look into Rosie."

"Thanks, Danny. Give Billie my love," Melissa said as she hugged him.

"Will do," he said before turning to walk to his car.

Danny's jaw set as his mind was running a thousand miles an hour. *Had Rosie been intercepted by the Ballencourt Security people if they went through the house? Had Garcetti or Franks gotten to Rosie?* "Will this Ballencourt crap ever go away?" he murmured as he opened the car door.

———

Billie entered Jake's Bar and Grill to see Danny seated at one of the booths. She waved toward Jake as she stepped over to join Danny.

Dressed in civilian clothes, wearing a raincoat, Billie stopped in front of the booth. "What did Melissa want?" she said as she hung her coat on the hook next to the booth.

Before Danny could respond, Jake stopped next to them. "What can I get for you guys?"

"Fish and chips with a Coke for me, Jake," Billie said.

Danny looked up at him. "That sounds good, Jake. Make that two," he stated.

"Comin' up."

As Jake walked away, Danny turned toward Billie. "She hasn't heard from Rosie for three months. Melissa said she sent an email to her saying she was going back to Mexico City and wanted to retire. Here, check out her email," Danny said as he passed his phone to Billie.

Billie scrolled through the email, then looked at Danny. "Just like that she leaves. Doesn't sound like something anyone would do, especially someone who worked for the Mortensons," Billie mused.

Danny pulled the sandwich bags from his pocket. "Melissa found this button by the front door. I found the other object in the floor vent," he said as he held out the bags.

"This is from a tactical vest," she said as she looked at the button. "The lab might be able to get DNA from the threads."

"Yup. But if I can find the vest, the lab can match it to the threads," Danny stated.

With a surprised look, Billie's eyes opened wide. "Danny, this is a fingernail."

"I know. I didn't tell Melissa that's what it was. I didn't want her to worry or speculate."

"You might be able to make a case if there's DNA on the threads or from the fingernail," Billie stated.

As they were talking, Jake brought them their meals. "There you go, you guys," he said as he set the food and drinks on the table.

"Thanks, Jake," Billie said with a smile.

After Jake left, Danny responded, "I know. Without a body, it'd be tough. Doable, but tough," Danny responded.

"But you know what you have to do, right?" Billie asked.

"Yes. I need a trip to the evidence room," he said with raised eyebrows.

Billie raised her eyebrows up and down as she looked at him. "Great minds think alike. Do you need a hand checking all the vests from Orcas Island?"

"No, but thanks anyway. You're tied up with your own work. Besides, we need to get ready for the trip up to Leavenworth tomorrow," Danny reminded her.

"Yeah, Mom and Dad are excited to see us," Billie said with a grin.

"Your sister and brothers too. We haven't seen them since the wedding," Danny responded.

"My brothers, yes. My sister just wants to see you. She thinks you're hubba-hubba, Lieutenant," Billie said with a broad smile.

"Well, she is kinda pretty, but I'm already taken," Danny responded.

"Oh really. Who got their hooks in you?"

"I got my eyes on this blonde bodybuilder in the department. She's way hot, and smart as well. She also does this hip bump thing to me whenever she's flirting. She makes my knees weak when I'm around her."

"Wow, she sounds amazing, Danny," Billie said as she placed the napkin on the plate.

Danny placed twenty dollars on the table as he stood. "She is," Danny said as they both walked to the exit.

As they waved at Jake, Billie swung her hip toward Danny, bumping him on his right hip.

"You better stop that, unless you want to embarrass the citizenry right here in Pike Place Market," he said.

"Nah, let's wait to embarrass the citizenry of Leavenworth," Billie responded with a laugh as she hugged Danny from the side.

Auguste Marchand answered his cellphone as he sat in the café Milano drinking a latte. "Yes?"

"Sir, this is Daniel from Landon Automotive. We just picked up Mr. Black's rental car from the Seattle impound lot."

Marchand sat up erect as he heard the news. "How were you made aware of the vehicle's location?"

"We received a call from the impound lot," Landon responded.

"Were the options in the vehicle, Mr. Landon?"

"No, sir, the vehicle was empty."

"I see." After a long silence, Marchand replied. "Were there any charges applied to the vehicle?"

"No, sir. It was turned in as a suspicious vehicle by one of the residents where it was left. We believe the options were removed prior to the impound."

"Very well. Charge the company for any fines, fees, or equipment loss you incurred. In addition, I'll need a rental car for Seattle. Plan for pickup at the airport in three days. If at all possible, I'll need the same vehicle Mr. Black rented. Is that possible?" Marchand asked.

"Of course, sir. We'll have it cleaned and serviced for you."

"Not necessary. Leave it in the condition it was delivered to you. I do *not* want it touched. I'll pick it up from the airport in three days," Marchand ordered.

"Very well, sir. The car will be ready when you arrive. Additionally, keep me advised if further questions are asked regarding the vehicle."

"I will. Thank you, sir."

Marchand terminated the call as he stood. He placed ten dollars on the table, then walked from the restaurant. Once outside, he dialed a number on his phone.

After three rings, a voice responded on the other end. "Yes?"

"I need you in Seattle. I'll be accompanying you, so make reservations for us to leave this coming Tuesday," Marchand ordered.

"Is this a package delivery, sir?"

"No, reconnaissance only. I'll brief you while we're enroute to Seattle."

"Yes, sir, I'll make the reservations immediately."

Marchand terminated the call as he stepped into a taxi.

11

anny and Billie turned onto the hotel driveway off North Road, one mile southeast of Leavenworth. As they were pulling up to the Alpine Haus Hotel, Danny's eyes opened wide.

"Wow, it looks just like it was picked up from Bavaria and dropped down here. This is really cool," he said with surprise.

The couple exited the car, standing next to each other as they looked at the hotel.

"The original lodge only had ten small rooms, built by my grandfather in the fifties," Billie responded as she pointed to the entrance. "It was just that small section where the lobby is."

"So your grandfather started out here?" Danny asked.

"My great grandfather immigrated here from Germany to work in the sawmills. When the logging and mining stopped, the town slowly started to die. Just a few of the residents stayed, my great grandfather being one of them.

"The residents had a vision to turn the place into a tourist destination to jumpstart the economy. It took them until the early 1960's to get the plan put together and to find the funding needed. They turned the whole town into a Bavarian Village to draw in tourists. The plan worked, cause this is the second most popular tourist destination in Washington after Seattle," she said proudly.

As they were holding hands looking at the hotel, Karl and Marva exited the hotel's main entrance followed by a pair of St. Bernard dogs. The dogs ran to Billie as soon as they saw her.

She knelt down hugging the two dogs as they excitedly licked her face. "Meet Hansel and Gretel, the hotel's mascots," she said with a big smile.

Danny held his hand out toward the dogs, receiving welcoming licks filled with drool. He petted them on their backs as they pushed against him.

Marva stopped in front of Danny, giving him a big hug and a kiss on his cheek.

Karl smiled broadly at his son-in-law. "Welcome to Leavenworth, Danny," he said as he shook Danny's hand.

"You have a beautiful place here, Karl," Danny said, while admiring the structure.

"Thanks. It's been a long journey, but we finally got it finished," Karl responded.

Karl and Marva kissed their daughter as Danny pulled the luggage from the car.

Karl grabbed two of the suitcases from Danny. "Come on, let's get you two inside. I'll give you the nickel tour."

Danny followed Karl and Marva into the hotel as Billie walked beside him, holding his arm.

As they entered the front entrance, Danny saw a massive stone fireplace at the far end of the lobby. He stood still as he stared up, looking at the massive exposed beams of the vaulted ceiling.

"I just may stay here after the weekend," he said with a grin.

Danny followed Karl into the office. They placed the suitcases against the wall, walking down the hallway to the restaurant. As they entered the eating area, Danny saw Billie hugging her brothers and sister.

Gunter and Hans stepped toward Danny as they entered the restaurant. They each greeted him with a handshake and a smile.

"Where's Jade, Brenda, and the kids?" Danny asked.

"They all went to Denver to see Brenda's family. They won't be back until next week," Gunter responded.

The thirty-one-year-old stunningly beautiful Astrid ran to Danny, giving him a big hug. Danny glanced over her shoulder at Billie with a questioning look as her sister held onto him tightly.

Billie laughed as she watched Danny's captivity unfold. "Come on, Astrid, let him breathe."

Astrid let go of Danny, kissing him on the cheek. "Come on, Billie, we miss you guys," she said with a smile.

"Okay, everyone, let's have lunch," Marva said with raised and open arms.

They all sat down as Marva walked around the table kissing her family members. "Thank you for this," she said as she hugged each one of her family.

Billie was beaming as she looked around the table. "It's good to be home," she said as she squeezed Danny's hand under the table.

"Okay, the buffet is full of all kinds of goodies, so help yourselves," Marva announced.

Danny's cellphone rang as he and Billie were sitting in their room. He sat up erect and answered the call. "Yeah, Rick, you here?"

"We're just pulling into town. The GPS shows we're only about a mile from you."

"Are the rest following you?" Danny asked.

"Yeah. The captain along with his friends are in the car with me. Larry is behind us, driving the van with the rest of the team."

"Thanks, Rick. We'll meet you in front of the hotel," Danny said as he terminated the call.

"They're here," Danny said to Billie as they stood to walk out of their room.

Once at the bottom of the stairs in the lobby, Danny looked over to the hotel desk, addressing Gunter. "The guests are here."

"Their rooms are ready, Danny. I'll take care of the luggage."

"Thanks, Gunter. I'll give you a hand," Danny replied as they exited the hotel.

They both watched as the black Cadillac limousine pulled up in front of the hotel, with the white passenger van following. The doors of the vehicles opened and all of the guests began getting out into the midday sun.

Capt. Graves started introducing his friends to the team. The five friends of Graves were all dressed in business attire, looking out of place in the mountain town of Leavenworth.

Once the introductions were complete, Graves turned to Danny and Billie. "Can we all meet in the conference room to get things started?"

"Of course," Billie replied.

Billie led the group into the lobby of the hotel, then down the hall to the conference room. Once in the room, she closed and locked the double doors.

After everyone took a seat at the conference table, Billie stood next to her seat. "On behalf of the Eck family, we'd like to welcome you to the Alpine Haus. Your luggage will be placed in your rooms. Your room keys are in the envelopes with your names on them. For security reasons, your rooms will not be entered by the cleaning staff unless you're there or have requested it," she said after pointing to the stack of envelopes on the table.

As Billie was speaking, Danny was walking around the room placing laptop computers in front of the five new people.

"The laptop computers have been loaded with the file and are for your use while you're here at the hotel," Billie stated. "If you need anything, please contact either Danny or me. No one outside of this room is aware of what this weekend is all about. My family, the employees, the hotel guests have no clue about these proceedings. There are only eight guests at the hotel, all of whom have been strategically placed at the west end of the first floor, so there should be no interaction with them other than at the restaurant, the lounge, or the gym.

"At this time, we need to turn the floor over to Capt. Graves, who can fill you all in regarding the agenda for the weekend," Billie said as she took a seat next to Danny.

Graves stood, looking at the occupants of the room with a half-smile. "I wish we could have met under better circumstances. It would have been nice to gather together and enjoy this beautiful setting rather than the weighty subject you've been brought here for.

"First, let me go around the room with formal introductions. To my immediate left is Sgt. Billie MacDougal, Government Liaison Officer for SPD. Next to her is Lt. Danny MacDougal, Chief of Detectives for the Central Precinct—and Billie MacDougal's husband.

"Next to them is Mr. Garrett Winters, Director and Pastor of the Rescue Mission, Seattle, a retired Army Delta Force Operative.

"To his left is Walter Killian, SPD Information Security and former Delta Force member.

"Left of Walt are Detectives Rick Barker, and Larry Colton of the SPD, former Army Special Forces and Marine Corp Sniper respectively.

"Next to them is Retired Navy Captain Bradley Forester, retired Deputy Director of Operations for the Defense Intelligence Agency (DIA).

"Immediately to his left is retired Navy Commander, Quinn Masterson, Naval Intelligence.

"Next is Dr. Glenn Packer, retired Operations Chief for the Central Intelligence Agency.

"Then, arguably the most intelligent of the group," Graves said with a smile, "Dr. Wanda Hale, former analyst and programmer for the National Reconnaissance Office.

"Finally, the only one of my former colleagues who's not retired, Ellis Hollabird, owner of Apex Industries, a government contractor specializing in communications.

"I briefed my five friends about the file on our way up here. Obviously, it was a condensed review, but enough to give them a heads up as to what's happening. With the exception of my five colleagues, has everyone read the file in its entirety?"

The Seattle team all nodded in acknowledgement.

"As it will take quite some time for them to complete reading the file, we need to meet back here again late Sunday afternoon. Are there any questions?"

Fifty-nine-year-old Ellis Hollabird responded while picking up a heavy bag from the floor, placing it on the table. "Mr. Killian, Mike told me you needed a portable computer for the task—something that was fast with a lot of storage." He opened the bag, pulling out a large portable computer.

"This started life as a Mega Pac L3 portable laptop. We've supercharged it. Only the military has this technology, so be extremely careful with it—it costs over thirty thousand dollars," Hollabird announced with raised eyebrows.

Walt stood and retrieved the computer with excitement in his eyes. "I'll take good care of it, sir," Walt said excitedly.

"If you're as good as Mike says you are, it'll be needed," he responded.

"Thanks, Ellis," Graves responded.

"The restaurant is first class, I'm told. The gym is also first rate, not to mention the setting is gorgeous. So, no excuses for not completing our tasks. Now, if there are no additional questions or comments, let's retire to our rooms and get to work," Graves said as the guests stood to leave.

The 59-year-old African American, Quinn Masterson, placed his right hand on Danny's shoulder as they were walking out of the conference room. "I'm told we have you to thank for the comfortable ride up here in the limousine."

"You're welcome, but I'm not the one to thank. It's a seized vehicle from the SPD Narcotics Division. The owner is in prison doing life for murder," Danny said with a grin.

Masterson laughed loudly as they walked into the hallway.

The sun was getting lower as Danny and Billie walked down the main street of Leavenworth. The smell of the evergreen and pine trees was strong in the air as they took in the beauty of the town.

"Man, it's pretty up here. I could get used to this," Danny said as his eyes scanned the street.

"Oh, Danny, you should see it at Christmas," Billie said excitedly. "The whole town is lit up with Christmas lights and decorations. Dad has the hotel decorated with lights everywhere. They have seven-foot-tall toy soldiers all around the hotel. They always pick out a fifteen-foot tree for the lobby. All the trees on the grounds are decorated. It's magical."

Billie wrapped both her arms around Danny's right arm. "Can we come up here for Christmas, Danny? Please."

Danny held his hands out palms up as he moved them up and down opposite of the other. "Gee, I don't know. Let me think about that. I could sit in Sean and Marylyn's pub, drinking myself into a stupor while listening to Christmas songs sung off key by drunken patrons. Or, come up here to be in paradise with my wife. Wow, tough call," he said with a look of indecision. Danny kissed Billie on the cheek. "I'll go with door number two."

Billie moved her hip sideways, bumping Danny on the right hip. "Good choice, MacDougal."

"You know, as pretty as it is up here, I imagine it would have been boring as hell for a kid. Nothing to do but get into trouble," Danny quipped.

Billie laughed before responding, "Not for the Eck family. That whole German work ethic thing was brutal. I was too busy with homework and my job at the hotel. The only relaxing was the occasional break for skiing."

"So, the town was settled by Germans?" Danny asked.

"No, my great grandfather was the only German in the whole town. It was settled by lumberjacks, miners, and railroaders from all around the country. They decided to transform it into a Bavarian Village because of the valley and the mountains around it. The whole area looks like Bavaria," she replied.

Danny's head tilted to the side. "Hey, how come your whole family has German names but you? Where the hell did you get the name Billie from? I mean, you have Karl, Marva, Astrid, Gunter, and Hans. Even the dogs have German names. How'd that happen?"

"I'm named after my great grandfather, at his request. He told Dad he wanted them to name their first born after him. Mom and Dad didn't want me growing up with the name Wilhelm, so they shortened it to Billie," she said with a smile.

"Well, ask a stupid question," Danny replied with a laugh.

Billie steered Danny into the coffee shop. "Come on, I want you to meet my best friend growing up."

The owner of the Kaffee Klatch looked up to see Billie entering the shop with Danny. She ran around the counter embracing Billie with excitement.

After they hugged, Billie held her hand out toward Danny. "Sharon, I want you to meet my husband, Danny MacDougal."

Sharon held Danny's right hand in both her hands. "I'm glad to meet you. I'm so glad she found you, Danny. I can see by the look on her face you've made her very happy."

"Thank you," Danny said with a smile.

Sharon turned toward Billie. "Your folks told me the wedding was huge," she said while looking at Billie.

"It was. The day was perfect," Billie responded.

Sharon spoke as she was walking back behind the counter. "Let me get you guys a coffee. What do you want?"

"Lattes for two, please," Billie stated.

"Sharon and I grew up together. Her parents have a hardware store here in town," Billie stated.

"Are you coming up for Christmas this year?" Sharon asked.

"Yes. We'll be here."

As Sharon handed them the lattes, Danny held out some cash. "No, on me," she replied.

"Thank you, Sharon. It was so good to see you. We'll stop by again before we leave," Billie announced.

As they went out the door, Danny took a sip of his latte. Once outside, he spoke softly. "You grew up with her?"

"Yeah, we went to school together. Why do you ask?"

Danny's eyebrows rose. "She just looks a whole lot older than you," he said as his head tilted to the side.

"Danny MacDougal, you just keep on saying things to make me love you even more," she said as she bumped her hip against his.

12

Barnes' ear-piercing screams filled the warehouse room as Danny shoved the dagger deep into his knee.

Danny bolted upright in bed, beads of sweat rolling down his face. His body was trembling as he tried to catch his breath.

Billie reached out, placing her hand on his leg. "Are you okay, baby?"

Danny didn't answer as he got out of bed. He pulled on his t-shirt, then opened the bar fridge, pulling out a bottle of water. Opening the container, he quickly downed half of the contents.

He pulled on his sweat pants and put on his flip-flops. Danny grabbed his hoodie, then stepped next to the bed. He bent down and kissed Billie on the forehead. "I'm gonna get some fresh air."

Billie sat up in bed as she watched Danny exit the room.

He walked down the stairs into the lobby. As he passed the desk, he nodded toward Hans, who was standing behind the counter. After exiting through the front doors, he turned to the right, walking down the wooden deck.

Danny stopped midway and leaned on the wooden handrail. He downed the rest of the water, then sighed heavily as he stared at the full moon in the sky.

"Having a hard night, Danny?" the voice back in the darkness asked.

Startled, Danny's head snapped to the right to see Reverend Winters leaning against the wall in the shadows. "You just scared the hell out of me, Gary. You're lucky I left my pistol in the room," he said with a grunt.

Winters stepped next to Danny. "That wouldn't have been a problem, son. Absent from the body—present with the Lord."

"Is there nothing for which you don't have a bible passage stuffed in your memory banks?" Danny asked.

"Nope. Tools for the job." Winters turned toward Danny. "What's eating at you, son?"

With his head hung down, Danny responded, "Nothing."

"Lt. MacDougal, you ought to know by now that you can't spread horse manure at my feet. I wasn't always this gentle, calm, sweet talking pastor you see before you now. Something is eating at you. It's written all over your face. Do you want to talk about it, or do I have to badger you while I'm sitting on your chest?"

Danny took in a deep breath, then chuckled as he exhaled. "What is it that keeps me from going off on you?"

"My cherub-like demeanor," Winters said, while continuing to stare Danny down.

"Gary, I just need space to get past some lingering issues with the Ballencourt case."

"Danny, when the mind suffers, the body cries out. You got something on your mind that has the potential to eat you alive from the inside out. It's written all over your face."

"Okay, okay, we'll talk. Just let me get through the weekend, then I promise we'll talk. I need to be on my game for tomorrow. Happy?"

"Alright, just for the weekend. But I'm holding you to it when we get back to the city. Now get back to your room and be with your wife."

Danny snapped to attention, saluting Winters. "Yes, sir," he said with a smile as he turned to walk away.

Danny and Billie sat in the restaurant across from each other as they ate the morning meal. Billie kept glancing at Danny as they ate. She was concerned, but didn't want to crowd him. She knew if the situation were reversed, she would want space to think as well. She had a becoming smile as she reached across the table holding his hand.

Astrid came up to the table and poured more coffee for the two of them. "Oh, you guys, get a room, will you? Isn't the honeymoon ever gonna end?" she said with a chuckle.

"Nope," they both replied in unison.

As she walked away, Capt. Graves approached the table. "Mind if I join you guys?" he asked.

"Of course not. Please, have a seat," Billie replied.

"Well, Billie, my hats off to you," Graves said as he sat down. "This was a great idea. The place is quiet, secluded, and stunningly beautiful. I slept like a log last night. Please thank your parents again for me."

"I will. It's a special place," she replied.

As they were talking, the three of them noticed Walt Killian enter the restaurant. He hurriedly gathered food into a to-go container and paid the cashier. He was almost at a run as he left the room.

"Wow, looks like Walt is enthralled with his new toy," Graves stated.

Danny chuckled at the observation. "Looks like Winters made a good choice in Walt."

"Have you seen any of your friends since last night?" Billie asked.

"Nope. Unless I miss my guess, we won't see them until later Sunday for the roundtable. I know these guys, they're like bulldogs. They won't let go until they're finished. Anal doesn't even begin to describe these guys."

"Captain, how do you know them?" Billie asked.

"We were all in the first gulf war together. Straight out of the farm."

"The farm?" Billie asked.

"The CIA. We were all assigned to an outpost in Iraq together. After we got back, we all went in separate directions with other agencies. Except Glenn—he stayed with the CIA."

"Sounds like you were all pretty tight," Danny stated.

"Yeah, we formed a pretty solid bond. Seems like it was just yesterday. That was thirty years ago." Graves shook his head slowly. "Where the hell does the time go?" he said softly.

Billie chuckled as she responded. "Yeah, Dad still lives in the sixties. He wishes we could go back to it."

"For me, it was the eighties. I was in college, thinking the world was my oyster. The economy was great, the government was smaller, and we believed anything was possible. That all changed in the nineties. We've been going downhill since." Graves took a sip from his coffee before continuing. "In many ways, I envy your parents, Billie. They had a wonderful life laid out for them by their parents. They've had long life, filled with great memories, thanks to the ethics instilled by their family. I truly envy them."

Danny leaned forward with his elbows on the table. "Everything good about me is as a result of my grandparents. They came to this country without a dime in their pocket, building a good life for themselves." He looked at Graves as he spoke. "The sixties destroyed my parents. Drugs, free love, and a lack of morals put them on a path of decline they had no hope of getting out from underneath. I suppose that's why I hate drugs so much to this day. It robbed me of a life with them."

Before continuing, Danny smiled. "That said, I now have a wonderful life. For the first time, I'm truly happy. I have a reason to get up in the morning," he said while winking at Billie.

Billie squeezed his hand as she stood. "Come on, I need to pick up some stuff at the store."

As Danny pushed the chair under the table, he looked toward Graves. "Thanks, boss. We'll see you later."

Danny and Billie walked out of the restaurant toward the lobby. As they passed the desk, they both saw Billie's father. Karl nodded toward them as they exited the hotel.

Once outside, they stopped on the deck. "Man, it sure is beautiful up here. I could live in this town for the rest of my life," Danny said as he stared at the valley.

"Danny, we could do both if you want," Billie responded.

"What do you mean." Danny replied.

"We could spend time at the house on Orcas, then come up here. The house is almost completely repaired up on the island. We could spend our time at both places if you want," Billie stated.

"Are you saying you're ready to throw in the towel with the PD?" Danny queried.

Billie sat at one of the chairs on the hotel deck. She looked at Danny as he took the seat next to her.

"I wanted to leave Leavenworth to get out into the world to make my mark when I was young. I've always been pretty independent. I gathered a bunch of trophies in my sport; I was at the top of my game. I married someone who was also a competitor. The match seemed like it was made in heaven.

"As I was walking down the aisle to get married, I remember thinking something just wasn't right. I went through with it anyway. I thought it was just the jitters. Turns out my instincts were correct. The only person Max Hardesty was in love with was himself. When I found out he was sleeping with every woman who smiled at him, I left as quick as I could. I had a few relationships over the years after the marriage, but none of them were right.

"I needed a new direction in my life, so I hired on with the PD. I set out to become the best cop I could. I put up a wall around myself ten feet tall. It took a stubborn but determined Scotsman to tear it down.

"Now, after all these years, none of my past dreams or goals seem important. I have someone who truly loves me, someone who makes me feel whole. I want to look into those baby blues every morning when I get up and again when I go to sleep," she said while holding his hand.

Danny grinned as he looked at his wife. "There's an old saying. 'When one leaves home to set the world on fire, they often return home for more matches.'

"If you want to come back home, I'm on board with it. We make decisions together, as a team. Truth is, I've been thinking about it since Winters and Graves told us to bail once we launch the plan we've been putting together. I can retire anytime now. I'll only get about seventy-five to eighty percent of my retirement, but it'll be enough to keep us afloat with what we both have in savings."

"I could cash out my retirement, Danny. Between the two of us, we could come up here with over three-hundred thousand."

"We could open a restaurant, a gym, or both, if you're serious. We could make this happen, baby, if that's what you *truly* want," Danny said.

Billie got up and sat in Danny's lap. "You've made me the happiest girl on the planet, Danny." She kissed him passionately. "We can do it as soon as the operation is put into action. We'll use up our vacation time after we kick it off, then go back down and put it all together."

"Then I can spend the rest of my life looking into *those* baby blues," Danny said.

Lying in the prone position, Monica Meyer looked through the riflescope at the MacDougals. Hidden from view by the thick trees, she heard a voice speaking into her earpiece.

"Unit three, status?" Carver asked.

"Quiet, nothing to report. I have eyes on the two primaries," she responded.

"Where are they?"

"Sitting together on the front deck of the hotel."

"Report if they leave the property," Carver stated.

"Copy," Meyer responded.

Three C-130s were strategically parked and chocked in front of the newly renovated hangar. The aircraft retained their overall white paint job, with newly applied tail art. On the large vertical stabilizer, a brown silhouette of a Texas Longhorn was displayed.

Under the longhorn silhouette, the words *Choice Texas Beef* was prominently displayed. The rear cargo doors for all three aircraft were open, readying the planes for loading.

Gordon Johnson was leaning against the side of his Mercedes G Wagon with his hands in his pants pockets. The afternoon sun was blocked from hitting his face by his wide-brimmed straw cowboy hat.

He stood from the vehicle, taking his hands out of his pockets as two tractor-trailer trucks entered the property through the nine-foot chain-link gate. The forty-foot containers were painted a rust brown color, with a large white asterisk painted on each side.

The trucks drove around the hangar, pulling up next to the building's west side. As the airbrakes hissed, the drivers stepped down from the cabs.

"Any problems?" Johnson asked the drivers.

"No, sir," they both replied.

"Good. Make sure Johnny checks all the cargo before they're fed. The other product will be off-loaded after the human cargo," Johnson ordered.

The high-pitched squeaks from the cargo doors being opened filled the area around the hangar. Three of the ranch employees jumped into the containers and began handing the children down to workers on the ground.

All of the children appeared to be under the age of ten and were dressed in torn and dirty clothes. Many of the Asian children didn't have shoes on their feet. Johnson watched as they were taken into the hangar.

The last child stepped to the edge of the container, looking down at the ground with tears in her eyes. Johnson looked up to see the Caucasian girl in her mid-teens, frightened and trembling.

Johnson stepped to the rear of the container as she was lowered to the ground. "Bring her here," he ordered.

The young girl was led to Johnson by her left arm. As she stopped in front of him, he looked her over. The attractive teenage girl was five-foot-seven, with blonde hair and an innocent face.

Johnson spoke, as he looked her over. "Large breasts, wide hips, in her prime for child bearing. Have Johnny look her over first, then take her to the ranch," he ordered.

"Mr. Johnson!" one of the workers in the container said loudly.

Johnson stepped to the open doors. "Yes?"

"We lost two," the man advised as his open right hand pointed to the two small bodies.

With an emotionless face Johnson replied. "Get the backhoe and take care of it. Make sure it's done far away from the property."

"Yes, sir," the man responded.

Johnson walked inside the hangar to see the one hundred fifty children being looked at by his employees. The terrified children were crying as the men stood around them.

Johnson turned to see the aircrews walking up to him. He looked at his watch before speaking. "We only need two of the planes for this shipment. Make sure we have three more aircraft for tomorrow's arrivals. We'll have four trucks coming in."

Johnson's chief pilot, Jerry Branson, responded, "I'll have the other planes here by nightfall."

"Good—wheels up in two hours, Jerry," Johnson ordered.

"Yes, sir," he replied.

13

The conference room was uncomfortably quiet as the twelve people looked around at each other with blank stares. Each of the attendees was dressed in ultracasual clothing, consisting mostly of jogging suits, hoodies, and tennis shoes. Danny locked the door, then sat next to Billie.

Everyone had loaded their plates with finger food, fruits and vegetables, waiting for Graves to open the meeting. With all parties present, he called the room to order.

"Well, with having two days to review the file, knowing each of you like I do, I'll turn it over to you for questions, comments, or ideas, as I know you have plenty of each," Graves stated.

The fifty-nine-year-old Quinn Masterson leaned back in his seat. "Well, it was certainly entertaining, I'll give you that."

Danny's back stiffened as his lips pursed. "Entertaining? Did you read it?" he snapped back.

"Every last word, Lieutenant. Watched all the videos as well," the African American man said with surprising calmness in his voice.

Graves' eyes rolled as he listened to his friend and former colleague. "Quinn, a little more warm and fuzzy please," Graves chided.

"Lieutenant, I'm here at this meeting for only one reason." Masterson pointed across the table at Graves while still looking at Danny. "I owe that man my life. Had I known fully what this was all about, I might not have come."

Billie leaned forward in her seat. "Mr. Masterson, please help me to understand. The first time I read that file, I wanted to go on a killing spree in Washington DC. Yet you take it as much ado about nothing."

Masterson turned to face Billie. "Mrs. MacDougal, I got enraged thirty-five years ago when I first found out about it too. The only difference between you now, and me back then, is you have documents, records, and video to back up what the file says. The only thing that *has* changed are the faces of the players.

"It's still the same old garbage. Man's inhumanity to man. Sin so immense you can't wrap your head around it. We took out a lot of them covertly back in the day. Seized their bank accounts, locked a lot of them up, thought we were making progress. Now, fast forward thirty-five years later and there's literally thousands more of them; they never go away."

Graves leaned in toward Masterson. "Quinn, what in the hell has happened to you?"

"I'm just tired, Mike. Like every other one of my friends here, I retired to spend my last few years with my wife, children, and grandchildren. Getting spooled up over this does me no good."

Masterson leaned forward, rubbing his face with his hands. "I'm not a robot, Mike. When I see people like that asshole Senator Gibbs or that useless bitch of a Congresswoman Alberts, molesting little girls and boys I want to throw up." Masterson's voice was getting angrier as he spoke. "These sick bastards have been doing this ever since the union was formed. The only difference is now they flaunt it. They throw it up in our damned faces.

"Every one of us who came here to this meeting knows all about this. We've known about it for decades. Tell him, Wanda," Masterson said as he pointed to the former National Recognizance Office (NRO) Deputy Director.

The bookish looking sixty-year-old Wanda Hale leaned to one side of her chair as she sipped at her coffee. "Lieutenant, Quinn's correct. All of us have known about this for years. It's one of the poorest kept secrets in Washington. We just haven't had the documentation or, quite frankly the juice to do anything about it. Now, all that we've ever needed to be able to throw a net over it is handed to us, but we're too old, too tired and too soft to act on it. I turned sixty this year. My joints creek, my bones ache, and my butt's gotten too big."

Wanda leaned in toward them. "Danny—if I can call you Danny?"

"Of course." Danny nodded.

"We're not cowards. There's not a one of us here who'd run from a fight. I don't speak for the others, but I'll help you in any way I can. I won't be on the front lines, but I'll be *in the rear with the gear*, as they say," Hale said with certainty.

Brad Forester, the former Deputy Director of the Defense Intelligence Agency (DIA), sat up in his seat. "Mike; Glenn, Ellis, and I already spoke about it this afternoon. We're in, just like Wanda. We can't be boots on the ground, but we'll be covering your back."

"Okay then. What about you?" Graves said to Quinn.

"I need to listen to all of your team, Mike, before I commit. Let's hear your plan," Masterson stated.

Graves looked at Danny. "The floor's all yours, Danny."

Danny opened the laptop in front of him. "If you would all scroll down to page 923 in the file, I'll show you our intentions."

As the group all got to page 923, Danny began to lay out their plan. "We have the names of all the people who are being blackmailed in the United States. Democrat, Republican, Independent, Socialist, even Communist. There are corresponding videos of them in compromising positions. Taking bribes, drug trafficking, sexually assaulting minor children, treason. Literally sixty to seventy percent of the house and senate are compromised.

"Our plan is to have Walt send them electronic copies of their activities; videos, records, etc. They'll be told to leave office, retire, quit, or just go away. They'll be given forty-eight-hours to leave.

"The file also contains people in the news media, Hollywood, and some of the largest corporations in the US. If there's anyone in this country who can influence an election, sway public opinion, or have an impact on society to benefit the Globalists, there's damning material there.

"Although we haven't been able to confirm it, we believe there are a total of ten such master files throughout the country, one in each of the ten regions. We were able to get ahold of the master file for region ten from a patriot who gave up his life, along with three of his friends, and two people from the Seattle Police Department to preserve it.

"Initially, we used the data from the file to expose their shipping routes, transportation companies, shipping and delivery points. We resurrected an old Russian mafia code to communicate with reporters and law enforcement throughout the west. Even though the code is still in place, the methods are no longer an option, as they've shut down their old methods and routes. We did a lot of damage to them at first, but they've since dialed back their operations.

"That's when we decided to push it to the next level and expose them publicly," Danny concluded his remarks.

Masterson took a bite of his croissant, then leaned in toward Danny. "And what if they don't leave office? What then, Danny? You gonna kill 'em?"

"Of course not! We have Walt put the data out to our contacts in the media. If we go around killing them, we become no better than they are." Danny closed his eyes tightly as he responded. "Killing them brings on a whole new set of issues." He opened his eyes as he addressed Quinn. "Trust me, I'm not in the mood for any more killing," Danny said with clenched teeth.

"Lieutenant, there's only about a couple dozen ways for your plan to collapse in a heap. You need to have a security team. You need a bottomless barrel of cash, a first-rate intelligence group, and a rapid response team. All that takes a butt load of cash, Danny. We all have access to people, equipment, and sources of cash. We can help, but it'll take time to set up. You can't trust anyone, Danny," Masterson said emphatically.

"The system and the agencies are so corrupted, you don't know who to trust. There are literally only six or seven agencies that *can* be remotely trusted. The street level people are the patriots. The CIA has been so compromised, it needs to be torn down and eliminated completely. Give all the files and data to military intelligence, then burn the buildings to the ground.

"The FBI needs to be completely rebuilt. Fire everyone above the second floor. Customs, Border Patrol, the DIA are the only ones who can be trusted. Eliminate the ATF, DEA, Commerce Department, three fourths of the State Department, then take the IRS apart brick by brick. Are you beginning to get the picture as to how difficult this will be? You need a hell of a team, Danny," Masterson stated.

"We have a lot of military experience in the room, Mr. Masterson, plus some of the best in law enforcement. We can put it together, and in a timely manner. Just give us the direction we need to move in. Everyone here is a dedicated professional and a patriot," Danny responded.

"Won't do you any good, Lieutenant. They'll come after you. Every one of you," Masterson said as he pointed to Danny's team.

"So, what would you have us do?" Danny asked sarcastically.

"Question is, what do you intend to do? What are you prepared to do?" Masterson stated emphatically.

"Look, Danny, your team bloodied their noses a few months back. You cost them a lot of money. You embarrassed them in front of their handlers. Quite frankly, I'm amazed you're all still alive," Masterson said with a cold stare.

"Your confidence in us is uplifting," Danny replied sarcastically.

Masterson's voice elevated as he stared Danny down. "Let me be painfully graphic so you can grasp the situation you're up against. If you launch this operation, you'll cause major damage to their Globalist machine. Your first operation just cost them a few billion dollars. No big deal, that's lunch money for them, petty cash.

"You do *this*, and it'll shut them down across the country for a long time. It'll do irreparable damage to their operation for a decade. They'll kill everyone in this room, then just for shits-n-giggles, they'll kill your family members. If you're lucky, Danny, they'll give you and your wife a heart attack. If not, they'll shoot her, then shoot you, setting it up to look like a murder suicide."

Masterson sat up erect as he became more animated. "They use master assassins, street thugs, even drug cartel enforcers to do their bidding. Lieutenant, they'll tie you down, raping your wife repeatedly, while you're forced to watch. Then they'll kill her, then carve you up with a machete!"

Billie was squirming in her seat as Masterson continued to speak.

Danny was getting angrier with every second that passed. "You asshole. Who the hell do you think you are? We've lost friends, colleagues, and all you can do is piss on their service and insult me and my wife?" Danny snarled, trying to control the rage building up inside him.

"I'm not trying to insult you," Masterson shot back. "I'm trying to give you a healthy dose of reality, Lieutenant. You're not dealing with sane people.

These individuals will bring down an airliner with two hundred innocent people onboard just to get the one passenger they want to eliminate. They've blown up fully occupied buildings to instill fear in people just to pass legislation they want enacted. Life means nothing to these people.

"I'm sorry to be so graphic, Lieutenant." He turned toward Billie. "I'm especially sorry for being so blunt, Mrs. MacDougal, but all of you need to know what you're up against."

"I can assure you, Mr. Masterson, we know what we're dealing with. We've all read the file, and we dealt with their enforcers face to face. I almost lost my wife, sir. Yeah, we know what we're up against," Danny replied snidely.

Masterson looked to the others on Danny's team. "And what about the rest of you?"

"You know I'm in," Graves responded.

Larry Colton and Rick Barker both nodded in the affirmative.

Reverend Winters looked at Masterson as he spoke. "I fall in the category you five do—I'm too old to mix it up. I'll be part of the planning stage, available to offer assistance when needed."

Walter Killian raised both his hands. "I'm all in. Have been since day one," he said with an emotionless face.

Masterson pushed the sleeves of his hoodie up past his elbows. "Okay then, let's get started."

Retired Navy Chief Corpsman Johnny Hurd stopped the Dodge Ram pickup inside the large barn on the Johnson ranch property.

He exited the truck, walking to the passenger side of the vehicle. He opened the door, grabbing the young woman by the right arm, then pulling her from the truck. The girl was bound at the wrists, her eyes covered by a mask.

Hurd walked her to the tack room, opening the door. He guided her through the door, then toward the back of the room. He reached under the saddle hanging on the wall, pulling down on the hidden latch. The door swung outward.

He turned the lights on, revealing a staircase going down into the basement of the barn. Stepping onto the landing, he closed the door. Carefully helping the young girl down the stairs, he stopped at the bottom, removing her mask.

The basement was massive, taking up the entire area underneath the property's barn. There were ten by twelve-foot cells all around the perimeter of the basement. Each cell had three concrete walls, a concrete floor and ceiling, with old style jail bars with doors at the front of the cell. All around the room were strategically placed support columns to bear the weight of the heavy concrete ceiling.

The entire basement was unbelievably clean and painted an antiseptic white, resembling a hospital room rather than a holding facility. At the back of the area, was a complete functioning hospital examination room, kitchen, and shower. Each of the cells had a full-sized bed, with throw rugs on the floor and clean linen for the beds. The enclosures looked more like hotel rooms than jail cells. Almost all of the cells were occupied by teenage girls. Some were caring for their newborn babies.

The girl trembled uncontrollably as she entered the examination area. Hurd helped her up onto the examination table. He went to the sink and began washing his hands.

After putting on a doctor's coat, he began taking the clothes off the girl. Once he had disrobed her, he led the girl to the shower on the back wall. Without speaking, he slid the curtain back, turning on the water. Once the water was at temperature, he handed the naked girl a bar of soap, and a small bottle of shampoo.

Without speaking, he let the girl see him hang a clean white towel on the hook next to the shower. He stepped next to the examination table, removing a cigarette from the pack in his pocket. He leaned against the table as he took a long drag from the smoke.

14

Masterson leaned forward with his fingers laced together and his elbows on the surface of the table.

"Most of what we know about the Cabals human trafficking operation has been learned from arrests we've made, people who've been covertly placed inside trafficking rings, and from documents we've obtained.

"The vast number of the children come from the far east. They tend to be healthier, lack birth certificates, or any other documentation of their existence. Less desirable, from purely a health standpoint, are the children from Mexico or South America.

"There's also the phenomenon of Haiti. Right after the 2010 earthquake, the human traffickers descended on that place. They gobbled up thousands of children under the guise of bringing them to the developed nations for their health and safety. Most of them have never been seen again.

"The race of the child has no apparent appeal one way or the other. As the demand for young children has exploded around the world, the traffickers are getting bolder and bolder. We've seen a rise in child trafficking inside our borders the likes of which haven't occurred before.

"With the border wall continuing to go up, the number of children being brought in has dropped significantly, along the order of seventy percent.

The downside to that is we are seeing a huge increase in child kidnapping within the US.

"The most highly prized children are girls or boys in their early teenage years, especially the girls. The girls can be used as breeding stock. The boys are either prostituted out or used in satanic ritual sacrifices. The girls are confined to holding facilities, kicking out a baby every nine months, just like clockwork.

For the most part, the conditions of the places the breeding is being done in are atrocious. Conditions comparable to what common livestock are kept in. The more sophisticated and better-funded operations have facilities that are kept clean and well-staffed. The girls are treated better than the usual breeding operations which are lesser funded. The girls are checked on a regular basis and carefully monitored."

As the young girl exited the shower, Hurd stopped her in front of the curtain. He took several pictures of her naked body, then handed her a set of clean hospital scrubs, along with hospital slippers.

After she was dressed, he helped her onto the examination table, lying her on her back. Hurd carefully rubbed the inside of her right elbow with an alcohol swab, then inserted the needle. The girl began trembling as the needle found a vein. Hurd looked at the girl with a smile, trying to comfort her as he withdrew the blood.

After removing the needle, he placed a swab on the needle mark, bending the girl's arm at the elbow, holding the swab in place. He pulled a penlight flashlight from his pocket, looking into her ears, then her mouth and eyes. He recorded his observations on the clipboard.

Masterson took a sip from his coffee cup before continuing. "Most of the girls burn out after about five or six years. As you might guess, psychologically it takes a toll on them. They give birth every nine months, then have their babies taken from them. They're bred again almost immediately, then the cycle continues.

"The lucky ones are the girls who've been taken by the elites. They're cared for at a greater level, as they're provided to the rich and powerful. If you can call being held captive lucky," Masterson said with a sneer.

Hurd finished his examination of the girl, then motioned for her to put her clothes back on. The fourteen-year-old had blonde hair, blue eyes, with an hourglass figure. At five foot six inches tall, Hurd recognized that the attractive teenager would be a highly valued prize for his employer, Gordon Johnson.

He stepped to the refrigerator and removed a plate with plastic wrap covering the food. He removed the wrap from the plate, then placed it in the microwave oven.

After the food was done, he placed it on the desk next to his computer. He pulled a box of milk from the fridge, placing it next to the plate. Hurd motioned for the girl to sit at the desk and eat. He lit a cigarette and smoked as he watched the girl ravenously consume the food.

Masterson's jaw set as he continued. "They're threatened with their lives if they attempt to escape. Most of the girls are kept in remote and secluded facilities, where they have no hope of ever escaping. The majority don't even know what state or country they're being held in. They're used for breeding for as long as they are viable, then sold off for prostitution, or sacrificed in any number of satanic rituals.

"The babies are oftentimes sacrificed at satanic events around the country. We know where most of their sites are, at least the ones being used by the elite. The toddlers are given to the sickest filth for sexual purposes. Some of the older children are tortured for the purpose of maximum fear, which produces adrenalized blood. That blood is more valuable than any drug being manufactured on the market today. Adrenochrome is the most expensive drug in the world."

Hurd picked up the tray from his desk, carrying it to the counter. He pulled a chair next to the seated girl, looking deep into her eyes as he sat down.

"This is your life now. If you behave yourself, you'll be treated very well. You'll be given nice clothes, good food, presents, with occasional trips out on the property. The facility here is clean, you'll be constantly cared for.

"There's no escape from here. Even if you were to get out of the facility, there's fifty miles of desert in all directions. It's filled with rattlesnakes, scorpions, wild boar, along with the occasional mountain lion. Behave yourself, and you'll be treated well. Misbehave, and the consequences could be deadly. Do you understand me?"

The shivering young girl responded in almost a whisper. "Yes."

"Good. Now let's get you in your room so you can get some rest," Hurd said as he led the girl to her cell.

Masterson appeared as though he was about to tear up as he concluded his remarks.

"I've seen some of the children who've been rescued from their captivity. They're damaged almost beyond repair. It takes years of therapy to get them back into society. Some never *do* come back. The suicide rate is off the charts. Alcoholism, drug use, promiscuity consume a lot of them. This is the result of the damage caused by the Globalists and their sick lusts. This is what the New World Order promises us if we don't eradicate it."

Hurd closed the cell door as the young girl sat on the edge of the bed. She watched as the man left the basement, turning the lights out, locking the door behind him. Her head fell into her hands as she sobbed uncontrollably.

Masterson lowered his voice as he turned to address Danny. "Let's define some terms here, shall we? <u>Shadow Government</u> describes the politicians who are working for the restructuring and ultimate destruction of the US. The <u>Deep State</u> is the bankers, the military industrial complex, <u>Technology Companies</u>. Cabal just refers to the group of people centered around the common cause of destroying this country. The term <u>Globalist</u> refers to those who wish to establish a <u>One World Government</u> with one central bank, one religion, no borders or nations, promising universal peace, as though they have any chance of obtaining *that*.

"The fuel that keeps the Globalist engine running is pedophilia, Lieutenant. Little children are what keep them satisfied and empowered. Organ harvesting, satanic ritual sacrifice, molestation, that's the kind of sickness you're dealing with. Conservative estimates are that eight million children worldwide are trafficked every year. There's six to eight hundred thousand here in the US alone. Hundreds of billions of dollars are generated by this trafficking.

"If the average American knew what their leaders were doing, they'd burn this place to the ground. Their minds are incapable of processing the heinous-ness of what's being done to the most vulnerable of our citizens. Do you really think your actions will make a difference? The citizenry can't wrap their heads around this and won't believe what you're telling them. They especially won't believe it about people they've turned into their heroes."

Danny frowned as he stared at Quinn. "If what we do about this doesn't matter—if no one cares about this, then we truly are finished."

Dr. Glenn Packer, the sixty-one-year-old retired CIA Deputy Director of Operations, held his right palm out toward Masterson. "Quinn, if I may." He turned toward Michael Graves. "Mike, I say this with love, brother. Get your ass out of Seattle. Your city, along with LA, San Francisco, and Portland, have been targeted for destruction; and that's just on the West Coast."

All of the Seattle team sat forward with wide eyes, as Dr. Packer continued. "The West Coast of the US has been slated to be turned over to the Chinese government. It was supposed to happen no later than 2023, but that's been delayed because of the current political environment.

"The Globalists will be making their long-awaited play soon. They'll start with riots, attempting to fracture the population around race. They'll then move into economic terror. You'll hear things like *eat the rich, kill Wall Street*. They'll demand the city defund the police. And then last, they'll present social demands so radical, it would tear the country to pieces if implemented.

"The people running this country don't even live here. They're not even US citizens. The politicians in the US are elected by the Globalists before the first ballot is ever cast. We think we're in charge—we're not! Our elections are decided in Brussels and Strasbourg.

"The New World Order has had China waiting in the wings. They were to be the next superpower."

"And what makes you think that could happen here?" Danny demanded.

"Because I've seen the invasion plans!" Quinn said, raising his voice. "China demanded that all the private weapons be confiscated from the American people right after 9-11. That way they would have virtually no opposition from the people. They plan to invade the West Coast at Portland, San Francisco, and Los Angeles. Moving east, the forces were to link up in Colorado."

"What about the United States military? Aren't you forgetting about them?" Rick Barker asked defiantly.

"Mr. Barker, all of the computer chips and software for our fighter planes, warships, tanks, and missiles are made in China. Do you really think they're so stupid as to not prepare for that contingency? Besides, just so you know, all the politicians who are being blackmailed in your file have been in on it. Twenty-six of the governors in the country have taken bribes from the Chinese government in the form of campaign contributions, speaking or consulting fees."

The group all sat silent with their eyes open wide after hearing Masterson's statements.

Masterson took in a deep breath as he looked at Graves. "Mike, the five of us are here for you—for all of you. You have to know that. Glenn's right, though, we're all on borrowed time." He turned toward Danny and Billie.

"When you do this, make sure you're five hundred miles from the city. Take that beautiful wife of yours and leave town as soon as you pull the trigger. You've done your part, Lieutenant. It's time to move on."

Masterson looked at the rest of the team. "Leave as soon as this operation is kicked off. Move to Idaho, Montana, Wyoming, Utah, anywhere but the coastal states. Your mayor is a complete moron. Your governor is a puppet in the pocket of the Globalists. Get out while you can."

He turned toward Graves. "Mike, come back to Virginia. Ellis can employ you at Apex Industries. I'm certain he can get all of the Seattle group jobs in the company. Come back to your real home. Grab Tracy and get out of this socialist hellhole."

Graves stroked his chin as he spoke. "Thanks, Quinn. We may take you up on that in the future. But for now, I haven't given up hope on my place of birth."

"The offer will always be available, Mike, just give me the word," Ellis Hollabird said with a smile.

Winters stood to stretch his back. "None of us know what God has planned. If He wants to destroy this place, you can bank on it being destroyed.

"If He wants to heal the place, putting destruction on hold, then that's what will happen. None of us, individually, or collectively, can stop what's coming.

"That said, as the pastor who married these two kids, I couldn't agree more. But for those of us who are believers, we don't get to choose our own path. If God wants us out of Seattle, He'll make it abundantly clear. Since the bulk of the team members here are believers, we'll have to decline your offer. Besides, if God wants this country healed, nothing can stop that either."

Rick and Larry gave each other a fist bump as they winked at Winters.

"Okay, I had an obligation to inform you, now I'm done," Masterson stated. Putting his glasses on, Masterson looked at the group. "Now that we've gotten the thunder and lightning speech out of the way, let's get to planning."

15

Danny and Billie sat in the Leavenworth town square drinking coffee and enjoying the view. The large clock in the square ticked over to eight a.m. as the shops began opening.

Billie reached into the paper bag, pulling out one of the croissants, handing it to Danny.

"Thanks, baby." He took a bite of the croissant, then rolled his eyes. "Man, your mother makes the best pastries."

"Yeah, that's why Dad's able to play Santa so well at Christmas," she said with a chuckle.

Danny took a sip of his coffee, then set the cup on the seat of the bench. "What do you think about the plan the captain's friends put together?"

"I think between what they said, and what we put together, it can work. The captain and Reverend Winters feel good about it." Billie grasped Danny's arm, pulling it to her chest. "What do you think?"

He crossed his outstretched legs as he looked out over the town. "It'll be fine. Has a better than average chance of success."

As she squeezed Danny's arm, she looked into his eyes. "Is everything okay, baby?"

"Yeah, it's fine. I'm just feeling a little selfish this morning. I want to leave the PD and start our new life together. Just being given pushback by my conscience."

"I know," she said while patting his arm. "I think we still plan on leaving, but remain open to change."

"Yup. We have three months to decide," Danny said as he finished off the croissant.

As they sat looking out over the town, Billie nudged Danny's side. "Look at that," she said with a giggle.

The two watched as Walter Killian and Astrid walked down the sidewalk. Astrid was smiling at Walter, listening intently as he talked. The two were oblivious to anyone else on the street.

"Looks like my sister has locked onto Walt," she said.

"Why not? They're both good lookin', smart, and the right age for each other. To quote my adopted mother, Marilyn, 'I think they make a cute couple'."

As Danny and Billie stood to leave, Astrid looked across the square waving at them. Billie smiled at the two as they began the walk back to the hotel.

"We have to get back to the hotel and pack," Danny said as he sighed.

"We'll be back up for Christmas, Danny. It's only a few months away. It'll go fast," Billie said as she bumped her hip against Danny's right hip.

Danny reached around her waist, pulling her in close. "I warned you about that hip bump thing. Looks like we may have to embarrass some squirrels on the way back to the hotel."

Billie grabbed his hand, leading him north. "It's too cold for that. Come with me, I've got something to show you first," she said with a wink.

A short walk north of the hotel put them at the Eck family house. Billie led Danny to the rear of the large craftsman home, through the Iron Gate at the back of the yard. She walked to the large cinderblock chicken coop standing alone in the center of the fenced in area of the yard. Opening the door to the coop, she pulled Danny inside.

The interior of the large coop was warm and clean, with more chickens than Danny could possibly count. "Why in the world did you bring me in here?" he asked.

Billie bent down, lifting the wooden rack from the center row of roosts. She turned her head toward Danny as she held up the rack. "Safest place on the planet."

Danny looked to see the disc holders for the Ballencourt master file. "Only three people know where they are—Dad, me, and now you," Billie said as she put the rack back in place.

Danny was moving his head side to side as he helped Billie back up. "Never in a million years would I have thought to put them in here." He smiled broadly as he held Billie. "You done real good, Kelli. You're like totally the best girlfriend anyone could ever have. I'm like totally in love with you."

"Oh, Chas, you like totally make my knees weak. Let's go to the soda shop for a milkshake," she said while fluttering her eyelashes.

After closing the coop, Danny put his arm around Billie's waist. "You know, if anyone ever heard us talking like that, they'd commit us."

"Well, at least we'd be committed together," she said while slapping Danny on the rear.

Graves was eating breakfast in the hotel restaurant as he scrolled through his phone, taking care of PD business. He looked up to see Quinn Masterson, dressed in a suit and tie approaching his table.

"Mornin', Mike. You up for some company?"

"For you, Digger, always," Graves responded.

"Wow, haven't heard anyone call me by my nickname for a long time now," he stated with a grin.

"Well, I didn't think it appropriate in front of the whole Seattle group."

Graves washed down the food in his mouth with coffee as he looked at his friend. "You were a little tough on my lieutenant during the briefing. Wanna tell me about it?"

"I don't think I was tough. If anything, I should have been tougher." Masterson took a bite of hash browns as he stared at Graves. "I like him, Mike. He and his wife look happy. And since I've *never* seen you be overly complimentary about anyone before, I speculate that he's special to you."

"He is; they both are," Graves replied. "He's a damned good detective, devoid of ego, and incorruptible. That kind of human being is hard to find nowadays."

"Mike, do me and them a favor. Usher them out of the department double quick. Let them go off and be happy while they still can. When you've done what we've done, for as long as we have, you're not fit to do anything else. Get them out before they become like us," Masterson said with concern.

Graves nodded. "Look, Digger, you're right. You're right about everything. Our mayor is an incompetent ass who will destroy the city with her progressive policies. The governor is an idiot who fancies himself intelligent, the worst combination for a leader. The police chief has been largely decent. She's capable, the officers like her, but between the mayor and the city council, they've neutered her. This city is going to hell.

"But if I pack Tracy and the kids up, go back to Virginia, I abandon some of the finest people I've known since I served with you five bozos. They don't have anywhere to go. I'd be putting them in the dragon's mouth. I can't do that. Don't worry, though, I'll leave before it goes south."

"You don't have much time, Mike. The Globalists are moving fast. They could have the West Coast destroyed by next year unless someone stops it. Don't wait too long."

"Thanks, Quinn, I won't," Graves said as he took a sip of his coffee.

As they continued to eat, Graves' four remaining friends came up to sit at the table. They were all dressed in their business attire. "Thought it'd be nice to have the last meal together," Brad Forester said as they sat down.

"Can't believe it's been eight years since we were all together. Where does the time go?" Graves said with raised eyebrows. "I want to thank all of you for this. With you guys on board, this has a better than average chance of success. We couldn't have pulled it off without you," Graves said humbly to his friends.

"Nonsense, you've got a good team, Mike. This'll work," Wanda Hale said.

Graves looked around the table. "I'm gonna miss you guys."

"Ah, we'll do it again soon. Maybe back up here. Make it an annual tradition," Ellis Hollabird replied.

Rick Barker approached the table. "The limo is all gassed up and loaded. I'm ready when you guys are," he said to the group.

"Thanks, Rick. We'll be out as soon as we finish," Graves responded.

The six friends continued to eat while reminiscing about the old days. Graves smiled as he watched his friends. He wasn't really even listening to what was being said he was just enjoying seeing them all together again.

Ellis turned his wrist, looking at his watch. "We need to get going."

"Yeah, we need to hustle. A person can only take so much of this horrible looking valley. Time to get back to DC, where the scenery is *so* much prettier," Masterson said sarcastically as he stood.

Graves slapped Masterson on the back as they all left the restaurant. "I'll walk you to the car."

As they entered the Lobby, the group stopped to say goodbye to the Eck family. They all shook Marva and Karl's hands.

Wanda Hale hugged Marva. "Thank you. This weekend was magical. You have a wonderful family and a magnificent facility. This is for you and your husband. Thank you," she said as she handed Marva an envelope.

"We were happy to do it. Please come back up anytime."

The group exited the hotel to see the Seattle team waiting at the car. As they were all shaking hands, saying goodbye, Ellis Hollabird pulled Walt to the side by his right arm. "Walt, I'm your point of contact. All correspondence to the team will be coming through me, nobody else. Do you understand?"

Walt nodded in agreement.

"If you need anything, let me know. If something happens to me, Masterson becomes your contact. Understand?" Ellis stated sternly.

"I do," Walt said as he shook Ellis' hand.

Masterson reached over and shook Danny's hand. "Thanks, Lieutenant. Hope I wasn't too much of a pain," he said with a grin.

"Nah, not even close. Looking forward to kicking this off," Danny responded.

Masterson gave him a thumbs up as he turned to get into the limo. The group all waved as Rick pulled away from the hotel.

As the limo drove out of sight, Marva opened the envelope to see a check for five thousand dollars, with a post-it note attached. *Thank you for a wonderful weekend. Brad, Quinn, Glenn, Wanda, and Ellis.*

She held the check out toward Karl. He raised his eyebrows as he looked at it. "Well, I'll be damned."

The Seattle team was loading their luggage into the back of the van as the Eck family came out of the hotel. Hansel and Gretel walked next to Billie as she made her way to the car.

Karl held onto Marva from the side as he looked at the group preparing to leave. Gunter and Hans shook Danny's hand, giving their sister a hug.

Billie nudged Danny with the back of her hand as she looked at Astrid and Walt walking to the van. Danny smiled as he watched Walt give Astrid a quick hug, trying not to be seen by the others.

Graves, Winters, Walt, and Colton all thanked the Ecks before getting into the van. Billie hugged her parents as the dogs began to whimper. Billie leaned down, patting the dogs on the head. "It's okay guys, we'll be back for Christmas."

Danny shook Karl's hand, then hugged Marva. "We'll see you guys at Christmas."

Karl nodded toward his son-in-law. "Yes, Christmas," he said as they entered the car.

Billie turned around in the seat to look at her parents as they drove from the property.

Brad Carver slowly pulled out from the hotel parking lot as he kept the van and Toyota in his sight. "Better settle in, we've got almost three hours of traffic to get through."

Carver pulled a cell phone from his pocket, punching in the number. Bernard Caron answered the call at the other end. "Yes?"

"Where you guys at, Red?" Carver asked.

"Just coming out onto the highway."

"Okay, keep eyes on them till they're on the plane," Carver ordered.

"Yes, sir."

"We'll all meet at the hotel when we're done."

"See you then."

Carver terminated the call, then twisted his body into the seat cushion, preparing for the long drive back to Seattle.

Auguste Marchand exited the Sea-Tac Executive Terminal with his wheeled luggage and umbrella in hand. He opened the umbrella as rain fell down hard. He stood with his feet together and a straight back as he waited for the car.

The dark green Lincoln Town Car stopped next to him as his employee exited the driver's side. "Sorry, Mr. Marchand, the car wasn't quite ready yet," Peter Wright stated.

"That's okay, Peter, apology not necessary," Marchand stated as Peter placed his luggage in the rear of the car.

Marchand opened the passenger door and folded his umbrella, quickly stepping inside the car. "Where do you have us staying, Peter?"

"We're at the Four Seasons downtown," Wright advised.

"Very Good. What about our subjects?" Marchand asked.

"Capt. Graves is signed out for four days. No destination or contact number, only a return date. He's due back in the office tomorrow morning. The rest of the crew left for four days as well, so they're in all probability gathered together somewhere.

"As soon as we can get a credit card for Graves, we'll do a search for where it was last used," Wright stated.

Marchand rubbed his face with his open right hand. "If they're gone for four days, maybe a flight. Check all the flights leaving Seattle four days ago, then all of them arriving today, beginning at noon. If they drove somewhere, it would have to be two-hundred-fifty miles or less, otherwise they'd fly.

"I'll check Amtrak and the ferry terminal. If they all left together for four days, it has to be important. Let me know as soon as they get back into the city. I need you going over this car with a fine-toothed comb. Let me know if there's anything out of place or suspicious," Marchand said as he stared out the side window. "What are you up to, MacDougal?" he muttered to himself.

16

Billie opened the back door to the house as Danny carried in the luggage behind her. She set the computer bags down as she saw Buster on the floor in front of her.

She tapped her chest as she looked at him. Buster responded by jumping into her arms. "Did you miss us?" she said as Buster purred in her arms.

After setting the luggage down, Danny looked at the food and water dishes. "Looks like the water and food held out for him. Kinda figured we put enough out. Missed you buddy," Danny said as he petted Buster on the head.

Danny rolled the suitcases into the bedroom, lifting them onto the bed. He sat on the edge, then hit the play button on the phone's answering machine.

"Hey, Danny, it's Brent down at the body shop. Looked the Camaro over, and I think it's doable. The right side has to be replaced, but new metal is available. If you want me to do a paint job while it's in here, now would be a good time. Let me know. Talk to you soon, bud."

He hit the button for the next message. "Hey, you guys, it's Mom. Sean and I are putting together a shindig down at the pub. Give us a call so we can talk about a date when everyone's available. Love you. Oh, by the way, Walter is a really nice young man and a big help for us. Thanks again, sweetie."

Danny hit the button again. "Lt. MacDougal, this is Dorothy Harris with the US State Department. There's an important matter we need to discuss with you and your department. I'm coming out to Seattle this week. I'd like to meet with you. Please call me at the number listed on your display so we can set up a time to meet. Thank you, Lt. MacDougal."

Danny picked the pen up off the nightstand, then scrolled down the call list on the handset. He scribbled the number down, then wrote the name next to it. He returned the phone to its cradle.

The hair on the back of his neck stood up as his eyes narrowed. He looked at the display to see the call had come in an hour ago. "My home phone, on a Sunday afternoon. State Department my ass," he said as he dialed Walter Killian's cell phone.

Auguste Marchand got up from the desk in his room as he heard a knock on the door. He looked through the peephole to see it was Peter Wright. He opened the door, letting the man in. Wright was a very fit forty-year-old retired Marine, and Marchand's right-hand man. Peter was never far from his boss's side.

"What did you find out, Peter?" Marchand asked as he sat back down at the desk.

"First off, sir, there's nothing out of the ordinary regarding the car. A forensic review could probably find something out, but I didn't feel that was necessary."

"Quite right, Peter," Marchand said sternly.

Wright opened the laptop computer and turned it on. He set the computer on the desk in front of Marchand. "Well, no one used their cellphones. This was clearly a clandestine meeting."

Marchand's left eyebrow rose as he looked at the floor. "And close to the city as well. I checked the ferry terminal, along with the train stations. Nothing showed up. Did you check their credit cards?"

"Only Graves and the MacDougals'."

Marchand opened his leather binder. He looked at the files for each one of the Seattle targets. He spoke as he thumbed through the pages.

"Check on him," he said as he pointed to Winters.

"Both of the detectives as well," he said while pointing to Rick and Larry.

"We need to keep a close watch on the MacDougal home and the police precinct as well. I'm quite certain they've expanded their numbers, Peter. It would be virtually impossible for them to mount any significant operation with only five people."

"Yes, sir. I'll get on them immediately."

"Thank you, Peter."

Danny was sitting at his desk going over the cases his section had been working on. He put post-it notes on the outside of each case file with his comments as he reviewed them.

He opened the next folder from the stack. Looking in the <u>Jane Doe</u> file, he read the cover sheet. He turned to the next section, containing the photographs. He snapped upright in surprise as he recognized the face of the dead woman.

Danny quickly grabbed his desk phone, punching in the four numbers. Rick Barker answered on the other end of the call. "Barker."

"Rick, it's Danny."

"Yes, Lieutenant, what's up?"

"I'm looking at your Jane Doe homicide at Arroyo Beach, Rick. She's Rosita Martinez, age 52."

"How do you know that, Lieutenant?"

"She was Francis and Melissa Mortenson's maid," Danny responded.

"I'll be right there," Rick said as he quickly hung up.

Danny carefully went over each of the photographs, studying them closely. He looked at the pictures of Rosie's fingers, but was unable to see if any of her fingernails had been broken. His concentration was interrupted as Rick enter his office.

"Are you sure that's her, Lieutenant?" Rick asked.

"Yes, positive." He pulled a post-it note from the pad, writing an evidence number on it. He handed the paper to Barker.

"Here's the evidence tag number. There's a military style button in one bag and a broken fingernail in the other. The fingernail was picked up by me at the Mortenson house. It was down in the heat vent by the front door.

"The button looks like it came from a tactical vest. It was picked up by Mrs. Mortenson. She found it while she was vacuuming by her front door. We know that the two FBI agents searched her house—maybe Rosie surprised them.

"In any event, we need to go over the clothing taken from the suspects at the Orcas Island raid," Danny stated.

"I'll go through the evidence boxes for Orcas and let you know," Rick stated.

Danny closed the file, handing it to Rick. "We need to put this on the front burner, Rick. I want it addressed before we kick off the operation. If you connect the button to one of the articles of clothing, let me know immediately," Danny ordered.

"You got it, boss."

Danny nodded at his friend. "Thanks, bud." He waited for Rick to leave the room before picking up the phone. He dialed Billie's office number.

"Sgt. MacDougal," the voice announced.

"Honey, we have some bad news."

With concern in her voice, Billie responded to her husband, "What's the matter?"

"Rosie Martinez's body washed up at Arroyo Beach," Danny responded.

"Oh no. We worried that something happened to her. Have you told Melissa yet?"

"No. I thought we'd both stop by tonight and tell her," Danny stated.

"Of course. Any leads on who did it?"

"Not yet. Rick's going through the evidence. I'll brief you when we get to the house," Danny stated.

"Okay, baby, see you then."

Danny terminated the call and dropped the phone onto the desk. "And the hits just keep on coming," he said as he slammed his folio closed.

Chief Hurd opened the cell door, entering the young girl's enclosure. "Come on, you're going to the main house tonight."

The tearful girl started to respond, "But I don't—"

Hurd raised the index finger of his right hand. "Quiet, no talking whatsoever. You're to remain silent!" he said sternly.

He led the girl out of the cell, to the back wall of the basement. "Take off your clothes," he said while he looked at the dresses laid out on the table. He selected one of the garments and held it out toward the girl. "Put this on."

The girl put the red satin dress on and stood trembling in front of Hurd.

He held out a pair of high-heeled dress shoes. "Here, these look like your size."

She put the shoes on and crossed her arms over her chest as she hung her head. "Nice, very nice," Hurd said with a smile. "Okay, time to go. You can have dinner when you get back," he said as he held onto the girl's left arm.

As they exited the tack room into the barn, the girl raised her head as they passed by the horse stalls. Once out of the barn, she winced as the afternoon sun hit her eyes.

"Remember, do as you're told and things will go well for you. If you create a problem or fight back, you'll be disciplined and privileges will be revoked. Do you understand?" Hurd said as his hand tightened around her arm. The girl nodded in agreement.

Hurd led her into the side entrance of the ranch house, then down the main hall to the master bedroom. They stopped in front of the door as he knocked softly.

The door opened, revealing the ranch's owner, Gordon Johnson, dressed in a bathrobe. Johnson only smiled at Hurd as he reached out, taking the girl's arm. "I'll call when I'm ready, Johnny."

"Very good, sir," Hurd replied as he turned and walked down the hall.

Danny and Billie walked down the sidewalk toward Melissa Mortenson's front door. As they stopped, Danny took in a deep breath, letting it out slowly. He reached up and pushed the doorbell.

Melissa came to the front door with a big smile as she saw Danny and Billie in front of her. Not receiving smiles from them in return, Melissa changed her demeanor. "What's the matter?" she said as she held the door open for them.

Billie reached out, holding Melissa's arms as she looked into her eyes. "Melissa, we found Rosie," Billie said with a frown.

"What? Then she's okay, right?" Melissa turned to Danny. "She's okay, isn't she, Danny?"

Danny reached out and hugged Melissa as she began crying. "We're sorry, Melissa, but Rosie's gone."

Melissa began sobbing as she melted in Danny's arms. "No, no, no, no, not Rosie too. Please, God, not my Rosie," she cried as Danny held onto her tightly.

Billie went into the kitchen and moistened a dishtowel with warm water as Danny helped the distraught woman to the couch. He helped Melissa sit down as Billie sat next to her, holding out the towel and putting her arm around her friend.

Melissa continued to cry as they sat with her. As she sobbed, trying to catch her breath, she asked Danny, "Was she murdered?"

"We believe she was, Melissa," Billie stated.

"How? How was she killed?" Melissa asked as she looked tearfully back and forth between Danny and Billie.

Sitting forward in the chair, Danny laced his fingers together with his elbows on his knees. "She drowned. Her body washed up on the shore of Arroyo Beach. The small half-moon object I found in your heat register was the tip of a fingernail from Rosie's right ring finger. It was matched up through her DNA.

"The button you found is most likely from a tactical military style vest. We have several possible leads we're looking into. It's pure speculation at this point, but we believe Rosie possibly surprised the team of people who went through your house. As you know, we found the cameras and microphones here. When we had you leave to go to your sister's, they came here and went through the house. That was verified by one of the subjects I interviewed. We'll find who did this, Melissa, I promise you."

"Is this ever going to end?" Melissa cried as she looked at Billie.

"It will, Melissa. It has to. The people who did this have been caught. Everyone who brought this into the city of Seattle has been dealt with. We're just sorry it wasn't dealt with before Rosie got caught up in it," Billie said while holding Melissa around the shoulder.

Melissa's face fell to her hands as she wept. "This home has been devastated. Please, no more, Lord. Please, no more."

Johnny Hurd led the young girl back to the barn, holding on tightly to her right arm. The evening gown she was wearing was torn in spots and draped unceremoniously over her body at the shoulders. She was beginning to show bruises on her face, arms, and legs. Hurd carried the high-heeled shoes as they entered the barn.

After opening the rear door of the tack room, he led the girl down to the holding area. Lifting the dress off, he walked her to the shower. "Make sure you clean yourself thoroughly," he said as he turned the water on.

Hurd opened the lid on the red burn container, throwing the shoes and dress into the thirty-gallon metal can.

As the girl exited the shower, he handed her a towel. He watched as she dried herself off, then put on the hospital scrubs she'd been given.

Hurd placed the dinner on the table next to his desk. "There you go. Eat it before it gets cold," he ordered.

The girl sat down with her hands on her lap as she stared blankly at the plate.

"Come on now, eat your dinner. Everyone else has been served. It's your turn."

She slowly placed small bites of food in her mouth as she cried softly. After she was done, he took the plate from her, placing it in the sink.

He led her to the cell, then opened the door. As she entered the room, Hurd locked it. "I told the cowboys to select a horse for you tomorrow so you can go for a ride. You've been good, and Mr. Johnson always rewards those who are good. You'll be taken for a morning ride after breakfast tomorrow," he said as he walked toward the exit.

After the lights were turned off, Hurd listened as the girl sobbed uncontrollably while sitting on her bed.

17

Brad Carver sat at the desk in his hotel room finalizing his daily report. As his cellphone rang, he looked at the display. Quickly sitting up, he answered the call. "Yes, sir."

"How was the operation up in the mountains?" the voice asked.

"Uneventful, sir. I was just finishing my report. I'll send it to you as soon as the call is terminated."

"Who do you trust there in the team to watch over the operation for a few days?" the voice asked.

"Any one of them, sir. They're all capable, but Bobby Higgins or Red Caron would be my choice."

"Very well, turn it over to either of them for the rest of the week. I need you in Dallas as soon as you can get there. You'll receive your orders when you get off the plane," he ordered.

"Yes, sir. I'll get the next plane out," Carver said as he terminated the call.

Rick Barker entered Danny's office carrying three evidence bags with raised eyebrows and a huge smile. Danny looked at Rick as he spoke. "I take it you have good news."

"The best, boss. As you already know, the fingernail matched up with the woman. The thread on the button had her DNA on it as well." Rick held up the large plastic evidence envelope. "The lab matched up the button thread with the remaining thread from where a missing button was on this vest."

"And?" Danny said as his head tilted to the side.

"The vest that's missing a button belonged to Terry Post, your best buddy from the café."

"Are you sure it was his vest?" Danny asked.

"His DNA was on it, and then there's this," Rick said as he turned the bag over, revealing the nametag sewn to the front of the vest displaying his name.

"God does reward the faithful," Danny said as he smiled broadly.

"I want to go with you for the interview, Lieutenant," Rick replied.

"Of course, it's your case. I just want to be there to see his face when you tell him about it. He's at the King County Jail, isn't he?" Danny asked.

"Yup, awaiting trial," Rick responded.

"Could you set up an interview for us, Rick?"

"Already scheduled. We see him tomorrow at 8 a.m.," Rick responded.

"Thanks, Rick, I'll pick you up here before the interview," Danny said as Rick left the office.

Peter Wright entered Auguste Marchand's room looking tired. He set his laptop in front of Auguste as he spoke. "I hit a dead end and decided to go back over the security footage from the airport." Wright scanned through the airport pickup area cameras, stopping on a limousine. "I couldn't see the driver's face, but thought it odd that a limo driver could get away with this."

Auguste watched as the limo driver stepped over to a Seattle Police Officer on duty at the airport. The driver shook the officer's hand, and slapped him on the back.

"I accessed the interior footage at baggage pickup and saw this." Marchand looked at the man's face, then glanced down at the photographs in the folder. "That's Detective Rick Barker, Mr. Marchand. And these are the people he picked up."

Marchand watched as the five arriving passengers shook hands with Barker. He paused the footage quickly as the camera showed an African American man standing in front of the others. His eyes narrowed as he spoke softly. "Capt. Masterson. It's been a long time," Marchand said with a frown.

"Do you know him, sir?" Wright asked.

"That's Capt. Quinn Masterson, US Naval Intelligence, retired. I remember seeing the others from time to time, but I don't recall their names."

Wright changed programs and opened camera footage on Interstate 5. "They left the airport, then drove on 405 up to Highway 90. I followed them as far as 90 and Highway 903." Wright backed out of the screen and pointed to the map on the computer. "There's only one place they could have gone— Leavenworth. The next large city on 90 after Leavenworth is Yakima. That's too far to drive for their purposes.

"I checked all the hotels in Leavenworth and finally hit pay dirt with the Alpine Haus. I found out they were all staying there for a long weekend. All of the police officers, including the five guests who were picked up at the airport, stayed there," Wright stated.

"Excellent work, Peter. You didn't happen to get them leaving, did you?"

"Yes, sir, four days later on Monday. A 12:15 pm flight to Dulles from Seattle. Barker dropped them off at the airport. I wrote down all five of their names," Wright said as he handed Marchand the file folder.

"Thanks, Peter. Excellent work." Marchand grunted as he looked at the picture of Capt. Masterson.

Everyone was busy loading the containers onboard the three C-130s, as Johnson watched from just inside the hangar. The three crews for the planes were checking over the aircraft as the final containers were loaded.

The loadmasters were securing the pallets as the ground crews were standing by. The crew chiefs for each aircraft had their headsets on as the communications cables were connected to the aircraft.

Now, with all the cargo secured, the planes began turning up their engines, each starting with engine number three. With all of the engines running and fully checked out, the crew chiefs secured their communications cables, then boarded their aircraft.

The ground crews began directing the aircraft from the apron, toward the flight line. Johnson watched as each of the three aircraft lifted off the runway, turning toward their West Coast destinations.

Standing next to Johnson, Lee Craddock turned to look at his boss as the last aircraft climbed out of the valley. "Well, they pulled it off," he said.

"No, Lee, you guys pulled it off. This wouldn't have been possible without your leadership. Thanks, I appreciate all you did," Johnson said as he placed his hand on Lee's shoulder.

Johnson nodded his head with approval as he watched as the last aircraft disappeared in the distance. "There goes twenty-two point three million dollars. We're back in business, Lee," he said with a big smile. "Let's get back to the ranch for a scotch."

Rick and Danny placed their service pistols in the lock boxes of the King County Jail. Dressed in civilian clothes, they walked down the hall to the sally port, then waited to be buzzed into the hallway to the interview room. After the deadbolt slammed open, they walked to the room, taking seats at the metal table, waiting for Terry Post to be brought in.

They watched as the Corrections Officer brought Post into the room. He limped from the shotgun pellets he'd been hit with at Orcas Island as he was led to the chair. Both men looked Post directly in the eyes as he sat across from them. Post leered at Danny. "Well, I'll be damned, if it isn't Detective MacDougal. Hey, Detective, is that girlfriend of yours as good in bed as I think she is? Man, I'd like a piece of that," Post said with a sinister grin.

Danny kept his focus directly on Post, staring him down, not saying a word. He watched as Rick began the questioning.

Rick opened his notebook as he thumbed through the pages. "Mr. Post, we won't take long here. This is strictly a formality." Rick pointed to the camera in the corner of the room. "We're recording this in its entirety. Mr. Terry Post, you're being charged with the murder of one Rosita Martinez. I further inform you that you have the right to remain silent. Anything you say can and will be used against you in a court of law. You have the right to an attorney. If you cannot afford an attorney, one will be provided for you. Do you understand these rights as they have been presented to you?"

"Who the hell is Rosita Martinez?" Post replied.

"Do you understand your rights as they've been read to you?" Rick repeated more forcefully.

"Yeah, I understand. Now who the hell is Rosita Martinez?"

"She's the maid you killed at the front door of the Mortenson house," Rick replied with a stone face.

Danny watched as Post's face turned ashen.

"I've never been to the Mortenson house. You're bluffing, Detective," he responded defiantly.

Rick opened the file, turning it around facing Post, showing the investigation photographs. "That button was matched to your vest, which is in the evidence locker, by the way," he said while pointing to the photographs. "The thread remnants were matched to the remaining threads on your vest where the missing button is. We found Ms. Martinez's DNA on the vest and the thread.

"We also found the tip of one of her fingernails by the front door. You see, Mr. Post, her body washed up at Arroyo Beach. We have it all. There's also a needle mark on her neck where she was injected with the poison. We have enough to put you away for life, even if you manage to escape the charges you're already facing. Now, do you wish to speak with us, or are you gonna take the hero's way out and take one for the team?" Rick said with a scowl.

"I want an attorney," Post replied coldly.

Danny and Rick stood. "Very good. Just keep in mind, we're on our way to speak with the rest of your teammates. You know the rules. Whoever speaks first gets the best deal," Rick said as he and Danny stepped to the door.

Rick knocked on the door, speaking loudly to the officer. "We're done here," he said as the door opened.

"Okay, okay! What do you want to know?" Post asked.

Rick looked at the officer. "Could we get some more time, please?"

"Yes, sir," the response came back as the door closed.

They sat back down at the table. "Okay, Mr. Post, let me lay it out for you. Based on Ms. Martinez' height and your angle while facing her, you're the one who shoved the needle into her neck. My guess is that your teammates would confirm that. How am I doing so far?" Rick said with a smirk.

"First, do you promise to speak with the DA about my cooperation?" Post asked.

"I promise to speak with someone, yes."

"Okay then, yes, I injected her," Post replied.

"With what?" Rick asked.

"Succs."

"Succinylcholine?" Rick asked.

"Yeah."

"And who made the decision to throw her into the Sound?" Rick asked.

"That FBI Agent—Franks," Post replied.

"And who disposed of the body?" Rick asked.

"Me, Ross, and Duncan."

"That's convenient. You're the only one of the three left alive after the raid on Orcas Island. How many were at the Mortenson house for the search?" Rick asked.

"There were twelve of us. Thirteen if you count the FBI guy."

"The three of you dumped her into the water? How'd that work?" Rick queried.

"We took some dumbbell weights from the house and tied them to her feet with rope. We waited until midnight, then took her out into the sound and threw her in," Post stated coldly.

"Who was controlling the operation at the house?" Rick asked.

"Agent Franks," Post responded.

"So, what were you looking for in the house?"

"Computer disc files, thumb drives, any kind of storage devices Mortenson could have used to store sensitive material on."

"What was on the files?"

"Don't know. They didn't tell us, only that it was related to National Security," Post answered.

"And which target were you assigned on the evening after the gala, Tillman or Bower?" Rick said in a low voice as he leaned in closer to Post.

Post's lips pursed as he looked around the room.

"Look, Post. William Barnes was interviewed before his untimely death. He admitted that you, Parker, and Udel were involved in the hit. So which one was your target?" Rick asked.

"Detective Tillman," he replied.

"Well then, you just won the lottery, 'cause Chuck Tillman survived. And who ordered the hit on the detectives? Was that the FBI agents?"

"No, that was Rushton, the Chief of Security for Ballencourt. The FBI guys weren't supposed to know about it."

"Okay, last question for today. Who did the FBI agents report to?"

"I don't know," Post answered. "I only heard a voice once while we were in the Federal Building. It was a woman's voice. They never used a name, just ma'am."

Rick opened his notebook, removing a statement form. "Mr. Post. We need to accomplish a signed confession," Rick advised.

"Okay," Post stated as he began writing the statement.

After finishing the statement, Post handed the document to Rick.

Rick reviewed the statement, then looked up at Post. "Good job. This'll do just fine."

Post looked nervously back and forth at Danny and Rick. "Are you going to talk to the DA about me? I cooperated. You'll speak to them, right?"

"I'll talk to my supervisor as soon as we get out of the facility. I promised you I'd talk to my supervisor, and I always keep my promises."

"Lt. Wade? You're gonna speak to Lt. Wade, right?" Post said with the slightest hint of a smile.

Rick and Danny stood, gathering their notebooks. Rick turned his head toward Post as he responded. "Lt. Wade got caught up in that whole Ballencourt Towers thing. He hasn't been with the department for months now. I got a new supervisor—Lt. Danny MacDougal."

Post's mouth opened as he looked at the two men.

"Have a nice day, Mr. Post," Rick said as they walked out of the room.

18

Billie walked out the back door of their house carrying a plate with a sandwich and bag of chips on it. In her other hand, she held a glass filled with Coke and ice.

She pushed the side door of the garage open with her foot, then walked toward the workbench. She set the plate and glass down on the bench, then looked at Walt Killian. "Thought you might like a sandwich, Walt."

"Oh, thank you, ma'am," Walt said as he picked up half of the sandwich with a napkin.

"What are you doing here?" Billie asked.

Walt waved his hand toward the Volkswagen engine placed on top of the bench. "I just got the block and heads back from the machine shop. I thought I'd put it back together while I had the time."

"How in the world did you get the engine here? You don't have a car."

"I borrowed the Mission's van," he responded.

"Walt, you're spending your time and money on this stupid Volkswagen. Does Danny know you're doing this?"

"Yes, ma'am. I told him I was going to tinker with it to see if I could get it running. I tried, but the engine was just too tired. I found a shop that gave me a good deal on the machine work."

"Walt, you shouldn't be spending your money on this thing," Billie stated with concern.

"It's okay, Mrs. MacDougal, I traded out some computer work for all the parts and machine work. I just thought it was sad to see a classic like this not running. The paint and interior are in really great shape. I just have to rewire it, put new tires on it, then get the engine back in, and this thing will be on the road again."

"You don't need to do this. I know Danny will appreciate it, but you should be spending your money on yourself," Billie said pleadingly.

"I don't mind, ma'am. I need something to do. Been a bum for so long with my head inside a bottle, I need something to keep me busy. Besides, you and Mr. MacDougal have been good to me. I owe the lieutenant a lot for the second chance he gave me."

"Well, I know I speak for him when I say you've been a blessing to us, and also to Sean and Marilyn. We're happy to have helped."

Walt nervously took a drink from the glass of Coke before speaking. "Mrs. MacDougal, would it be okay if I asked you a personal question?"

"Sure, what is it?" Billie replied.

"I was wondering if you, ah, your family would mind if I, well, if I could, you know, ask—"

"Walt, it's okay if you want to see Astrid. She likes you, you like her, no problem," Billie responded.

Walt's eyes opened wide. "You really think she likes me, Mrs. MacDougal?" Walt said with a boyish grin.

"Trust me, Walt. I know my sister, she likes you. I'll see if we can get her to come down for a weekend. As for the family, they won't mind. Astrid is divorced, Walt. She's had a pretty difficult time. Her ex was abusive and a cheat, who spent them into oblivion. The family will get along with you just fine," Billie said reassuringly.

"Thank you, Mrs. MacDougal," Walt said with a goofy look.

"No problem. There's about an hour before the meeting starts. Do you need anything else, Walt?"

"No, ma'am. I just have to put the heads on the block, then I'll come in," Walt responded.

"Okay, see you in a bit," Billie said as she turned to go back to the house.

Walt hurried into the house from the back door. He started washing his hands in the mudroom sink to get the grease off.

Danny's bellowing voice was heard from the dining room. "Hurry up, Walt, while we're still young!"

"Too late for that," Winters responded equally as loud.

Walt grabbed the portable computer from the floor, hurrying into the dining room. "I'm sorry, everyone, I had to finish putting the heads on the Volkswagen's engine," he said as he set the computer on the table.

The dining table had the entire Seattle contingent present. They all smiled as Danny gave Walt jazz for being late.

As Walt set the computer up, Danny passed the plate of snacks around the table.

Capt. Graves was first to speak. "Well, Walt, are we ready for the big show? After all, this is game day."

Graves winked at Danny and Winters as Walt hurried to get set up. "Sorry, you guys, just a little nervous here," he said while opening the screens. He finally finished setting up, and looked up to see the entire table staring at him with smiles. "Sorry."

Graves chuckled as he responded, "That's okay, Walt, we're just giving you a hard time. Why don't you bring us up to speed," Graves stated.

"Yes, sir. We have two classified messages that came in; one from Mr. Masterson and a second from Dr. Hale.

"The message from Mr. Masterson tells us to look at communications surrounding the Gordon Johnson ranch in Texas.

"The message from Dr. Hale is a result of an inquiry from Lt. MacDougal about a State Department employee," Walt advised.

"Why don't we discuss the message from Wanda first, Walt," Graves stated.

"Yes, sir, I'll forward it to all of you. Dr. Hale said Dorothy Harris is a mid-level department employee, who was appointed to her post in 2016.

She described her as highly partisan, extremely intelligent, and motivated by upward mobility.

"She's 32, with a Master's degree in Political Science from Yale. She's originally from Massachusetts. I did some further digging on her and found out she was sponsored for her current position by Senator Harold Gibbs. Who, as we all know, is Governor of Region 2.

"She's single and isn't seeing anyone at the moment. She makes regular trips to Brussels with Senator Gibbs and has a one-bedroom flat in DC. No vices, and Dr. Hale said she's only focused on her career. Dr. Hale advised for you to proceed with caution regarding a meeting with her. I agree with her, Lieutenant. From what I dug up, everything you say to her goes directly to Gibbs. And we all know where it goes from there," Walt advised.

"Well, no time like the present. Since we're all here, let's find out," Danny said as he set his phone on the table and turned on the speaker mode.

He pulled the post it from his wallet and dialed the number. They all listened as the phone was answered.

"Dorothy Harris," the deep sultry voice announced.

"Ms. Harris, Danny MacDougal returning your call."

"Yes, thank you, Lieutenant. As I mentioned in my previous call, I'd like to speak with you when I come out to Seattle. Would it be possible to meet for about an hour?"

"Not a problem. Can I ask what this is about, Ms. Harris?"

"I'm afraid I can't discuss it over the phone. It's a matter of National Security," she replied.

Danny looked to the others and raised his eyebrows as he smiled. "I understand. Are you opposed to meeting for dinner?" Danny said as he winked at the others.

"Not at all, I suppose we could do that. Do you have a place in mind?"

"I do. We have a nice little restaurant here the locals seem to like. It's called Canlis. When will you be arriving?"

"I get in Thursday at noon. Shall we say seven pm Thursday for dinner?"

"That works for me. We'll see you then," Danny said as he hung the phone up.

"Danny? A nice little restaurant the locals seem to like—Canlis, really? The most expensive five-star restaurant in the Pacific Northwest," Billie said sarcastically.

"Hey, if I'm gonna have my dinner paid for by the government, I just as well have it from Canlis."

"What makes you think they'll pay for your dinner?" Graves asked.

"They want something from us, they want it bad. Not to worry, they'll pay. And something else, my wife is going to be sitting in the restaurant with her date for the evening listening, keeping an eye on me," Danny replied.

"And who might that be?" Billie asked.

"Why Rick, of course. I assume that'll be okay, Captain?" Danny asked.

Graves' head was nodding as he spoke. "Why not? If we're going to bust the department's monthly budget, it just as well be at Canlis," he said with a frown.

Rick raised his eyebrows as he looked at Danny. "She sounds pretty hot, Lieutenant. Killer voice," he said with a wink.

"That's always deceptive, Rick. My money says she looks like an accountant with a hundred extra pounds on her.

Rick pulled ten dollars out of his wallet, waving it at Danny. "Ten bucks says you're wrong."

Danny smiled as he responded. "You're on." He turned to look at Walt. "And what was the message from Masterson about?" Danny asked.

"He gave us eight drop locations to place the confiscated funds in. The funds are to be sent to accounts in Washington, then routed back to us as needed." Walt smiled at Graves. "So not to worry, Captain, the trip to Canlis will be taken care of.

"And last, he gave us Intel regarding the Bar Ten Ranch in Texas. This is information that's not in the original file. There's new activity surrounding the ranch that needs to be investigated. The Bar Ten Ranch is owned by Gordon Johnson, Governor of Region 6," Walt stated.

Danny turned toward Larry Colton. "Larry, I know you're busy, but can you work with Walt on the ranch?"

"Sure thing, Lieutenant. Consider it done," Larry stated.

"Thanks, Larry." Danny turned to face Walt. "Have we received the go ahead from everyone yet?"

"All five of the DC members have given the thumbs up. We only need the word from all of us."

Danny took in a deep breath, then let it out slowly. "Does everyone here give the go ahead?"

He watched as everyone nodded in the affirmative. "As we all agreed during the meeting in Leavenworth, the decision needs to be unanimous." Danny looked at Walt and nodded. "You have the go ahead, Walt. Initiate."

Walt selected the names, then hit enter. As the upload completed, he looked around the room at the others. "Last chance," he said as his finger hovered over the 'yes' icon.

Everyone nodded. Walt hit the icon, then looked at the words <u>files sent</u>.

All of the members sat silent as they stared at the center of the table. The destruction that had just been unleashed on people's lives couldn't be taken back.

The actions taken by the twelve had been agonized over. Each of the members had voiced their disgust at the horrific conduct by the recipients of the messages. Now, they were almost feeling guilty for their actions. How ironic that people of conscience would feel badly for punishing those who were devoid of morals *or* a conscience.

Danny stood, looking at the group. "Well, for the first time in three months, I'd like a drink. Who's up for a scotch?"

Everyone agreed, with the exception of Walt and Winters. "We'll take a Coke, Danny," Winters said as he slapped Walt on the back.

"Comin' up," Danny replied as he went into the kitchen.

Senator Allan Brighton walked down the hall of the Senate Office Building with his satchel over his shoulder, carrying his morning coffee. He smiled pleasantly at people in the hall as he made his way to the office.

As he entered the space, he nodded toward his receptionist. "Morning, Linda. What's on the sheet for today?" he asked.

"You have a meeting with the Chairman of the Senate Armed Services Committee at ten. After that, your schedule is clear for the day, Senator," she replied.

Opening his office door, Brighton removed his satchel, placing it on his desk. He set his cup of coffee down next to the bag, then, taking off his suit coat, draped it over the back of his chair.

As he turned on the computer, he depressed the intercom button. "Linda, could I get a fruit plate, please?"

"Of course, Senator. I'll have it brought right up."

Brighton opened his email as he leaned forward in the chair, sipping from his coffee cup.

The first email in the folder caught his eye. *Your next career move.*

Opening the email, he began reading it as he scrolled down. *Senator, Brighton, full knowledge of your actions both in the Senate and after hours, has been obtained. You will leave office within the next 48 hours or your most closely guarded secrets will be placed out in the open for everyone to see. You must make an announcement of your immediate departure from office or the documents, including the videos below of you with your victims, will be placed in the open on the web, distributed to all news outlets. We are awaiting your resignation.*

Brighton scrolled down to see the video of him sexually molesting a three-year-old little girl. His heart raced as he looked at four other videos of him molesting little children. The sixth video was of him having sex with his receptionist, Linda Patterson.

With his heart pounding and his hands trembling, he reached into his satchel, removing the 2" Smith & Wesson Chief's Special. He placed the barrel under his chin and pulled the trigger. The loud report echoed through the hall of the building.

Congresswoman Gretchen Fornier stood behind her desk looking at the large 27" computer screen. Her arms were wrapped around her chest as she trembled at the videos before her. Her face was ashen with fear as the three videos continually streamed of her having sex with two young pre-teen children. The third video was of her in a black robe, standing over a baby with a dagger in her hands at a satanic ritual.

Fornier turned the computer off, then left her office. She walked past her executive assistant without saying anything, then into the hall. After leaving the building, she continued to walk with a blank stare as she made her way to the Washington DC Mall.

As hearings were being conducted in the house chamber, cell phone email signals went off throughout the room. In the middle of the proceedings, eighteen house members gathered their notebooks, computers, personal items and rushed from the chambers without speaking or looking at anyone. The room fell quiet as the members departed.

Senator Gibbs was on the phone when Senator Marvin Rockwell blew past his assistant, flinging his office doors open. "Of all the low-down dirty tricks I've ever seen in my life, this has to take the prize. You son-of-a-bitch, Gibbs, you said no one would ever see those videos if I played ball with you guys," Rockwell screamed.

Gibbs quickly hung up the phone and stood from his desk. "How dare you come into my office shouting at me. Who the hell do you think you are?" Gibbs replied as he closed his office doors.

"I'm the asshole who's gonna take you down. That's who the hell I think I am. You put those classified videos out for everyone to see. You went back on our agreement," Rockwell shouted.

"I don't know what the hell you're talking about, Marv. And you better dial it back a notch, son," Gibbs said angrily.

Senator Rockwell held out his iPad to Gibbs. "THAT'S what I'm talking about."

Gibbs hit the play button to see the video of Rockwell having sex with his sixteen-year-old Senate aide. "How the hell did this get out? I mean, that's about—. Wait just one damned minute." Gibbs turned toward Rockwell. "Have a seat, Marv. We're gonna fix this right now," he said forcefully.

"What do you mean fix it, Harold? This gives me forty-eight hours to leave office or that goes public. Are you trying to tell me you had nothing to do with this?"

"That's right. But I know who did. I need you to relax and let me see if we can stop this before it goes public. Marv, I'm asking you to stand down for forty-eight hours. I promise I'll stop this. Can you do that for me?"

"You've got forty-*six*-hours, Harold. After that, I go to the nearest CNN reporter and spill the whole damned thing, including *your* involvement," Rockwell said as he grabbed his iPad and stormed out of the office.

19

anny and Capt. Graves sat in his office watching the flat screen TV hanging from the office wall. A CNN reporter was announcing catastrophic political news out of Washington. *One hundred and thirty-five members of the house and senate were stepping down immediately. Nine members of the house, and three members of the senate have committed suicide.*

"Well, Danny, I don't think even Francis Mortenson could have known how devastating this would have turned out to be," Graves said with a stone face.

"I know. It's one thing to postulate what's going to happen. It's an entirely different thing to see it come to fruition. Eighty CEOs, over two hundred Hollywood actors, actresses, and executives were hit as well. It ain't over yet, Captain."

"I know. We'll see what happens, Danny. By the way, did you and Billie get taken care of by the lab?"

"Yes, sir. Ryan took care of Billie yesterday afternoon. I'll get in there tomorrow or the next day. Just been too busy," Danny replied.

Graves turned his head toward Danny. "Make sure you get in there, Danny," Graves said sternly.

"I will, Captain. I'll get it done before we leave," Danny replied.

"So then, we're all good to go for you two, right? When are you leaving? You know, two days ago would have been too late for me," Graves said nervously.

Danny nodded in agreement as he responded, "Captain, it's okay. Billie and I will be heading out right after my meeting with Ms. Harris at Canlis. Between you and Masterson, you convinced us."

"Okay, just a little paranoid. You two are the preeminent targets. The rest of us are just secondary. They want you guys *bad*."

"We're all set up with secure phones and laptops. Walt's taken care of us. You know where we're gonna be in case of an emergency. Nothing to worry about; it's gonna be fine, Captain," Danny said with a smile.

"Okay, Danny, get home to your wife," Graves said as Danny stood to return to his office.

As the sun was setting over the Bar Ten Ranch, the cowboys were getting ready for the evening routine. The security staff were closing down to the usual three officers on horseback for the night while the remainder of the men were settling in for dinner.

Riding next to each other, the three security officers rode out of the barn toward the north to begin their rounds. Each was making small talk as they settled in for the long ride.

The door to one of the empty horse stalls slowly opened as Brad Carver exited into the barn. He was dressed in tactical clothing, wearing a backpack. He quietly closed the door, then moved down the side of the eastern horse stalls. As he reached the door to the tack room, he quickly ducked back behind two of the quad ATVs.

Carver watched as Johnny Hurd came out of the tack room, leading a young Asian girl by the hand. He watched as Hurd led the girl out of the barn toward the house.

He opened the door to the tack room to see saddles, bridles, blankets, and harnesses. *This doesn't make sense*, he thought. He looked around the room, unable to find another exit door. He walked around the room, looking at the floor and ceiling. On the back wall, he saw scuff marks on the wood in front of a blank wall. He slowly ran his hands around the tack hanging on the wall until he found the hidden lever behind a saddle.

Pulling on the lever, a door opened next to him. Carver stepped in and onto the landing. As he slowly moved down the stairs, he heard young girls talking while some of them were crying. Before reaching the bottom of the stairs, he quietly peered around the corner. His jaw set as he saw cells around the perimeter walls of the basement of the barn.

He saw young girls tending to their babies inside the cells, while others sat on their beds softly crying. At the far end of the massive room was a medical examination area, along with a kitchen and full bathroom.

He took several pictures of the basement while tucked back behind the stairwell. The lights were on in the basement, which meant someone would be returning soon. He quickly went up the stairs, then out into the barn, before anyone could see him.

Carver then made his way to the house, staying close to the exterior walls. He took pictures of the area, mapping out in his mind the layout of the house. Carver moved away from the house, into the bushes. Once out of view, he texted the pictures and notes to his boss. Carver stood, tightening his backpack, readying himself for the long walk back to his car.

Danny opened the garage door to see Walt working on the Volkswagen. The engine was back in the car and Walt was filling it with oil.

Danny stopped next to Walt. "So, what's the verdict, doctor?" Danny asked.

"Give me about two minutes and we'll know, Lieutenant," Walt responded.

"Did you have to do anything else to it?"

"Nothing major. I cleaned out the gas tank, fuel lines, put new brakes and tires on it. I also put a new wiring harness in her. The mice had gotten to the old one." Walt stood as he wiped his hands with a shop rag. "She's in really good shape. No rust, and it doesn't appear to have ever been wrecked. You got a nice bug here, Lieutenant."

"Well, fire it up, Walt," Danny said with a smile.

Walt sat in the driver's seat, pumping the throttle several times. He turned the key, and the engine cranked, but failed to start. Walt went back to the engine, adjusting the timing. "Could you please start it?"

"Sure," Danny said as he sat in the seat and turned the key. The engine cranked and sputtered. Walt advanced the timing and hollered to Danny. "Okay, again."

The engine fired and coughed as Walt adjusted the timing, getting it just right. He adjusted the carburetor, then listened as the engine smoothed out. He stepped back from the car and looked at Danny with a smile. "See? She's a sweetheart."

Walt got into the driver's seat and revved the engine as Danny looked on. Walt turned the key, and the engine stopped. He handed Danny the keys. "There you go, Lieutenant."

Danny reached into his back pocket, pulling an envelope out. He handed Walt the envelope and the keys. "No, Walt, there *you* go. She's all yours."

Walt's mouth was open with shock. "No, I can't take this, Lieutenant. Please, this is too much," he said pleadingly.

"Look, Walt, the car is yours for three reasons. First, because you can't keep borrowing the mission's van. Second, because we may need you in an instant, and without a car, we'd have to wait precious minutes for you to respond. Third, if you're going to be traveling to Leavenworth, you need a car to get there, and to drive a certain lady around town," Danny said with a smile.

"Thank you so much, Mr. MacDougal. I can't begin to thank you enough," Walt replied. "Please thank Mrs. MacDougal for me too."

"I will. Just do me a favor. Pay it forward someday, will you? Billie and I have been blessed with so many incredible friends since all of this unfolded, especially one in particular. Walt, we both have a pretty formidable mentor. Reverend Winters saved my life. If not for him, I'd still be drinking myself to sleep every night. Instead, I have a wonderful wife, wonderful life, and a relationship with God that I never thought I would," Danny said pensively.

"Yeah, I'd be dead if it wasn't for Reverend Winters. He pulled me out of the gutter. I'm serious, I was in the gutter, completely passed out, when he picked me up and carried me into the mission. Two weeks of tough love later, he got me on my feet. I owe him everything."

"Yup, we both owe him our lives." Danny patted Walt on the back. "Can you stay for dinner?"

"No, thank you anyway. I have to get the van back down to the mission," Walt replied.

"Well, the bug is here once you get her registered. Pick it up anytime."

"I will, Lieutenant. Thanks again," Walt said with a huge smile.

Danny waved his hand toward Walt as he walked back into the house.

Auguste Marchand dialed the cellphone, placing it to his ear. The voice on the other end responded, "Yes?"

"I've discovered the reason for our delivery interruptions," Marchand stated coldly.

Peter Cornell responded, "Is it a competitor?"

"Of sorts. An old acquaintance and former colleague," Marchand replied.

"Do you need our assistance?" Cornell asked.

"No, I'll deal with this without cost to you, as it's already interrupted our operations far too much. I'll be returning to Washington this evening."

"Very good. I'll see you when you get back," Cornell stated as he terminated the call.

Brad Carver removed the cellphone from his pocket and dialed the number. He took a long drink of his beer as he sat in his hotel room.

"Yes?" the voice on the other end stated.

"Sir, I completed the surveillance of the ranch," Carver announced.

"Very good. What did you find?"

"I got the plans for the ranch house, barn, and all of the out buildings from the county. I'll send them to you when the call is over. Did you get the photos I sent?" Carver asked.

"Yes. What are the photos of the cells all about?"

"It appears he's running a breeding operation. Each of the cells I could see were occupied by young girls. They also had cribs in them. The cells are nice inside, complete with bathrooms. There would have to be a doctor, midwife, or some sort of healthcare professional on staff to take care of the girls.

"If he's breeding his own babies, he doesn't have to worry about birth certificates. Also, all of the young girls I could see were of Asian descent, except one Anglo," Carver advised.

"And the site in the middle of the trees? Tell me that isn't a sacrificial grove," the caller asked.

"Yeah, that's what it looks like, sir. Right down to the large statue of Molech. The statue is made of steel, with a chamber at the base for a fire. Looks to be about fifteen feet tall. The site is approximately three miles north of the ranch house," he advised.

"How many cells were in the barn?"

"Not sure. I could only see ten. There were probably more out of view. If they were lining the back and the opposite wall as well, twenty to twenty-five. I kept out of sight. I didn't want to be seen by the occupants," Carver stated.

"Were you able to get a count of staff at the ranch?"

"The house has seven. Twenty-eight cowboys and thirty security personnel. Five for his helicopter; two pilots, and three ground crew. There were construction crew listed, but I couldn't find anything on them," Carver stated.

"I looked through his financials. He's spending a buttload of cash on a construction project somewhere on the ranch or close to it. Nose around and see if you can find out anything about it."

"I will. Is there anything else, sir?" Carver asked.

"I need you on the point of this until it's resolved. I'll be going out to Seattle first thing in the morning to be there in your absence. Let your team know I'm coming. The news coming out today in Washington has made it clear that our primary has made his move. We need to be there to cover him and the others. The opposition is spooled up for sure."

"Understand, sir. We'll be ready."

"Keep me appraised."

"I will," Carver said before terminating the call.

Danny bounded up the steps of the mission with his leather notebook in hand. As he opened the door, Rhonna Collins ran to Danny, giving him a big hug.

"How's my favorite cop doing?" she asked.

"Fantastic. How's my friend doing?" Danny asked with a big smile.

Rhonna kissed him on the cheek. "Always at the top, Danny. You here to see the reverend?"

"If he's in."

"He sure is. Help yourself."

He walked to the rear of the mission and knocked on Winters' door. "Enter," the booming voice stated.

As Danny opened the door, Winters greeted him with wide eyes as he stood. In unison, they both hit their chests twice with their right fists, then fist bumped each other. "Booya," Danny said as he spread the fingers of his right hand out toward Winters, then snapped his fingers.

"You know, if people saw us clowning around like this, we'd empty out the mission. They'd run down to that soup kitchen on fourth," Winters said while chuckling.

"Aw, Gary, you have to laugh every once in a while. If you don't, the job will crush you."

"And on that, we can both agree. Now, why are you here and not with your wife?" Winters asked.

Danny leaned forward with his elbows on his knees and his fingers laced together. "Gary, outside of Billie, you're my most trusted friend. I need your insight and your friendship."

"You already have that, Danny. What's up?"

"Billie and I decided while we were in Leavenworth, we were going to leave the force after we kicked off the operation. We thought it best to pack it in. I was going to take an early retirement, and Billie was going to pull her retirement out. We thought maybe we'd move up to Leavenworth. Between the two of us, we have enough savings to open a restaurant, a gym, or a coffee shop.

"I suppose that watching my soon-to-be wife fighting for her life in ICU was the tipping point. I certainly wasn't going to tell her to retire. That choice belongs to her. I mentioned how much I loved Leavenworth, the next thing I knew, we were picking out the curtains."

Winters grinned. "It sounds like you guys made a decision together. What's the problem?"

"By leaving, we'd be hanging all of you out to dry. And this comes from both of us, by the way, not just me," Danny stated.

"Danny, we're all grown-ups. No one paid their dues for this more than you and Billie. We launched the operation, so leave. Leave with all of our blessings. Is this what's been bothering you at night? Is this what's giving you nightmares?" Winters asked, concerned.

"No, that's a separate matter, Gary. I just don't want to see anything happen to you guys. If it did, I don't think I could live with myself. I just don't know if that's what the Lord wants of me, or of us for that matter," Danny said humbly.

"Danny, focus on the job he gave you. Do it with passion and dedication. If you want to change careers and be with your wife, just ask Him. You two are going to be on a 'leave of absence' for three months. That should be enough time to clear your heads and make a decision. Ask Him. He'll respond," Winters stated.

"Thanks, Gary, you're probably right. I might be stressing too much. We'll talk about it while we're gone," Danny said with a half-smile.

Winters sat back in the chair, arms crossed, with a smirk. "So, if this isn't what's been keeping you up at night, what is?"

"Ah, Gary, please give it a rest. It'll work itself out in time," Danny said while tilting his head back.

"Danny, my experience in these matters is they almost never work themselves out in time. Don't ignore this for long. Whatever is eating at you, deal with it quickly," Winters said sternly.

"I will. Now, I need to get back to the station, pronto! I have a date tonight with a strange and mysterious woman," Danny said while rolling his eyes at Winters.

"Have the lamb for me. I've always heard it's the best in the country. Never could afford to go there," he said as Danny stood.

"I will. I'll let you know what the meeting turns up," Danny said as he turned to walk away.

On the west side of Lake Union, just off Aurora Avenue, sat Canlis, Seattle's most exclusive and arguably finest restaurant on the West Coast.

Although he had nothing to do with the 1950 design, Frank Lloyd Wright certainly could have been the architect. Appearing to hang over the hill's edge, the restaurant had the most spectacular views of Lake Union and downtown Seattle.

Each section of the seating area had walls of windows placed at an angle leaning out toward the lake, supported by stone pillars around the inside. The open beam wooden ceiling was beautiful, giving the impression the structure could have been part of an early Alfred Hitchcock movie.

Danny sat at a small table for two, next to the window, providing an excellent view of the city. He wore a suit and tie and tugged at the necktie in protest as he waited for his guest.

Seated at the opposing corner of the room, Billie and Rick watched over Danny as they enjoyed a plate of appetizers. "Boy, Danny, these calamari are incredible," Billie chided as Danny listened in his earpiece.

"Man, the stuffed mushrooms are to die for too, Lieutenant. Too bad your date is late," Rick said with a smile.

"Keep it up, you two. Just remember, payback is bit—" Danny stopped talking as he saw the maître d' walking toward him. Danny couldn't help but have his mouth hang open as he saw the woman following.

Dorothy Harris was five foot ten inches tall and had legs that appeared to be five feet of that. She was dressed in a form-fitting dark blue dress that only came down halfway to her knees. Her beautiful olive complexion was outlined by long thick black wavy hair cascading down her back and front. Every eye in the restaurant was on her as she walked to the table. Across the room, Danny saw a stunned Billie sit back in her chair as she stared at the woman.

"Damn, someone owes me ten bucks," Rick muttered into Danny's earpiece, shaking his head. Danny saw Billie glaring at Rick. "Not funny," she snapped.

Danny stood as she approached the table. He reached out to shake her hand as she stopped in front of him. "Danny MacDougal, Ms. Harris. Nice to meet you."

"Nice to meet you as well, Lieutenant." The two sat down as Harris continued to speak. "I didn't expect someone so good looking, Lieutenant," she said.

For the first time in a long time, Danny didn't have a snappy comeback. "Thank you. Ditto," he said clumsily as his head tilted to the side with his eyebrows going up.

The waiter stopped at the table, placing menus in front of the two people. "Can I get you something to drink?"

"The house Cabernet for me," Harris replied.

"Make that two," Danny stated.

Danny heard Billie's voice in his earpiece. "You're so handsome, Lieutenant," Billie mocked. "Why, thank you, Ms. Harris—ditto."

Danny tugged at his ear as he heard the words.

"Beautiful restaurant. And the location is stunning," Harris proclaimed.

"We're very proud of it. It's been here for seventy years," Danny stated.

He was having a difficult time not looking into the woman's eyes. They were dark and deep. He couldn't believe that this was a typical State Department employee.

The waiter placed glasses of wine on the table. "Are you ready to order, or do you need more time?" he asked.

Harris looked at Danny. "I don't know. Suggestions, Danny?"

"The dry-aged Ribeye is incredible," he responded.

"That sounds good. Medium rare, please."

"And for you, sir?"

"The lamb please—chef's prerogative," Danny responded. The waiter nodded and walked away.

"So, are you from here, Danny?" Harris asked.

Danny heard his wife in his earpiece in a high-pitched voice. "Are you from here, Danny?" He tugged at his ear as he responded to Harris. "No, San Francisco originally."

"Oh, Danny, please call me Dorothy," she said with a smile. "Why did you move up here?"

"Okay, Dorothy," he said clumsily. "I came up here with a high school friend of mine after we graduated. He had family here, and I fell in love with the place. Been here ever since."

Twenty minutes later the waiter brought the meals while the two people continued with small talk. "So, I understand you were promoted to lieutenant three months ago, is that right?" Harris inquired.

"Yes, three months," Danny replied.

As she put the piece of ribeye into her mouth, she closed her eyes. "Oh, wow. This is incredible. You're right, this place is amazing."

As Danny swallowed the piece of lamb, he looked across the table. "So, Dorothy, why me? Why am I so special that you want to meet with me?" he said while continuing to eat.

"Oh, Danny, I think we both know why I came out here to speak to you," she said as she took a sip of her wine. "There are a great number of people who are upset with you."

"Your employers, possibly?" he asked.

Harris chuckled as she responded. "Oh goodness no. I don't work for them. The State Department just wants this whole thing gone. It's messy business, especially so close to an election. I was just asked to see if I could negotiate a conclusion to the whole thing. I assure you, Danny, I'm just a disinterested third party."

"So, what are they proposing?" he asked.

"They have documents that can be helpful to the Seattle Police Department. Although I haven't seen them, I'm told they can clean up a great number of problems the department has had for a long time."

"And?" Danny said as he leaned in toward her.

"They're proposing compensation at a level that you can't imagine," she said with a smile.

"Or believe, I'd bet. That's bribery, Ms. Harris," Danny said with raised eyebrows.

"No, it isn't, Danny. It's a gift. Nothing was mentioned about a quid pro quo. It's merely a gift from a generous benefactor. Use it as you see fit," Harris responded.

"I take it I have time to think this over?" Danny asked.

"Of course. I've been authorized to give you one week to come to a decision. In the meantime, I'm to give you the file as a gesture of good faith."

"And this file, I assume you don't have it with you?" he said as he looked at Harris' tight dress.

As she fluttered her hand over her chest, obscuring the view of her cleavage, she smiled coyly. "No, it's back at the hotel."

"And how am I to get this extremely important and helpful file?"

"Danny, I took an Uber here. I was hoping you could give me a ride back to the hotel. I can give it to you there."

"Okay," he said as he raised his hand for the waiter.

"No, no, Danny, this is on the government. This is my treat," Harris said as she gave the waiter four one hundred-dollar bills. They walked to the lobby where Harris retrieved her coat.

The waiter handed her the receipt, as she handed him fifty dollars. As they were walking out to his car, Harris placed her left arm around Danny's right arm.

"Where are you staying?" he asked.

"The Sheraton Grand," she responded.

"Sheraton Grand it is," he said as he opened the door for her.

As he sat in the driver's seat, he started the car, then backed out of the stall. "It's not that far. Just down the road a bit."

After a short ride, Danny turned onto Sixth Avenue, pulling into the hotel valet parking. They both exited the car, walking to the lobby. Harris grabbed Danny's arm, pulling it close to her. "Why don't you come up to the room for a drink, Danny?" she said while pulling his right arm into the side of her breast.

"I'd like to, but I need to get back to the station. I'll wait down here in the lobby for you," he said with a smile.

"Come on, Danny, I like you. I was hoping we could spend some more private time together." She smiled and winked while she brushed his leg with her knee.

"Maybe next time. I really need to get going."

"Okay," she said with faux pouty lips as she turned to walk to the elevator.

"You're so busted, MacDougal," he heard in the earpiece.

"Come on, I turned her down, didn't I?" he responded.

"Boy, I'm glad that was you, Lieutenant. Not sure I could have resisted her. I've never seen a woman so, so—"

"Okay, both of you clowns shut the hell up," Billie's voice blared into the earpiece.

Danny saw Harris approaching from the elevator lobby. As she stopped in front of him, she smiled. "Here you go. A gift from them," she said as she handed Danny the folder. "I hope it's useful, Danny," Harris said as she kissed him on the cheek.

"Thank you, Dorothy, I'll be in touch," he said. As he turned around, she blew him a kiss.

Danny handed the ticket to the valet attendant, then walked to the exit ramp of the valet parking lot. As he fumbled through his pocket to retrieve a tip for the attendant, a hand from behind pulled his head back as a needle was stuck into his neck. Danny's body went limp as the two men dragged him to their car.

The two men threw Danny into the back seat. As one of the men sat next to Danny, the other man got behind the wheel of the car.

The man removed Danny's earpiece, pistol, and cellphone. As the car passed by the large trashcan, the man in the rear threw Danny's gear into the receptacle, as the vehicle left the hotel.

Rick and Billie sat parked on Sixth Street, waiting for Danny to contact them. They had a clear view of the hotel parking entrance as they waited for him to exit.

"Something's not right, Rick," Billie said as she rubbed the back of her neck. "He called for his car ten minutes ago." She pulled up her handheld and called Walt.

"Walt, we've lost Danny. Do you have a signal on him?"

"No, I don't, Mrs. MacDougal. The lieutenant never got in for his implant. All I can do is track his cellphone," Walt responded.

"Dammit, Danny, you procrastinating ass. You're in so much trouble," Billie shouted out loud as she hit the dashboard of the car. "Can you track his cellphone, Walt?"

"Yes. I show it as still at the hotel," Walt replied.

Billie looked at Rick with concern. "What do you think?"

"Billie, it's not like Danny to keep silent. He's always in communication," Rick responded.

Billie was nodding in agreement as she looked at the garage exit. "Let's get in there. Something's wrong."

Rick placed the gear lever in drive and stomped on the accelerator, quickly closing the one city block distance to the hotel. As he pulled into the valet area, they saw Danny's Crown Victoria sitting at the valet's stand. Billie exited the car running before it was fully stopped. She stopped in front of the attendant as she pulled her badge out.

"Where's the man who belongs to this car?" she demanded.

The young man leaned back away from an obviously irritated Billie. "I don't know, ma'am. I took his ticket and went to get his car. When I got back, he wasn't here."

"Was anyone with him when he gave you the ticket?" Billie asked.

"No ma'am," he answered.

Billie pulled the radio from her belt. "Walt, where do you show his phone?"

"You're almost on top of it."

Billie began walking around the parking area as she held the radio to her ear.

"You're getting farther away, Ma'am," Walt responded.

She turned back and started walking to the exit of the parking area. "Getting closer. Closer yet. You're right on top of it," Walt stated.

Billie and Rick turned around in a circle as they looked at the ground. Rick stopped as he saw the trash can. He quickly picked it up and dumped the contents out onto the concrete.

The two began moving garbage aside as they searched the contents. Billie held up an earpiece as she looked at Rick. In response, Rick held up Danny's cellphone and pistol.

"They grabbed him, Billie!" Rick blurted out.

Billie called out on the radio. "Walt, we need you searching anything and everything you can think of. Traffic cameras, bus stops—anything. Larry, we need you ready to respond in an instant once we locate him."

Both men responded in the affirmative. Billie looked at Rick. "We need every cop within a ten-mile radius looking for him. Call out the cavalry, Rick. I'll get ahold of the captain and find out what I can here at the hotel. I need you to go back to the restaurant and comb the area. We need to retrace our steps," Billie said, her breathing labored as she began to panic.

Rick placed his hand on Billie's arm. "We're gonna find him, Billie. Don't worry, we're gonna find him."

"I know," she said while frantically looking around the area. "Let's get going," Billie said as she stood and hurried toward the hotel entrance.

21

Danny slowly opened his eyes as his nostrils filled with the smells of old fish entrails and saltwater. He blinked several times, trying to fight off the monster headache he was having.

He glanced down to see water below, between the spaces of the old wooden floor. The area was dimly lit by two overhead lamps thirty feet away. He found himself tied to an old wooden chair by nylon ropes. His legs were secured to the two front chair legs, with his wrists tied to the armrests. He was almost completely undressed as he sat in the chair, wearing only his boxer shorts.

Turning his head to the left, he heard hard soled shoes walking toward him. As the figure got closer, coming into the light, he could see it was Dorothy Harris. She stopped in front of him as she held a bottle of water in her right hand.

"Here, this will help with the headache you're undoubtedly experiencing," she said as she held the bottle out toward him.

As Danny drank from the bottle held to his lips, Harris looked him over. "Wow, Danny, you're in great shape," she said as she slid her right leg between his legs. "Too bad you didn't want to come up to the room. We could have had such a great time together," she said while running her right index finger across his chest.

"Is this the part where I'm granted an evening of passion before my death?" Danny asked with a smirk.

"Oh, baby, it's too late for that," she said coyly. "I'm afraid I have to leave. I have to turn this over to someone else, sweetie." Harris spread her legs and sat on Danny's right leg as she grabbed his crotch, kissing him hard on the lips. "Too bad," she said as she turned to walk away.

As she was leaving the building, Danny heard her speak to a man standing in the shadows. "He's all yours."

Danny squinted to see the man now walking toward him. There was something familiar about the dark figure approaching. Rage filled him as he saw Lt. Phillip Wade stopping in front of him.

"Well, it's true what they say, the biggest rats are down on the wharf," Danny said with a smirk.

Phillip Wade clenched his fist, hitting Danny hard in the face. "Too bad you had to be such a boy scout, MacDougal. You could have had a comfortable life. But instead, you decided to rock the boat."

"What, work with you, Ballencourt, and that puss-gutted troll of a mayor? I'd rather have a root canal."

Wade hit Danny in the face again as he grunted. "Look what it got you. You're about to go the way of the Dodo, MacDougal."

Danny spit blood from his mouth before responding. "What, from you?" He chuckled as he responded. "A fifty-year-old grandmother could clean your clock, you metro-sexual piece of shit."

Wade crossed his arms as he looked at Danny. "No, not from me. From him," he said as he pointed to a large man coming out of the shadows.

Danny looked at the big man approaching him. His chest was massive as he flexed his large biceps in front of Danny. He was wearing denim pants, heavy weight engineer's boots, with a sleeveless summer weight t-shirt. The bald man had a full beard, with dark lifeless eyes.

As he stopped next to Wade, he sneered at Danny. "This is The Caretaker, or at least that's what they called him at San Quentin.

"Let's make this easy, Danny. You tell me what I want to know, and The Caretaker gets to have the evening off." Wade sat at another chair in front of

Danny. "I need that Master File, Danny. Tell me where it is, and we can avoid all this unpleasantness," Wade said with a smile.

"I don't know where it is. We made some copies, then gave the master to Arnie Bower to secure. And since you trolls killed him, the secret went to Arnie's grave with him," Danny said with a blank stare.

"Oh, Danny, you can't expect me to believe that a detective of your caliber didn't have a backup plan. Now one last time. Where is the master file?"

"Shove it, Wade," Danny said defiantly.

Wade stood, nodding toward The Caretaker. "Looks like you're up."

Capt. Graves slid his department car to a stop next to Rick Barker. Furious, he fought the urge to scream at his teammate. "We look like a bunch of rookies right out of the academy. Now exactly what in the hell happened?"

"Billie and I decided to retrace our steps. We agreed that I'd go back to the restaurant while she would look at the hotel. After I finished at Canlis, I tried to contact her but got no response. We had two of the uniforms take the valet and the desk clerk down to the station for questioning. That's when—"

Walt interrupted the conversation over the radio. "GOT HER!" he said loudly. "She's five miles north of you. Looks like she's on the water's edge. I'll keep you informed as you get close," he stated.

"On my way," they all heard from Larry over the radio.

Without further conversation, everyone jumped into their vehicles, speeding away, heading north.

Danny's head was slumped to the side, pointing toward the floor. His left arm was broken above the elbow, with bruises all over his chest. His face was beaten badly and his left eye was swollen completely shut. Blood dripped from his mouth and nose as he fought to take air into his lungs.

The caretaker stood over him as Wade got up from his seat. "You're one tough son-of-a-bitch, MacDougal. Never seen anyone take a beating like that before. It's clear we're not going to get the information from you the traditional way. We're going to have to take a more drastic measure."

Wade turned to his right, snapping his fingers. Out of the shadows three heavily tattooed Hispanic men appeared leading Billie by the arms. Her hands were tied behind her with her eyes covered by a blindfold.

Danny fought to raise his head to see out of his one good eye as he heard more people entering the room.

When the three Hispanic men laid Billie on the floor in front of him, he heard her voice. "What's going on? Who the hell are you people?"

Danny raised his head, forcing his right eye to focus. He saw his wife lying in front of him ten feet away. With all his strength mustered, he fought to get the words out. Muffled through swollen lips, he cursed at Wade. "You bastard. If you don't let her go, I'll kill you."

Hearing Danny's voice, Billie sobbed as she cried out, "Danny! Are you okay?"

"I'm here, baby," he replied through swollen lips.

Wade nodded toward the three Hispanic men. They spread her legs, looping ropes around Billie's ankles, tying off the ends to posts in the floor. They stretched her arms out to her side, tying them off with ropes as well.

Danny was shaking with rage as he spoke as loudly as he could. "Wade, you bastard, I'll KILL YOU!" he said as he fought to see through his one good eye.

Wade looked at Danny as the three men tore off Billie's evening dress, leaving her wearing nothing but her bra and panties. "Wow, MacDougal, you lucky son-of-a-bitch. She's really hot. I sure would like to have had some of that, but I promised my friends here they could have her."

Danny was fighting against the ropes as he struggled to free himself. He cried out as he heard Billie begin screaming. He turned his head toward Wade as he bellowed at the man, "Let her go, you bastard!"

He saw one of the Hispanic men throw a machete to the floor, sticking it into one of the planks.

Wade smiled as he looked down at Billie, then turned to Danny. "They'll each have a turn raping her. Once they're done, they'll carve her up into little pieces. All of this, of course, while you're watching."

Danny saw Wade step next to Billie and pull the blindfold from her face. She raised her head to see Danny, bloody and beaten, wearing nothing but his shorts. "Danny!" she cried out as she looked at her badly beaten husband.

Wade continued, "These three men are drug cartel enforcers, Danny. They're *very* good at what they do. They'll have sex with Billie until they can't stand up anymore. Then, they'll each enjoy some cocaine, then start all over again. After a couple of hours, when they're finished, they'll cut her up and throw the pieces into the sound, just before they disembowel you.

"Now you can stop all of that. All you have to do is tell me where the master file is. See how easy this can be? Just tell me, and this all goes away."

Danny heard his wife cry, "Don't tell them, Danny. They're gonna kill us anyway!"

"Honey, I'm so sorry. I love you more than you'll ever know," Danny said while tearfully responding.

"I love you too, baby," Billie said, sobbing defiantly.

Danny raised his head slowly, fighting the pain, looking at Wade. "Stick it, you worthless piece of shit."

He watched as Wade turned to look at the three men, nodding. Danny locked eyes with his wife as tears ran down their faces.

One of the men looked down at Billie, smiling as he took off his trousers. Getting down on his knees between her legs, he reached out for her waist with his left hand.

The muffled shot was barely heard as the left side of the man's head exploded, splattering blood all over Danny and Billie.

Before the other two men could even respond, two more suppressed shots came so fast they almost sounded like one report. The men's heads nearly vaporized from the impact.

The Caretaker turned to run away, but only made it two steps before Danny saw his body pitch forward from a bullet to the back of the skull.

Startled, Wade pulled his pistol, pointing it toward Danny. As the bullet entered Wade's chest, his reflexes pulled the trigger of the pistol. The bullet whizzed past Danny's head, hitting the back of the chair. Danny saw Wade drop to his knees in front of him, then watched as Wade fell over to his side, dead.

"Billie! Are you okay?" Danny screamed.

"I'm okay, baby," she cried as she tried to raise her head to see him.

Weak and dizzy, Danny tried to free himself. With his head tilted to the side, he looked toward the other end of the building. He saw a lone figure walking toward him, outlined from the moonlight entering the building. The figure was out of focus, but Danny could see he was dressed all in black, with a black tactical mask on his head, only revealing his eyes. The scoped M-4 rifle was strapped to his chest.

Danny desperately fought to free himself, not knowing if the figure was coming to finish them off. The man stopped in front of Danny, pulling a knife from his vest. He cut Danny's right hand free, then raised the knife above his chest. Throwing the blade at the chair, it stuck in the wooden arm next to Danny's right hand. The man's eyes glared at Danny as he turned to walk away.

Danny pulled the knife from the chair and cut his left arm free. He cried out in pain as his broken arm fell to the side without the support of the chair's arm. After cutting away the ropes around his ankles, he slowly stood, limping toward Billie.

With his left arm hanging at his side, he reached down and cut the ropes from Billie's wrists. As he tried to get up, he dropped the knife, falling over on his right side, groaning from the pain.

Billie quickly retrieved the knife, cutting the ropes from her ankles. She reached out and cradled Danny in her arms as she sobbed uncontrollably. Kissing Danny on the forehead and rocking him, Billie heard Capt. Graves and Rick calling out to her from the darkness.

"We're down here!" she screamed as she continued to hold Danny. "Hurry, we need an ambulance!"

As Graves came running, he stopped next to her and Danny. Billie saw him look around at the carnage in front of them. She saw his face grimace as he saw Lt. Phillip Wade lying on his back with a bullet hole in his chest.

Rick dropped to one knee in front of Danny, looking at his injuries. Billie continued sobbing as she held onto her unconscious husband.

From the opposite end of the building, she saw Larry Colton approach the group holding his sniper rifle across his chest.

Graves turned toward Colton. "Nice shooting, Larry, and just in the nick of time," he said with a nod.

Larry raised his left eyebrow as he stopped in front of the group. "I didn't shoot, Captain. I just got here."

There was complete silence as the four people slowly scanned the dimly lit room.

Quinn Masterson walked up the sidewalk toward his Georgetown townhouse. He was tired after a day of doing research for an old colleague. He was looking forward to a hug from his wife, a Seagram's and Seven, and a hot meal.

He inserted the key into the deadbolt, opening the door. As he was hanging his coat on the rack by the door, he called out to his wife.

"Janice, I'm home." He took off his dress shoes and slid on his house slippers. He smiled as he called out again. "Woman, the master of the house has arrived and needs a hug."

Holding his daily <u>New York Times</u> under his arm, he walked toward the kitchen. He was talking to his wife loudly as he rounded the corner into the dining room.

"You know, a fella could get—" He stopped mid-sentence as he saw his wife bound and gagged, in one of the dining chairs. There were two men at her side, one holding a gun to her head.

He slowly turned his head to see an old acquaintance sitting in the easy chair, Auguste Marchand. He slowly sat down across from his wife.

"How very nice it is to see you again, Quinn. How long has it been, my old friend?"

With a deadpan expression, Masterson responded, "Thirteen years."

"How sad that we didn't keep in touch. I so enjoyed our conversations. You were always the best conversationalist out of the team. Although Martin was always fun to talk to as well," Marchand said with a big smile.

"What are we doing here, Auggie? What's this all about?" Quinn asked soberly.

"A minor issue, Quinn. It occurs to me you've been stepping on my territory. Twice now I've had employees fail to return to the office with their tasks completed."

With a stone face, Masterson responded with an overly soft tone to his voice. "Auggie, I don't have any idea what you're talking about. I haven't worked in almost twelve years."

"How nice it would be if that were true. I'm just having a hard time believing you. You know, that *was* a nice touch, sending my men's clothing back to me. You always did have a flare for the dramatic."

"Auggie, you're not making any sense. I don't know what you're talking about," Quinn stated.

Marchand slapped the arm of his chair as he angrily responded, "You've been running cover for two of my targets, Quinn! I've seen you with them. All I'm looking for is some professional courtesy here. Just admit what you're doing, then we can get on with our business," he said in a lower voice.

Quinn knew the man seated before him extremely well. He was about to be eliminated, and based on past professional interactions with Auguste Marchand, there was nothing that could stop him. "Who are you talking about?"

Marchand crossed his legs as he looked at his old friend and colleague. "Danny and Billie MacDougal. I saw you with them," Marchand said softly.

Masterson leaned forward. "Look, Auggie, I had no clue they were your subjects. Please let my wife go so you can deal with me however you wish. Please just let her go as a favor to an old friend," Masterson pleaded.

"Okay, as a favor to an old friend." Marchand nodded to one of his men.

The man stepped around the table and quickly placed the barrel of the suppressed pistol to Quinn's temple. The weapon discharged, and Quinn fell over onto his side.

Quinn's wife cried out through the gag on her mouth as she watched her husband die. Her eyes slammed shut as she cried out uncontrollably. While she was sobbing, the man shot her in the chest. He placed the pistol in Quinn's hand as the other man removed the restraints from his wife. Marchand pulled an envelope from his pocket, placing it on the table.

All three men quietly and swiftly left the townhouse.

22

Billie sat in the chair next to Danny's hospital bed as she watched him sleep. Her eyes were red and puffy from crying.

She looked at the window to see Capt. Graves staring back at her on the opposite side of the glass. Billie stood quietly, exiting the room to greet him.

"So, what's the verdict?" Graves asked.

"The doctor said he's rarely seen a more severe beating. Danny has a concussion, three broken ribs, a broken left arm, and two teeth knocked out. Not to mention multiple contusions and abrasions all over his body. The doctor said he should fully recover if he has complete rest," Billie stated with tears forming in her eyes.

"What about you? Are you okay?" Graves asked.

"I'm fine, Captain. Aside from a bruised ego for getting taken, I'm alright."

"How'd they get to you?"

"I went back into the hotel after Rick left to talk to the desk clerk. As I was in the hallway, someone grabbed me from behind. Next thing I knew, I was being dragged into that old warehouse," Billie explained.

"Had you seen them before?" Graves asked.

"No. The first time I got a look at them was at the warehouse when they took the blindfold off me. Wade was the only person I recognized."

"Well, you and Danny are lucky to be alive. The big gorilla who put a thumping on Danny was one Gregory Pastrel, AKA The Caretaker. He was paroled two months ago from San Quentin. Stone cold killer.

"The three tattooed tough guys were cartel enforcers. The Cabal use them for hits here in the states. And, of course, you know the douche bag who was in charge of the whole thing.

"My guess is once we sort this out, the perp who tried to take you out downtown is tied to these guys," Graves stated.

"What about the clerk and the attendant at the hotel?" Billie asked.

"The desk clerk wasn't involved. The parking attendant was clueless. He said a 'Mexican guy with a lot of tattoos gave him a hundred dollars to stall getting Danny's car up to the valet station, and to keep his mouth shut."

"We haven't been able to put together how Wade survived all this time living off grid, right here in Seattle under our noses. It'll take time, but we'll find out. Then there's the issue of who took out the bad guys. Did you get a look at them?" Graves asked.

"I saw a figure dressed in tactical gear approaching us. The way the figure walked, stood, and was built, indicated it was a man. A tall man at that. Full face mask with eye slits. He didn't say a word, just cut Danny's right hand loose, then left the knife for him. There could have been others with him, but I didn't see anyone else."

"Well, we don't have anything to go on. They even picked up the spent brass. No footprints or fingerprints. Not even clothing remnants. It's like they were never there," Graves stated.

"We do have one lead, though. That long-legged tramp from DC," Billie stated.

"Maybe not," Graves responded.

"What?" Billie said with a puzzled look.

Graves opened his cell phone and went into his mail. "I requested the file on Dorothy Harris. This is what they sent me," he said as he showed Billie the document.

"You're joking," Billie said as she looked at the file photo. "*This* is Dorothy Harris?"

The picture was of a plain looking woman with no makeup, blonde hair, weighing 210 pounds.

"That's what my wife would say happens when you don't use makeup or product in your hair."

"This doesn't make sense. We did a search of the State Department web site. That is *not* the person who showed up," Billie said, surprised.

"We have photos from the hotel and the restaurant of our suspect. They're running them through facial recognition as we speak," Graves stated.

Billie took in a deep breath, then let it out slowly. "Well, we sure screwed this one up, Captain," she stated.

"There's no getting around the fact that we got complacent. We didn't think they would come after us so soon. I thought we'd have enough time to get you guys out of town. My fault; I'm sorry."

"Not your fault. We all have to share in the blame," Billie responded.

Graves pursed his lips as he turned to leave. "We got lucky. The good Lord looks out for fools, cripples, and the Seattle Police Department."

Billie shook her head as she watched her boss leave.

Brad Carver looked through the binoculars at the airfield hangar as the sun was going down. He watched the employees leave for the evening. When the last car drove through the chain-link gate, one of the two remaining employees closed and locked it. The two security officers went back into the hangar.

Carver scanned the south side for cameras, but found none. Rising to his knees, he swung his rifle around to his chest. He pushed up on the center of the fence from the bottom as he lay on his back. Sliding under the chain-link, he rolled onto the asphalt.

With his pistol held out in front of him, he quickly moved to the wall of the hangar. He slowly raised his head up and over the window sill. The two security officers were sitting in the break room drinking coffee.

Carver moved around to the front of the hangar to find the main doors open. Squatting, he looked to see multiple refrigerated containers around the hangar floor. He kept low as he entered the space, making his way to the closest one. He took pictures of the interior of the container, then backed out of the building.

Moving to the opposite side of the building, he quickly made his way to the outbuildings. Carver stopped next to the warehouse, looking through the window. His jaw set as he saw small children locked inside cages with nothing more than a blanket on the concrete floor. Calculating the large warehouse would hold at least a hundred and fifty cages.

He dropped back down to the ground, removing his backpack. After pulling out the small cylindrical device, he put the backpack on, quickly moving toward the three C-130s parked on the tarmac in front of the hangar. He stopped next to the first aircraft, getting down on his knees under the wheel well. He stretched his arm out, placing the magnetic tracker at the top of the well.

Carver carefully worked his way back to the perimeter fence where he entered the property. Crawling up under the chain-link, and quickly moving away from the property, he worked his way back toward the car.

After getting back, he entered the vehicle and pulled a cellphone from his vest. Dialing the number, he started the car, then turned the AC on Max.

Opening the bottle of water, he took a drink as the call was answered. "What do you have?"

"Sir, I found out where he's spending all the money. They have an old airfield about ten miles north of the ranch. The hangar and the outbuildings are newly refurbished. There were three C-130s parked on the ramp in front of the hangar," Carver stated.

"You think he's moving the human cargo out in the open in a C-130?"

"No, sir. There were about a hundred refrigerated containers in the hangar. I got up close to one of them. There's no insulation on the interior. My bet is they're transporting the cargo in the containers."

"How many containers per aircraft?"

"Six. Twenty to twenty-five children per container, or product, or both. This is no small operation, sir. Johnson is moving a shit load of product. He's got to have more aircraft, based on the number of containers I saw," Carver stated.

"What markings are on the aircraft?"

"Dark brown silhouette of the head of a Texas longhorn on the tail, with the words Choice Texas Beef underneath. All the containers have the same logo," Carver stated.

"I'll check on the operation once I get back to DC. There was an attempt on the MacDougals last night," the voice announced.

"Were they hurt?" Carver asked.

"The woman wasn't, but the man was beaten pretty badly. He's in the hospital as we speak."

"Do we know who did it?" he asked

"We're pretty sure we know who it was. I should have a definitive answer by tomorrow. Are you finished there?"

"For the most part, sir. There's not much more I can do for now, unless you have additional work for me," Carver replied.

"No, not at this time. Let's have you get back up here as soon as you can. They'll try for the MacDougals again, probably sooner than later. Your team can fully brief you once you're back up here."

"Yes, sir, I'll leave immediately," Carver said as he hung the phone up.

Walter Killian sat at the kitchen table having his coffee as he reviewed the morning emails. He took a sip from the cup, then opened the secure communication from Ellis Hollabird.

Walt slammed the cup back down onto the table as he reached for his phone. He quickly punched in Capt. Graves' number.

"Good morning, Walt, what's up?" Graves stated.

"Sir, we received a secure communication from Mr. Hollabird. He said Mr. Masterson and his wife were found dead in their home last night," Walt stated solemnly.

The other end of the line was silent for a full thirty seconds. Walt could hear Graves take in a deep breath before speaking. "Does the email give any details?"

"Yes, sir. Mr. Hollabird said it's being investigated as a murder suicide."

Graves grunted on the other end of the line. "Walt, can you set up a meeting of the members as soon as possible?"

"I will, sir. I'm sorry, Captain. I know you were very close with Mr. Masterson."

"Thanks, Walt. Get that meeting together as quickly as you can," Graves said as he hung up.

Danny sat in the hospital wheelchair waiting for Doctor Clement to come to the room. His left eye was no longer swollen shut, but still black from the beating.

His left arm was in a cast, bound to his chest preventing movement. His legs ached from being kicked repeatedly by the caretaker. He ached all over, but was not about to say so. He wanted to be discharged.

Doctor Clement approached Danny and Billie carrying a large plastic bag. As he stopped in front of them, he looked at Danny. "Lt. MacDougal, are you sure you're feeling up to speed?"

"A hundred percent, Doc," Danny replied.

Clement handed the bag to Billie as he looked back and forth between the two. "For the first time in my career, I'm going to say something that's absolutely none of my business.

"Almost four months ago, I pulled a bullet out of your chest, Mrs. MacDougal. I really didn't think you were going to pull through, but very relieved when you did.

"Then, I'm given the distinct pleasure of treating your husband for the third time. The first two, I treated him for gunshot wounds. This time, he's beaten so badly that I thought he might have permanent damage to his mobility and cognitive functions.

"Now you guys do as you see fit, it's your lives after all. But at your age, it's time to move on and find better vocations and lifestyles. Get a grownup job, a job where you interact with adults, go off and be happy. Golf, crochet, collect stamps—I don't care what it is, so long as it isn't in law enforcement.

"Now, I've said my peace. In the bag are dressings enough for a week. There are meds in there for three days, plus prescriptions for more. No, and

I do mean *no,* strenuous activity until that cast comes off. I'll see you in one week for a follow-up," Clement said as he frowned at Billie and Danny.

"Thank you, Doctor. I'll make sure he stays still for at least thirty days," Billie responded.

"I'm counting on that, Mrs. MacDougal," Clement said as he turned away.

"Man, that guy's bedside manner sucks," Danny stated.

The nurse standing next to Billie looked down at Danny. "He cares about his patients. What he just said to you, I've never heard him say before. He likes you guys," the nurse said as she started to push Danny's wheelchair to the main entrance.

At the hospital exit, Billie ran to the parking lot to get the car.

Danny carefully adjusted himself to be able to stand once the car arrived. As Billie pulled the car up to the curb, the nurse helped Danny get up. He grunted with pain as he stood from the wheelchair.

As Billie opened the door, the two women helped Danny sit in the passenger seat. After exhaling hard, Danny settled into the seat.

He turned to the nurse. "Thank you for all your help," he said.

Billie hugged the nurse before hurrying around to the driver's side. "Thank you," she said to the nurse from over the roof as she entered the car. Once buckled in, Billie pulled out into the street, pointing the car toward home.

"Well, guess this answers the question about leaving the department," Billie said as she negotiated the traffic of downtown Seattle.

"I agree. There's just one last thing I need to do before we leave," Danny said as he stared out the windshield.

"Oh no you don't. That's what got us *into this* trouble," Billie said as she waved her right hand toward Danny.

"This isn't dangerous or stressful. I made a promise to Melissa to put Rosie's death to rest and find those responsible. I only have one more interview left to do that. It's one of the FBI agents in lockup at the Federal Detention Facility at SEATAC," Danny replied.

"Can't you have Rick or Larry do that? I don't like it, Danny," Billie replied.

"No, *I* have to do it," he replied.

"Okay, but after that, we're outta here," Billie said forcefully.

"I do need to have Ryan get me that implant, though," Danny said with a smirk.

"Already done. He came up to your room when you were sedated and put it in you," Billie said with a big smile.

"Oh yeah? Where?"

"I'll never tell," she responded.

"You're really not gonna tell me, are you?" Danny protested.

"Serves you right for not getting it when you were supposed to," Billie stated.

Danny groaned as Billie went over a bump in the road.

She frowned as she looked over at her husband. "Be nice to me. I can find a whole lot more bumps on the way home."

23

Peter Cornell walked along the path of the Washington Mall holding an umbrella as a gentle rain came down. Auguste Marchand approached Cornell from behind as they passed the Museum of Natural History. Also carrying an umbrella, Marchand slowed as he caught up to Cornell.

"Chaos has erupted as a result of not fulfilling this contract," Cornell stated.

"The problem came from your end, Peter. The responsible party was one of yours. At least he used to be one of yours," Marchand stated.

"And this is why I saw Quinn Masterson and his wife in the news?" Cornell asked.

"Yes."

"I find it highly unlikely he was responsible, as he hasn't been active for over a decade now," Cornell protested.

"I placed him with our targets at a location in the Washington mountains. When confronted, he admitted it."

"You'd better be right. Your immediate attention is required, Auguste. This delivery must be completed. You're authorized to make deliveries on all of the Seattle items as soon as possible, irrespective of collateral damage. Is there anything you require from us?" Cornell asked.

"Senator Gibbs has become a problem that has gone beyond the stage of an annoyance. He's responsible for a failed attempt on the principal targets.

As a result, he's brought unwanted attention to us all. Is this a problem that you can control?" Marchand asked.

"Not at this particular time. We'll review your request in the near future."

Marchand looked at Cornell. "I shall be in touch soon," he stated as he turned to walk away.

The MacDougal house was filled with the entire Seattle team. The members had brought food and drinks, knowing Danny was unable to cook.

Danny sat in the reclining chair of their living room as the remainder of the team sat around in a circle. Clearly concerned for Danny, Buster remained curled up in his lap.

Danny's lips were no longer swollen, but still bruised badly. The same was true of his left eye. He winced from the pain in his chest every time he moved. He and Billie had remained mostly silent as the group interacted among themselves. Danny was having a hard time focusing on the tasks at hand.

Capt. Graves leaned forward in his chair. "Before we get started, I need to address our failures surrounding Danny and Billie's abduction. This is not your fault," Graves said as he waved his hand around the room. "The blame rests completely and solely on my shoulders. We got complacent, and it nearly cost Danny and Billie their lives—something we promised wouldn't happen.

"Also, we lost Quinn and his wife. The media is calling it a murder suicide. That's a lie of the highest order. I spoke with Ellis, Wanda, and Glenn. They're pulling out all the stops to find out who did this." Graves was becoming angrier and angrier as he spoke. "There are a limited number of people who have the skills to fulfill tasks at this level. Eventually we'll find them.

"Walt has confiscated three hundred eighty million dollars from the accounts of the targets we identified. We'll receive back a sizeable portion of those funds for current operational expenses. Before his death, Quinn was putting together a group of operators for us. Wanda said she and Ellis will finish up on that. She said they'll get back with us ASAP.

"To date, only eight people in politics, media, and the entertainment industry have refused to step down." Graves looked at Danny. "Is the Russian code still operational?"

"Yes," he replied.

Graves turned to Walt. "And our contacts in the media are still in place?"

"Yes, sir," Walt responded.

Graves looked out over the group. "Is everyone in agreement?"

All the members of the group agreed.

"Then send out the data on the eight who haven't left, Walt," Graves stated with an emotionless face.

Unable to sit still anymore, Graves stood and began walking around the group. "The thug who was tailing Billie downtown, Alex Rodriguez, has been identified as being with the Gulf Cartel. Thanks to Billie's contacts in DEA, he was identified. This ties him to the three cartel enforcers who were with Phillip Wade at the old cannery," Graves stated.

"Walt and I recognized the tattoo on his arm immediately. The crossed arrows with an upright sword through the center is a special forces logo," Winters said with an emotionless face. "The Latin phrase on his arm, *De Oppresso Libe* means *To Liberate the Oppressed*."

"That's rich," Danny said with disgust in his voice.

"The picture is starting to come into focus. Wade has been controlling this all along. The question is, who was bankrolling and covering for him?" Graves stated.

"Walt, get what you can on him. I'll have everything he had on his person available for you down at the station. It'll be ready for you first thing in the morning."

Graves turned to Winters. "Sergeant Major, this is what you did for a living before the ministry. Can you join Walt on this?"

"Affirmative, Captain. Consider it done," Winters replied.

"Thank you, Gary," Graves replied. He turned to Danny with his eyebrows lowered. "Now to the issue of Danny's dinner date. Facial recognition has identified her as one Jeri Patronne. She's an independent contractor, currently working for the Justice Department," Graves stated.

Danny grunted as he slowly readjusted himself in the chair. "The captain is wrong. This is my fault. First of all because I didn't get the implant when I was supposed to. Second, because I was careless at the hotel.

"She was working with Wade; of that you can be sure. She made it a point for me to see her with Wade at the cannery," Danny said.

"Wait a minute, she was there with Wade? Danny, you didn't tell us that," Graves protested loudly.

Danny leered at Graves as he stared him down. "Had a lot on my mind since that night. Guess it just got past me," Danny said with a stone-cold stare.

"Look, Danny, I know you're hurting. They beat you up pretty bad, but—"

Danny quickly but painfully sat upright as he interrupted Graves. "You seriously think I'm worried about *my safety*! You're not the one who had to watch three filthy sleazebags tear the clothes off your wife, preparing to rape her."

The others in the room stared at Danny with sober faces as he responded.

Danny scanned the room with fire in his eyes. "If it takes me the rest of my life, I'm going to hunt every one of these bastards down and kill them. Especially the freaks who are calling the shots.

"When Quinn told me what could happen to me and Billie, I was laughing inside. That kind of evil doesn't happen in a civilized society, I told myself. Well, I was wrong. Gang raping women, then chopping them up into little pieces. You can't reason with animals who would do something like that. They're not even from the same species."

Danny winced as he stood from the chair. "Had it not been for the mystery people interceding over these past weeks, we wouldn't be here." Danny turned and walked to the kitchen.

"Well somebody is covering us, that's for sure," Larry Colton stated emphatically.

"Do we have any clue who it could be?" Rick asked.

Danny returned from the kitchen with a beer, slowly sitting down. "No clue. But someone is most certainly covering our butts. They stopped what we assume was an attempted assault at our house. They stopped an attempt on Billie's life. And this last time, they killed everyone involved in our abduction."

"I'll get the DC contingent involved. Maybe they can shed some light on this," Graves stated.

Winters stood as he looked at the others. "Come on, guys, we need to get going so Danny and Billie can have some time with each other."

"Yeah, I gotta get going too," Rick said as he stood.

Danny remained seated while the others gave him half smiles as they were leaving. Danny watched as Graves gave him an almost apologetic wave before walking out the door. He nodded in response.

After the group had left the house, Billie threw the door's deadbolt, then turned to face him. She pulled one of the dining room chairs in front of him and sat down. "Do you want to talk about it, baby?" Billie said softly.

"Talk about what?" Danny responded with a frown.

Billie reached out and held Danny's right hand. "The dressing down you gave Graves."

"I didn't dress him down," Danny said with a frown.

"Honey, you stomped on him." Billie reached out and kissed him on the cheek. "What's going on?"

Danny kept his head down, remaining silent as he held Billie's hand.

"Honey, look at me, please," Billie said softly.

Danny lifted his head, turning toward her.

"Baby, nothing happened. The Lord took care of us. He kept us safe. I'm fine, so you can stop worrying. We just need to get you healed up." Billie kissed him tenderly.

"Have I told you yet today how much I love you?" Danny said as he sat back in the chair.

"At least a dozen times," she replied with a smile. Billie leaned forward. "Danny, I didn't want to say this while the others were here."

"What?" he said with furrowed eyebrows.

"You know who saved us, don't you?" she said most directly.

Danny took in a deep breath before responding. "What makes you think that?"

"The look on your face when the topic was brought up," she responded.

"That's pretty good detective skills there, Sergeant," Danny responded.

"I was trained by the best," she replied. "Not to mention the fact that your four-inch folding Gerber knife has been missing for three months. Imagine my surprise to see it taken in as evidence. I watched the big guy who cut you loose stick it in the arm of the chair you were tied to."

"Billie, do you know how many millions of those knives Gerber has made? That's pretty thin, Detective," Danny said with a frown.

"You should have never let me use it over the years, because I would see the initials DM on the blade every time I used it. Now cut the crap, MacDougal. How'd that guy get your knife, and who is he?"

"Nicholas Garcetti," Danny said abruptly.

"The FBI agent?" Billie said with surprise.

"Yup," he said while looking Billie in the eyes.

"Danny, you gotta help me out here. You gave your knife to an assassin—why? What in the world happened?"

Danny took a long drink from his beer. "After you were shot, I went to a pretty dark place. I knew they had to kill us both. I waited in your hospital room after hours, and, sure enough, William Barnes showed up.

"He tried to inject the contents of a syringe into your IV. I stopped him, took him down to the old Decker Building, and had a 'one on one' with the little troll.

"He told me he reported to two FBI agents, Nicholas Garcetti and Todd Franks. Barnes additionally said Franks killed Mortenson, he killed Lambert, and Garcetti killed Rowland and Crossland.

"I caught up with Garcetti a few days later and had a chat with him in the basement of the Pike Place Market. I tied him to an old chair with duct tape and talked with the asshole. After the conversation, I got the feeling he didn't have a clue what was in the file. I let him read it from my iPad. He actually got pissed. He didn't know what was on the disks he'd been killing people for. He was told it was for National Security reasons.

"I gave him some thumb drives with the file on them, then cut his right arm loose. I stuck the knife into the arm of the chair and told him to leave us alone. Now you know everything," Danny said with a sigh.

"And your interview with Terry Post; where does that come in?" Billie asked.

"The evidence obtained at Melissa's house tied him to Rosie's death. When we interviewed him, he implicated Franks in her disappearance. My next stop was going to be Franks at the SeaTac Federal Detention Center, but then this happened," Danny said as his right hand waved over his body.

"Do you need me to go with you for the interview?" Billie asked.

"No, this is something *I* need to do on my own. I want him looking directly into my eyes. But there is something you *can* do. With your federal contacts, could you find out where Garcetti's at and what his position is?" Danny asked.

Billie placed her right hand on Danny's leg. "Of course. But, Danny, there's something that doesn't add up. If Franks killed Barnes, that would have had to be after your interrogation. And all of that took place in the Decker Building. How'd that happen?"

Danny stared into Billie's eyes intensely with a blank look. "Best not to ask that question," he said coldly.

"Baby, if what I think happened, happened, I understand. With all that's unfolded over these past months, the rulebook has gone out the window. I can't point my finger at someone because of what they've done while my own desires are to do the same thing to the sick people we're dealing with. I only say this because I know you're suffering.

"You're a decent man, Danny MacDougal; your nightmares attest to that. If you weren't having nightmares, I'd be worried about you. Just know that I'm here for you," she said as she bent over, kissing him on the forehead.

After Billie left, Danny stared out the front window. His eyes narrowed as his jaw set. "I'll find every last one of you. You will *never* be able to hide from me," he said in a low whisper.

Senator Gibbs stood in front of the flat screen television mounted on the wall of his office. His arms were folded across his chest as he watched the news media try to spin the damaging reports coming out about his friends and colleagues. His office manager came into the room with a tray of coffee and pastries.

She turned to Gibbs after placing the tray on the table. "I just saw the news about Senator Rockwell. They said he overdosed on cocaine. I didn't have any idea he used drugs. What a shame," she stated.

"Yes, it was a shame," Gibbs responded with a monotone voice as he continued to watch the television.

After his manager left the room, he heard a knock on the door jamb. Gibbs turned to see Congresswoman Janice Alberts standing in the doorway. He spoke as he turned back toward the television. "Come in, Janice. Close the door behind you."

The bookish fifty-three-year-old congresswoman spoke while standing at Gibbs' side. "We're losing our power base, Harold. We're watching our demise unfold before our very eyes," she stated.

Still facing the television, Gibbs grunted. "There's always more where they came from. We just find more idealistic drones and compromise them as well."

Alberts' black hair was cut in a pageboy style. Her brown suitcoat and ankle-length gray skirt gave her five-foot-two-inch frame a librarian type of appearance. She was anything but a librarian, however. She had the distinction of being Gibbs' attack dog in the House. She held tight reigns on those politicians they controlled. She was known as The Enforcer. "This is a disaster. It'll take years to recoup the ground we just lost," she stated.

"Janice, slow down, will you? This is a setback, nothing more. It doesn't matter who gets elected or appointed. Let's get our people activated so we can place who we need in the vacancies. I don't care what party they're with, get our choices submitted," Gibbs ordered.

Alberts took in a deep breath and grunted as she exhaled. "Whoever's doing this, will just do it again. They need to be stopped, Harold. They need to be stopped or we'll all go down."

"Neither you nor I will go down. This will all go away soon," Gibbs reassured her. "Now get the people on our list warmed up and in the bull pen."

Alberts slowly turned and walked to the door. As she turned the doorknob, she looked back at Gibbs before opening the door. "They'll find out about us, Harold. They always do."

Gibbs didn't respond. He only continued to look at the television. Alberts opened the door and slowly left the office.

24

Danny looked up the driveway to see the Uber vehicle drop Walt off in front of the house. He stepped back into the garage, setting his coffee cup on the workbench. Danny nodded as Walt entered.

"Well, did you get her all registered?"

Walt quickly replied back at Danny. "Sure did. She's all legal."

"Well, I'm happy she's going to someone who loves classic cars and will treat her right. Enjoy," Danny said with a smile.

"Lieutenant, when are they coming for your household goods?"

"Saturday," Danny responded.

"I'll be here to help," Walt responded.

"That's okay, Walt. The movers can take care of it. If all works out well, we'll be outta here Sunday morning."

"I'm gonna miss having you guys here."

"We'll see you all the time, Walt. I'm sure Astrid will see to that," Danny said with a smile.

"Lieutenant, I know I could get in trouble for this, but I wrote down some information for you. The coroner pulled an implant out of Wade's body. I scanned it and found out it was manufactured by Lintel Industries in Silicon

Valley. I got into their records and found out it was one of a batch sold to Ballencourt Enterprises two years ago," he said while handing Danny the card.

"Since the Seattle PD doesn't implant their employees, present company excepted, I thought it may help you," Walt stated.

"What did it have on it?" Danny asked.

"It was coded with Wade's personal data. It also is coded for access to restricted area entrances. Where, I don't know."

Danny's eyes opened wide. A huge smile formed as he stared at Walt. "You did good, Walt. I'll look into it."

"Sorry if I messed up, Lieutenant," Walt said apologetically.

"No, not at all. If anything, you should be one of my detectives instead of working in IT," Danny replied.

"Lieutenant, there's something else I wanted to ask you about if I could," Walt asked.

"What's that?" Danny responded.

"It's the master file. It makes no sense that they keep trying to obtain it. There would be no reason to focus on the master file, because you guys said you made well over a dozen copies. They'd be pulling their hair out trying to find all the copies."

"We just assumed they wanted it because it was the original, which it is by the way. From a legal standpoint, we have the original, which is unalterable. In court, that's a slam dunk," Danny said.

"That makes sense, sir, but there's also another possibility."

"Oh?" Danny said curiously.

"If there are ten master files which represent the ten regions here in the US, there would have to be a way to download data into the master files from a central point. Otherwise, you'd have to do it the old-fashioned way by constantly updating it manually."

The light went on in Danny's brain as he listened to Walt. "Of course, that makes perfect sense. Can the files be coded to automatically retrieve updated data?" Danny asked with excitement in his voice.

"Of course. But there's a downside to that as well. If we link up and download the new information, they'll be able to track *us*," Walt stated.

"So why didn't they chase us down when we downloaded it in the beginning?" Danny asked.

"My guess is they hadn't created a new master for Region Ten yet. And since you were in such close proximity to Ballencourt Towers, it went unnoticed," Walt posited.

"But they've undoubtedly created another master file for Region Ten by now?" Danny asked.

"That would follow," Walt stated.

"So, then we should be able to have our master file updated, right?" Danny asked.

"In theory, yes. If we could get the master file in close proximity to the tower, it stands to reason we could piggyback for the download," Walt said.

"That requires two conditions to be true. First, that the master file is in Ballencourt Towers. They could have moved their headquarters. Second, that we know the time of the automatic download," Danny said with a smirk.

"Typically, downloads happen at around midnight, or possibly one AM. As to the new master being there, that's your area, Lieutenant," Walt stated.

"Well, we know Waterston is the new replacement for Ballencourt, so we'll just have to assume the new file was placed there as well," Danny stated.

"I can load the master onto our new computer and get it close to the tower. In theory, it should work," Walt stated.

Danny was thinking hard as his eyes darted around the garage. "I reviewed the plans for the tower a while back. The computer mainframe is in the basement. There's an entrance to the tower just out from the Pioneer Park tour. I can have Rick or Larry get you right at the foundation of the tower. Would that work for you?"

"Sure. I can get into anything with our new toy. But, Lieutenant, I don't need to be with someone. I can do it by myself," Walt stated.

"No! You're going in with one of the guys. We lost a good detective and friend because he went in there alone. I'm not losing you too. You go in with an escort," Danny said forcefully.

"Roger that," Walt replied.

"Okay, I'll get you the master file. It's in our secure location. It'll take a while to retrieve," Danny said.

"Glad you have it in a secure location, sir," Walt said with a serious tone as he opened the driver's door on the VW.

"Oh, it's secure alright. It's being watched by over a hundred guards," Danny responded.

Walt closed the door, then started the car. "Thanks again, Lieutenant."

Danny waved at Walt as he drove out of the garage and down the driveway.

The C-130 touched down on the Southern California Logistics Center Airport in Victorville, California. SCLCA occupied the facility formerly known as George Air Force Base.

The airport had little traffic, mostly limited to civil aviation. Almost all of the buildings at SCLCA had been abandoned since the military turned the property over to the city of Victorville.

The C-130 taxied to the apron at the end of the taxiway. As the aircraft stopped, the rear cargo doors were opening. The pilot had parked the aircraft close to the two flatbed tractor trailer trucks. The crew unstrapped the cargo containers as the forklift approached the cargo ramp.

The forklift operator skillfully extracted the six Texas Beef containers, placing them on the trucks. As soon as one of the containers was placed on the flatbed, the drivers were strapping it down. The operation was like a well-oiled machine.

As soon as the flatbed trucks pulled away, the two fuel trucks pulled up to the C-130, beginning the refueling process.

Once the refueling was complete, the crew began preparing the aircraft for the return trip. The efficiency of the operation was a testament to Governor Gordon Johnson's demands for perfection. The aircraft had unloaded its cargo in under an hour and was taxiing for the return trip in under two.

The entire operation from landing to takeoff was witnessed by only eight people. Johnson had been true to his word to <u>have as few people involved in the process as possible.</u>

Dressed in a suit and tie, Danny entered the Federal Detention Center, SEATAC. His left arm was in a sling tied around his neck. The left sleeve of his suit coat was hanging empty as it draped over his left shoulder.

He was forcing himself to ignore the pain from his ribs as he was escorted down the corridor of the holding facility.

Danny nodded toward the guard while entering the interview room. "Thank you," he said as he stepped inside. His face grimaced when he slowly sat in the hard metal chair behind the table.

He heard the deadbolt slam as the echo from the door opening bounced off the walls of the room. He saw Todd Franks enter the room wearing an orange jumpsuit, chained at his wrists and ankles. Franks had clearly been involved in altercations while in the facility. Danny could see scars on his face that weren't there before. He also had a large gauze bandage on his right forearm. Franks had lost weight and looked haggard.

Franks smirked at Danny as he sat opposite of him. "There has to be a god, 'cause my wishes have been fulfilled. Too bad they didn't finish the job. You look like you finally got what you deserve," Franks said as he leered at Danny.

"You should see the other guy," Danny responded.

"Bet he doesn't look as bad as you. I'd like to buy him dinner," Franks said with a scowl.

"Don't know, haven't seen him since he went to the morgue," Danny returned. "Well, enough of this family reunion crap. Time to get down to business. Todd Franks, you are being charged with the murder of Rosita Martinez. You have the right to remain silent—"

Franks interrupted Danny. "What's this all about, MacDougal? I don't even know a Rosita Martinez. What kind of bullshit is this?" Franks said angrily.

"Oh, no bullshit, Todd. Martinez is the woman you ordered to be disposed of after your henchmen stuck a needle into her neck at the Mortenson house. Your wanna-be tough guys from Ballencourt Enterprises gave you up; at least the ones still alive. They cut a deal."

Franks squirmed uncomfortably in his chair as he heard the words.

"Now continuing, if you will. You have the right to remain silent. Anything you say can, and will, be used against you. You have the right to council. If you cannot afford council, one will be appointed for you. Now, do you understand your rights as having been read to you?"

"Yeah, I understand," Franks stated with a smirk.

"Do you want to talk to me, or do you want an attorney?"

"I got nothing to hide, MacDougal. Now, what's your game?" Franks said matter-of-factly.

"I'll talk to the assistant US attorney after we're done here. He either gets a glowing report or more information to dig a deeper hole to put you in. Your choice."

"What do you want?" Franks said in a lower voice.

"I want the people who ran you and Garcetti. I want to go so far up the ladder, I'll get a nose bleed. I want the head of the snake, Franks."

Franks shrunk down low in his chair. "These walls have ears, MacDougal."

Danny got up and knocked on the door. The officer opened the door. "Yes, sir?"

"We need to go outside in the yard. Do you have a place we can be alone?"

"Yes, sir, I can arrange that," the officer responded.

Danny and Franks walked together as the corrections officer remained behind them. Once outside, they found themselves in a small grassy area surrounded by a nine-foot chain link fence.

"If you want to walk down the grass, you can be alone. Just wave at me when you're ready."

"Thank you, Officer," Danny said as he and Franks turned to walk to the other end of the small yard.

"Okay, what do you have, Franks?"

"I want complete immunity, MacDougal. No screwing around. If I give you the information I have, they'll kill me. I need immunity *and* protection," Franks said nervously.

"We can protect you. I'll set you up in a remote location with enough money to last you a lifetime. This, of course, depends on the information we get," Danny said reassuringly.

"No US marshalls! No government anything. Can you cover me, MacDougal? I mean *really* cover me?"

"Yes. I would be the only person who knew where you were going. Franks, I can have a new driver's license, new credit cards, Social Security card, a completely new identity. No one would find you. I'll put you in the most remote place on the planet if that's what it takes."

Franks nodded, sitting on the bench while he looked up at Danny. "There were ten of us on the team. At least there *were* ten. They may have transferred or restructured the team after I was arrested.

"Garcetti and I were controlled by Margaret Rosen at FBI headquarters. The rest worked for other agencies."

"She's the one who committed suicide, right?" Danny said.

"Yeah, right," Franks said with a smirk. "She was taken out. After the whole thing fell apart and you guys got your hands on the file, they wanted the whole thing cleaned up.

"It would have all fallen into place had that arrogant bastard Ballencourt not ordered the hit on you and your department.

"You have to believe me, MacDougal, Nick and I had no idea they were coming after you and your partners. We had complete surveillance at your houses, but we didn't know anything about the hit until you screamed into the camera that day."

Danny remained stone-faced as he continued to look at Franks. "And?" he asked.

"Someone got to Garcetti, and he went underground. They set me up for the murder of our asset, Barnes."

Danny shifted uncomfortably as he listened.

"They blew Ballencourt's yacht to pieces and killed Rosen. They'll get you and your friends, MacDougal, you can make book on it," Franks said nervously.

"Okay, who's they?" Danny said impatiently.

Franks nervously looked around the yard before speaking. "Senator Harold Gibbs for sure—"

Danny interrupted Franks. "Do I look stupid? You're giving me information I already have. We found the file, Franks! Gibbs' fingerprints are all over that thing. I need names of people who aren't in the file." Danny pulled his notebook from the right front pocket of his coat. He handed the notebook and pen to Franks. "Write their names, positions, and locations down."

As Franks began writing, Danny continued questioning him. "So, then you've seen the file?"

Franks spoke as he continued to write. "Yes. We weren't supposed to look at it, but I needed to find out what they were getting all spooled up about. It didn't make sense as to why they were doing what they were doing. It all fell into place once I looked at the file."

"And Garcetti, did he see it?"

"Nick? No way. He's too dedicated to the cause."

"So, who did Rosen report to outside the Bureau?"

"Gibbs, Congresswoman Janice Alberts, and CIA Chief of Operations Peter Cornell. There were others, but I never had contact with them."

"Now we're getting somewhere. Who does Cornell report to?"

"I don't have names. Some guy in Brussels and some billionaire on the East Coast in Virginia. I was too low on the totem pole. These are the only ones I have personal knowledge of. I can guess, but your guess would be as good as mine. But I do know that nothing happens here in the US unless those two approve it," Franks said.

"Okay, Franks," Danny said as he held his hand out for his notebook. He opened the book, looking at Franks' writing. "Looks good. I'll tell the DA you gave us invaluable information. Until I can get you out of here, I'll make sure they put you in solitary."

"MacDougal, these people set me up for murder. They won't stop until I'm gone. They've already tried to kill me twice now. I don't know why they went after me so hard. Maybe because they found out I read the file; maybe because you guys found it, I just don't know. But one thing is clear—they want me dead," Franks responded.

Danny pursed his lips before he responded. "I'll take care of it. Let's get you back inside." Danny raised his hand toward the corrections officer as they walked toward him.

"Thanks, MacDougal, I owe you one," Franks said as they entered the facility.

Danny remained silent as he continued to stare ahead.

25

Brad Carver picked up his cellphone as it began ringing. "Yes, sir."

Nicholas Garcetti responded on the other end. "I take it your team members briefed you?"

"Yes, sir. From what I can see, we got lucky," Carver stated.

"Nah, we had plenty of time. I just wanted to see all the players involved," Garcetti replied.

"He took a hell of a beating, sir."

"I owed him one," Garcetti responded coldly.

"MacDougal and his wife are eventually going to figure out what's going on, sir. We need to be more careful," Carver warned.

"He already knows. I left him a calling card," Garcetti replied.

"Are you sure that was wise? That could jeopardize our operations."

"MacDougal isn't your average flatfoot. Don't underestimate him. I did, and it nearly cost me my life. He would have figured it out sooner or later anyway. This way we're in a better position to control it."

"Very well, sir." Carver paused before continuing. "I received a phone call that may or may not be of concern for us."

"Oh?" Garcetti said curiously.

"An old friend and colleague of mine reached out to me about a job. We've worked for each other on and off many times over the years. He said he needs a dozen people for a protection job in Seattle," Carver stated.

"Really? Did he say who the employer was?"

"No, he would never reveal that. We worked together in the teams when we were in the Navy. He's a good egg, sir."

"Well, let me do some digging. I'll see if I can find out who the customer is. Text me his data."

"Can do. He's already on site and in contact with the Seattle group," Carver responded.

"By the way, the C-130 you put the tracker on flew to the Southern California Logistics Center Airport. The SCLCA is the old George Air Force Base in Victorville, California. It was on the ground for one hour and forty-nine minutes. It lifted off, then returned to the airfield in Texas.

"We need to get trackers on all the aircraft under their control, the containers as well, but you said there's almost two hundred of them, right?" Garcetti asked.

"Best as I could determine, sir. I can get maybe thirty of them. The ones up by the hangar doors are most likely to be used next," Carver stated.

"I can't do that. I need you right where you are until further notice."

"I can brief Red on it. He'll get the aircraft and the containers covered," Carver responded.

"Okay, make it happen. Did you go over the plans for the operation?" Garcetti asked.

"Yes, sir. It's doable, but it isn't going to be cheap. It just may break the bank, sir," Carver stated.

"Not to worry. The credit card just had its limit raised," Garcetti replied. "How much time do you need before initiating it?"

"Once we get the word, wheels up in eighteen hours," Carver stated.

"Very good. Keep the phone next to your ear."

"Will do. Anything else, sir?"

"No, just keep close to them, Brad. They'll try again," Garcetti warned.

"We're on it, sir. I'll be in touch."

After Carver terminated the call, he texted Red Caron. *Need you in my room asap.*

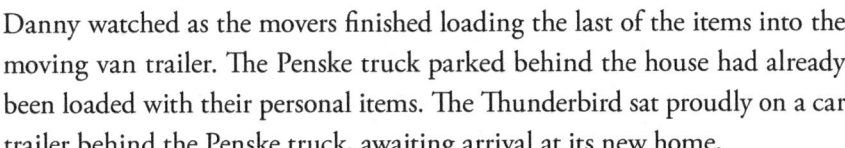

Danny watched as the movers finished loading the last of the items into the moving van trailer. The Penske truck parked behind the house had already been loaded with their personal items. The Thunderbird sat proudly on a car trailer behind the Penske truck, awaiting arrival at its new home.

He entered the garage to make the last walk around before closing it. As Danny latched the garage door closed, Billie came out of the house.

"Well, I've walked through the house three times. Opened every drawer, cupboard, and storage space. I can officially announce that there are none of our things remaining behind," Billie said with a grin.

As she stopped next to Danny, he reached around her waist, looking at the house. "Gonna miss the place."

"Me too. It was our first home together," she said as she kissed him on the cheek.

The driver stepped over to Danny and Billie. "We're all done here, folks, unless you have some other items?"

"No, you have it all." Danny pulled a piece of paper and a hundred-dollar bill from his wallet. "Here's the address for the storage units. Thanks for all the help," Danny said.

"And thank you, sir," the man said as he held up the bill with a smile. "We'll see you in three days, sir," he said before turning to leave.

They both watched as the moving truck drove down the driveway, then out onto the street. "Well, that closes the first chapter of our life. Let's get on with the next one," Billie said as she kissed Danny.

"Yeah, time to get to it," Danny said as he opened the door of the Penske truck.

"Honey, you sure you can handle the truck?" Billie asked.

Danny's mouth curled up at the corner. "That's why we got an automatic with power steering. I'll be fine, just follow me and keep an eye on the Thunderbird. If anything happens to that car, my wife will kill me."

"You can count on it," Billie said with a smile as she got into her car.

After starting the truck, Danny reached over and opened the door to the cat carrier. Buster exited the container, then curled up in Danny's lap. "You ready, Buddy?" Danny said with a smile as he placed the gear lever in drive. He drove slowly down the driveway, with Billie following. Pulling onto the street, he looked in the rearview mirror as the house disappeared when he drove around the corner. Danny took in a deep breath and slowly let it out as he settled in for the long drive. "Man, I hope we're doing the right thing," he said quietly as he headed toward Interstate 405.

Twenty passengers exited the Executive Terminal of the SEATAC Airport and walked to the two black Mercedes Benz passenger vans parked in the rear of the building. All of them were wearing cargo pants with mountaineering boots and lighter weight North Face jackets. Each carried canvas duffle bags for their personal items, with the red letters <u>RT</u> embroidered on the sides.

They all threw their duffle bags into the rear of the vans, then entered the seating area. The older bald-headed Allan Nowack stopped next to the car rental specialist, holding out his right hand toward the man.

The rental specialist handed the clipboard to Nowack. After checking the paperwork, he looked at the specialist. "And everything we requested is in the vehicles?"

"Yes, sir. Option twelve, for twenty people, as requested."

"Very well," the bald-headed Nowack said as he signed the papers.

Taking the clipboard, the specialist looked at the man. "Should you need anything else, please don't hesitate to contact us. And thank you for choosing Landon Automotive Rentals. Have a nice day."

Without responding, the man entered the van, putting his seatbelt on. Not saying a word, he started the vehicle and drove to the airport exit.

Driving east on Interstate 90, Danny took a sip of his Coke, placing the bottle back in the cup holder. He quickly reached over and grabbed a handful of French fries as his left knee kept the steering wheel straight. He dropped one of the fries onto the seat in front of Buster, which the cat quickly devoured.

For the first time in months Danny was relaxed, and excited to start over. A peace fell over him as he saw Billie following.

As he was looking in the mirror, he saw his old Volkswagen Beetle passing Billie, then him in the fast lane. Walt honked the bug's horn several times as he passed them, holding his left hand out the driver's side window, waving frantically.

Danny turned onto Highway 970 off of I-90 as his cellphone rang. He put the earbud in his ear, then lifted the cellphone up to see it was Capt. Graves calling. He rolled his eyes as he answered the call.

"Captain, what's up?"

"Just got a call from the assistant district attorney. He said his two star witnesses both committed suicide last night," Graves announced.

"What?" Danny yelled into the phone. "Dammit! They were locked away in solitary for their protection."

"Yeah, well, apparently they didn't get the memo," Graves responded.

"How'd they commit suicide?" Danny asked.

"They both hanged themselves," Graves stated.

"Of course, they did, sitting in solitary. What did they use, a length of rope no doubt?" Danny said mockingly.

"Extension cords."

"Well, ask a stupid question," Danny said sarcastically. "No use in asking for the camera footage. That's probably disappeared I'll bet," Danny replied.

"Of course, the footage is lost. This is just a courtesy call, Danny. Look, we both know why and how they died. We'll follow up on the leads you gave us. I just wanted to let you know rather than have you blindsided."

"Thanks, Captain. I'll tell Billie," Danny stated.

"Good deal. I'll be in touch," Graves said as he terminated the call.

Danny grunted in protest as he pulled into the town of Leavenworth. After driving the one mile to the hotel, Danny and Billie pulled up in front of the Alpine Haus. He put Buster back into the carrier, then stepped down from the truck.

Billie looked at the Volkswagen parked in front of the hotel. "Well, no keeping those two apart, huh?" she said with a giggle.

Karl and Marva came out of the hotel to see Billie and Danny walking toward them. Marva hugged her daughter as Karl shook Danny's hand. "Good grief, Danny, you look like you went through a buzzsaw," Karl stated.

Billie reached over, placing her hand on her father's arm. "Daddy, no questions; you promised."

"Okay, okay, sorry," Karl said as he patted Danny on the right shoulder. "Let's get you kids inside for some lunch, then we'll get the truck unloaded," Karl said.

"We put you two in the Presidential Suite. It has a lot more room and a bigger working space," Marva said to Billie.

"Marva, don't do that. We'll be fine with a smaller room," Danny protested.

"Not to worry, Danny, we've only rented it three times in the last five years," Karl said with a chuckle.

"Besides, Billie said it's only for ninety days. If it's any longer, we'll find you a house up here," Marva stated.

"If it all works out, we'll be up here permanently. If not, we'll be here at least through Christmas and New Year's," Billie said as she squeezed Danny's hand.

The four people entered the dining room to see Walt and Astrid sitting at the largest table. Walt immediately stood as they came in. "Mrs. MacDougal, Lieutenant," he said with a smile.

Danny spoke as he gently sat in one of the chairs. "Walt, I think we can dispense with the formalities, especially in light of the current situation. Please, just call me Danny," he asked with a grin.

"Okay, I will, Mr. MacDougal," Walt responded.

The others at the table laughed as they listened to Walt's stumbling.

Danny shifted the conversation toward Marva. "I'd like to help out in the kitchen, if that's okay?"

"Sure, if you're up to it. We could use the help. With the summer vacation over, our summer help has all gone back to university."

"Good. I won't get this cast off for another five weeks, but there's still a lot I can do," Danny replied.

"I'll help out with cleaning the rooms and helping at the front desk, Mom," Billie offered.

Tears began forming in Marva's eyes as she listened to her family. "You okay, Mom?" Billie asked.

"Just so happy, sweetie. I have the whole family back here now. It's just like it was twenty years ago," she said as she began to cry.

Danny looked toward the entrance of the restaurant to see a bearded man dressed in khaki cargo pants and a dark green wool pullover sweater looking back at him. The man had his hands clasped together in front of him, looking directly at Danny.

Danny excused himself as he walked toward the man. He had a forced PR smile on his face as he waited for Danny to stop in front of him.

The man reached out his right hand. "Mr. MacDougal, I'm Roger Dent. I'm the team leader for your security detail."

Roger Dent was a solidly built man, standing at five-foot-nine. Danny guessed him to be in his mid-forties. "Nice to meet you. Capt. Forrester told me you'd be meeting us here."

"I'm sorry about the loss of Capt. Masterson. He was the one who originally hired us," Dent stated.

"Yes, we've been dealing with a lot of loss for quite some time now. He'll be sorely missed," Danny responded. "Where's your team at?"

"I have them set up at the Comfort Inn. I'd like to stay here at the hotel close to you guys if that can be arranged?" Dent responded.

"Of course, I'll see to it. How many men do you have?" Danny asked.

"Fifteen, counting me, with four down in the city covering your people there. We'll be here as long as you need us, Mr. MacDougal," Dent stated.

"How will we know you and your people?"

"We'll all be in tan watch caps. Can't miss us," Dent responded.

"Very good. Come on in, I'll introduce you to the family, then we'll get you fed."

"I knew I was going to like this assignment," he said with a grin.

Led by Allan Nowack, the group of men entered the lobby of the downtown Seattle Hilton. As his nineteen men stood quiet behind him, Nowack stepped up to the hotel's main desk.

"Can I help you, sir?" the front desk clerk asked.

"Yes, a reservation for Allan Nowack. Twenty rooms for two weeks," he stated.

The clerk looked at the computer screen. "Yes, Mr. Nowack, your rooms are ready. Do you want the rooms kept on your corporate credit card for Rexlan Technologies?"

"Yes, that would be fine," Nowack stated as he signed the paperwork.

Nowack tossed the room keys to each person as they were given to him. After all the rooms were assigned, Nowack nodded toward the clerk as he walked away from the desk.

After getting off on the fourth floor, Nowack looked at all of his team. "My room in thirty minutes." The team left to go to their rooms, as he opened his door.

Once inside the room, he threw his suitcase onto the bed, then took off his coat. He removed the shoulder holster holding his Heckler and Koch VP9 with two spare magazines. He took off his shirt and stretched his back as he groaned from the effects of his past injuries. Even with his T-shirt still on, one could see the scars on his body.

His wounds came from decades of conflict. The forty-eight-year-old retired Green Beret was built like a slab of pig iron. He sported a salt and pepper crew cut hair style with a five-o-clock shadow beard. The scar on the right side of his face ran from the top of his right eye socket down to his neck. He killed the man who gave it to him with his bare hands.

Anyone doubting his resolve would pay a severe price. His dedication to his job could be described in two words: Never Married. Anything that took focus away from his vocation was something he couldn't be bothered with. Allan Nowack was not someone to be messed with.

He pulled three mini bottles from the bar and poured two of them into a glass. He threw his head back, downing the scotch. He poured the third bottle into the glass and set it on the table as his cellphone rang. He answered the call in a low monotone voice.

"Yes?" he answered.

Auguste Marchand spoke forcefully on the other end. "Are you ready to make the delivery?"

"We are. We'll deliver the package as soon as we receive the information from you about the address," Nowack stated.

"The primary deliveries have changed addresses. We're awaiting an update. The remaining deliveries haven't changed, but they all need to be delivered at the same time. Total surprise is mandatory. Our deliveries have been thwarted too many times," Marchand stated.

"Very well, we're waiting for the word from you."

"I'll let you know immediately," Marchand stated.

With the Thunderbird safely tucked away in the Eck family garage, the moving truck unloaded and taken to the Penske facility in Wenatchee, Danny and Billie began unpacking the suitcases in their room.

"Oh, I almost forgot to tell you. As we were coming into town, I got a call from the captain. He said that Post and Franks both committed suicide last night in their cells."

Billie's head snapped up. "What?"

"And before you ask the question, they both hung themselves with electrical cords. And no, there's no camera footage. It was lost," Danny said with sarcasm in his voice.

"Well, they're nothing if not consistent," she said while moving her head side to side. "I hope they gave you enough valuable information, 'cause going back to the well is no longer an option," Billie stated.

"They did. It's a trigger I don't want to pull just yet. Best not to show our hand until we're in a stronger position," Danny replied.

"Just don't wait too long. You know how you like to procrastinate," Billie said while slapping him on the rear.

Danny chased Billie around the room as she laughed loudly. He pushed her down on the bed, tickling her on her waist with his free hand as she screamed. "No, no, no, Danny, no tickles, please," she said as she writhed on the bed on her back. "Please, no!"

As they held each other on the bed, they heard a knock at their room. An out of breath Danny got up and walked to the door. As he opened it, he saw a red faced and clearly embarrassed Walt standing on the other side of the door, carrying the computer.

"I'm so sorry, Lieutenant, but you asked me to stop by the room to talk about the master file," Walt said shyly.

"It's okay, Walt, we were just letting off some steam. Just getting used to being unemployed," Danny said with a chuckle. "Come on in."

"Sorry, ma'am," Walt said as he entered the room, looking at Billie.

Billie chuckled as she straightened her hair. "Walt, it's quite alright." She handed him the bundle of disc containers wrapped in a blue and white checkered hotel dishtowel.

"Wow!" Walt said as he saw the large number of storage discs. "Good grief, there's enough storage room here to put the Library of Congress on."

"Really?" Danny said with surprise. "I guess I never noticed. But you're right, there's only thirty-eight-hundred pages of text. Even factoring in the videos and documents, that's a half a dozen discs at most."

"Exactly," Walt responded. "There has to be a lot more data hidden in the program. I'll see if I can dig it out," Walt said as he gathered the discs.

"Thanks, Walt. Keep me posted, will you?"

"I will. This shouldn't take too long," Walt said as he left the room.

Billie locked the door and turned back toward Danny. "Well, I've gotta dig in and start helping with the maid service. Will you be okay here?"

"I thought I'd dive into the kitchen and start putting up some ideas for meals your mother could use," Danny said as he placed the last bit of clothes into the drawers.

Billie kissed him on the cheek. "Thanks, baby. Mom will enjoy the help. She may fight you at first, but she secretly wants you helping in the kitchen."

"Hey, I'll win her over I've had tougher cases," he said with a smile.

"Her daughter for instance?" Billie replied.

"Just to name a few," Danny said as he winked at his wife.

Red Caron lay in the prone position as he looked through the binoculars at Gordon Johnson's aircraft hangar. Dressed in a ghillie suit, Red blended into the tall grass and sage brush around the airfield.

He was taking pictures with his telephoto lens camera as he surveilled the airfield through the noonday sun. With his pocket notebook in front of him, Red meticulously gathered information on the property, the buildings, and the airfield personnel.

A seasoned combat veteran, Red was used to lying still for long periods of time, waiting to engage the enemy. He wanted to observe the employees performing their daily routine, getting a lay of the land for his report to Brad Carver.

Red slid a piece of Jerky into his mouth as he watched the ground crews secure the eight C-130s parked on the tarmac. He wrote the tail numbers down in his notebook, taking photos of each of the crew members.

His concentration was interrupted by Lee Craddock whistling at the men inside the hangar. He listened as Craddock yelled at the crews. "Come on, you guys, let's get to the barbeque. Mr. Johnson doesn't like it when we're late," Craddock ordered.

Red took a picture of Craddock, writing in his notebook, *Probably the supervisor.*

He watched as eleven people walked out of the hangar toward their cars. Red saw them slapping each other on their backs and laughing. He turned the binoculars back toward the hangar to see one person walking back into the building.

After all the employees had driven away from the field, Red deployed a small drone. The palm-sized drone flew to the warehouse, hovering outside the windows, giving Red a view of the inside. He could see cages inside the warehouse, each of which was occupied by a small child.

Once he had flown around all of the buildings, he determined that the lone security officer was the only person on the property. Returning the drone to his location, Red carefully stored the vehicle, then moved toward the hangar.

Once at the hangar, he looked through the window in the personnel door to see the security officer sitting in the office watching television. With the main hangar door open, Red lowered his body, entering the building. He quickly placed tracking devices on the shipping containers. The magnetic devices attached quickly to the inside of the hollow metal legs. Once done, he moved out of the hangar working his way to the aircraft.

Red placed trackers on each of the C-130s in the top of the wheel wells, then moved quickly back to the perimeter. Before leaving, he checked one last time at the hangar window, to see the security officer still watching television. Red moved back outside the fence line, retrieving his gear before departing the property.

After a three-mile hike, he arrived at his van, parked at the bottom of a wash, out of view of passersby. Once inside, he threw the ghillie suit into the rear of the vehicle. Removing his cellphone, he punched in the number to Carver.

"Yes?" Brad Carver answered.

"Just finished checking out the airfield, boss. I'll get a report to you as soon as I get back to the hotel," Red stated.

"Is everything in place?"

"Affirmative. I got thirty containers and eight aircraft covered," Red stated.

"They had eight aircraft there?" Carver asked.

"Yes. Do we know how many aircraft they have in total?"

"We put a best guess at ten, but that may be inaccurate. Eight may just be the bulk of it," Carver stated.

"It appeared that operations were suspended for the day because of some company function. They were talking about a barbeque at the ranch.

"I got drone footage of the property. There was only one security guard there after the others left. A check of the warehouse revealed approximately fifty kids in cages inside the building. It looks like they're getting ready to transport either tomorrow or the day after."

"Okay, Red. Stay there for another two days in case we get any further intel. I'll be in touch."

"Copy that," Red said before terminating the call.

Danny was standing next to a banquet display in the hotel restaurant with his right hand on the table, his right foot crossed over his left leg, resting on the tip of the shoe. He was waiting for his mother-in-law to come into the restaurant.

He was wearing a chef's coat, with his arm in a sling outside the coat. The table was full of different dishes he had prepared throughout the day.

Danny smiled as he saw Billie leading Marva into the restaurant's banquet room. Billie held onto Marva's left arm as she guided her mother into the room blindfolded. Astrid, Gunter, and Hans followed.

Billie stopped her mother in front of Danny. "Okay, Mom, you can take your blindfold off now."

As Marva removed the scarf from her eyes, her mouth fell open. The table had entrees, hors d'oeuvres, desserts, breakfast items, with dishes of various comfort food laid out in front of her. It was all presented with impeccable garnishes. The centerpiece was made up of flowers from the grounds of the hotel.

Tears filled Marva's eyes as she walked around the table looking at the beautiful display of food. "Danny, this is incredible. When you told me you wanted to present some ideas for a new menu, I had no idea," she said as she continued to look at the dishes.

She looked up at Danny with a beaming smile. "I'm blown away. How did you do this with only one arm?"

Danny pointed to the opposite side of the room. "Your two daughters-in-law helped, along with Astrid and Walt, and of course, my wife," Danny replied while winking at Billie.

Jade, Brenda, Astrid, and Walt stepped up to the table. "Isn't it beautiful, Mom?" Astrid said with a huge smile.

"It sure is. Danny, why don't you guide us through the menu?" Marva said as she stepped back.

"Every meal you see here has a cost point lower than what you're currently serving. I believe it's important to keep some of the German dishes on the menu, but offering a trendier selection should bring in more customers.

"The pastries you serve are beyond good. They're brilliant. The whole city needs to be eating them. You should be marketing to the entire town, locals included. You could invite the chamber of commerce, along with the town council up here for their next meeting. We'll blow them away with dishes they've never had before," Danny said.

"Easy for you to say. Two of the town council members own restaurants," Marva said with a grin.

"Leave that to me," Danny said while winking at her. "I printed up six different menus with various options on them for each day of the week and all four seasons," Danny said while handing the examples to Marva.

Billie and Danny waited with anticipation as to what Marva was going to say. They watched her get in close to the plates of food as she smelled each offering. When she got to the plate of Coq Au Vin, Marva picked up a fork, taking a taste from the plate. She closed her eyes, groaning with delight. "Danny, that Coq Au Vin is really good."

Danny held his right hand out toward the loaf of his Rosemary Focaccia bread. He poured some olive oil into a small plate, then poured some balsamic vinegar into the oil. Try this," he asked.

Marva took a slice of the bread and dipped it into the oil. "Oh, Danny, stop it. This food has to be sinful." Marva turned toward her family. "Come on, you guys, taste this and let me know what you think," she said.

Billie looked at her mother. "Now you know why I've gained five pounds," she responded.

Hans spoke through a mouth full of food. "Danny, this potato salad is killer."

Astrid stepped up next to Marva. "Mom, you've got to try this salmon. The sauce is unbelievable," she said as she held out a fork full of the fish.

Marva put the fish into her mouth, letting it sit on her tongue. "Okay, okay, you're hired, Danny. The kitchen belongs to you." She kissed him on the cheek, then whispered into his ear, "Thank you, Danny. You're a blessing to this family." She stood on her tip-toes, reaching up to kiss him on the forehead.

Billie reached her arm around her husband as tears fell down her cheeks. "Thank you, Danny, thank you for this day," she said as she looked at her family walking around the table sampling the food.

"No, baby, thank you. I finally have the family I've always wanted." Danny kissed Billie on the mouth as he hugged her with his one good arm. "I'm the happiest man on earth."

Garcetti sat at his desk sipping on his morning coffee. The three computer screens he was watching were connected to his desktop computer and were tracking six of Johnson's C-130 aircraft.

As he took a sip from his cup, he looked at one of the C-130s flying over Utah. The aircraft was descending as it approached the small South Valley Regional Airport in West Jordan, Utah.

He pulled up his database, entering the airfield's name, time, date, and location. He looked at the center screen to see that another plane was landing at Ryan Field in Tucson, Arizona. He frantically began entering the data as the planes were touching down all around the West.

Eagle County Regional Airport, Gypsum, Colorado, George AFB, Victorville, California, and the Nut Tree Airport, Vacaville, California, rounded out five of the six C-130s that had left Texas in the early morning hours.

Garcetti watched the sixth aircraft as it flew toward the Puget Sound area of Washington. "Okay, hotrod, where you gonna land?" he said out loud as he sipped his coffee.

The screen showed the last aircraft descending as it approached central Washington on the I-5 corridor. He watched as it slowed, approaching the Chehalis-Centralia Airport, Chehalis, Washington. Once the plane touched down, he entered the data into the database, then leaned back in his chair, waiting to see where the containers were going.

Garcetti ran some quick numbers as he scribbled on a sheet of paper. Drugs, human cargo, guns, he quickly wrote down estimates of what he believed each plane was carrying based on the six containers in each aircraft, times six for the number of planes. He added his estimates, then looked at the total at the bottom. His eyes opened wide as he saw the twenty-one-million-dollar figure.

He sat back as he whispered. "And that's at three to four times a week," he said while shaking his head.

Looking at the screen, he saw that the containers were now showing movement toward their final destinations. Without exception, each container was traveling toward the nearest major city.

Garcetti dialed Carver's phone number. He leaned back in his office chair as he put his right foot on the desk.

"Yes?" Carver said as he answered.

"I've tracked six of the aircraft to their destinations. They all landed outside the major cities. Seattle, San Francisco, Phoenix, Denver, LA, and Salt Lake City.

"And as I'm talking to you, two more planes just lifted off from Texas. These guys are banking a shit load of money every day they fly. Even if they only fly three days a week, they're making over three hundred million a month!" Garcetti exclaimed.

"They've been able to put together a hell of an operation over a short period," Carver stated.

"This is nothing. Before MacDougal's gang of six got involved, the operation was massive. So if it's any consolation, three hundred million a month is a pittance compared to what it was. But you're right, in only three months they've managed to bounce back to just under a third of what it was," Garcetti explained.

"So, you got your old partner all squared away?"

"Yes, sir. Dent's on site with his crew. There'll be three from our team remaining here as well," Carver stated.

"How did you get him to agree to it?" Garcetti asked.

"I told him he could keep the fees from the Seattle group, and we'd pay him as well."

"Isn't capitalism amazing?" Garcetti said with a chuckle.

"Once I told him we were also involved in security for the Seattle group, he agreed. The only stipulation he had was that he not violate the agreement he had with the MacDougal group," Carver stated.

"Good. Do you need me to do anything else?"

"No, sir, Roger's good with a handshake. By the way, thank you for the bank transfer for his crew."

"You're welcome. Were you able to put together a plan for the interdiction?" Garcetti asked.

"Yes, sir. We'll be ready when you need us."

"Okay then," Garcetti stated.

"I'll see you when you come out here next week," Carver stated.

"See you then," Garcetti replied.

27

Billie looked up to the doorway of the office as Walt knocked on the jamb. "Hey, Walt, what's up?"

He handed Billie the blue and white hotel towel with the discs wrapped inside. "I'm finished with these and wanted to return them."

Billie took the discs from him. "You leaving soon?" she asked.

"Within the hour. I just needed to get those back to you and say goodbye."

Danny came into the office as they were talking. He slapped Walt on the back. "You outta here?"

"Yeah, leaving soon." Walt looked around the office to ensure they were alone.

"No one else is here, Walt," Billie responded.

Walt spoke in a lower voice. "I broke the firewall that was on the discs."

Danny's eyebrows rose as he leaned in closer. "What was on it?"

"Our guess was right. The program allows all the hosts to communicate with each other. It also allows for daily downloads. We don't have to be next to the tower to get the downloads, but if we want to fly under the radar, we'll need to be there."

"Are you going to the tower tonight?" Billie asked.

"I already talked to Larry. He said he'd go to the base of the tower with me tonight. I'm banking on the theory that they download every night at midnight," Walt mused.

"Good work, Walt. I'm excited to see what happens. Can you give me a call once you get the updates?"

"Can do. It may be after one a.m. Is that okay?" Walt responded.

"No problem," Danny stated.

"Okay. I'm going to say goodbye to Astrid and your parents. I'll let you know," Walt said as he turned to go.

"Thanks, Walt. Be safe," Billie said.

Danny gave Walt a thumbs up as he left.

Rick Barker, two other detectives, and three uniformed officers exited the elevator on the penthouse office level of The Dantermoor Group (TDG) tower.

Rick approached the Executive Assistant, Jennifer Clausen, holding out a search warrant. "Detective Rick Barker with the Seattle Police Department. These two gentlemen are Detectives Warren Harrison and Don Beasley.

Jennifer Clausen held her hand up. "I'll need to have our chief of security here before you go in, Detectives."

"No, that won't be necessary," Rick responded.

"Gentlemen, Mr. Waterston is out of town. I'm afraid I won't be able to let you in," she protested.

"That's okay, Ms. Clausen, we'll let ourselves in." Rick held up the small evidence bag containing the implant from Wade's body. He passed it in front of the glass door. To her surprise, the door opened.

"Okay, you guys, let's get to it," Rick announced.

As the detectives and the uniformed officers entered Waterston's office, Jennifer Clausen was already on the phone.

As all the group began looking around the office, Rick walked to the rear. He passed the implant in front of the door, and the deadbolt failed to open.

He exited the office, walking to the main entrance to the vice president's office. He passed the implant in front of the door, and the deadbolt slammed open. Before entering the office, he looked back at a frowning Jennifer Clausen. Entering the space, he found it to be vacant. All the furniture, paintings, and shelves had been removed. It hadn't even been vacuumed since occupied by Carlton Lambert.

Rick went to the door at the rear of the office. He passed the implant in front of the door, and it unlocked. He kicked the throw rug over to block the door open. Entering a foyer between the two offices, he saw the door to Waterston's office, and a third door.

He passed the implant in front of the third door, and the deadbolt slammed open, leading to a set of stairs going down. He also blocked that door open. Rick pulled his pocket flashlight out, shining it down the stairs. Seeing a light switch, he turned it on, illuminating the stairwell.

There were two opposing doors at the bottom of the stairs. The one to his left was under the president's office. The one to the right was directly under the vice president's office. He passed the implant in front of the reader on the left door, and it failed to unlock. He then tried the implant in front of the other reader, the deadbolt slammed open. Rick slid a chair in front of the door.

The lights turned on in the room as the switch was flipped, revealing a one thousand square foot living space in front of him. The room had a small kitchen, bedroom, bathroom, and living area.

The small quarters had all the amenities anyone could want. The bed was found to be unmade, and the counter in the kitchen had dirty dishes stacked on it. Rick looked around the living room to see food containers, along with empty soda bottles littering the space.

He put on a pair of latex gloves and began going through the space. As he was looking at the countertops, Rick heard Harrison behind him.

"I got the uniforms going through Waterston's office. Don's keeping security and Clausen busy," Warren said with a smile.

The two men began placing dishes, cups, utensils, and items of clothing into evidence bags. Rick looked down at a leather-covered, eight by eleven notepad. He whistled at Warren while he held up the pad.

Warren took the pad and looked at the cover. The inscription read *Lt. Phillip Wade, Seattle Police Department.* "Bingo. If we get his prints and DNA from these items, we're golden," Warren stated.

"He was protected here for over three months. I can't imagine he got out much. Just about every Seattle cop could have identified him," Rick stated.

"Well, he got out the night someone put a bullet in his chest. Not too difficult. He would have just taken the elevator down to the parking garage, then drive out," Warren replied.

Rick stopped as he looked at a glass candy bowl on the counter. The dish contained a ring of keys, a tube of Chapstick, a pack of gum, and a thumb drive. Rick pulled out a small evidence bag, dumping the contents into it.

"Did you find something, Rick?" Warren asked.

"Maybe. It was a thumb drive. Need to have the IT Department look at it," Rick said as he pulled out his phone, texting Walt.

In his hotel room, Nowack pulled on his shirt and began buttoning it. With his pants on, he sat on the edge of the bed, putting on his shoes. As he stood, he tucked the shirt into his pants.

While straightening his clothes, the call girl sat up in the bed and grabbed her dress from the chair. As she was pulling the dress on, she looked at Nowack. "Will you be wanting me again?"

Without looking at her, he responded. "Saturday night at ten," he responded.

"See you then," she said as she pulled her coat on, then left the room.

Without looking at her, or speaking, he pulled two scotches from the bar. As he poured the bottles into the glass, he heard a knock on the door.

He opened it to see one of his men. "Come in," he said as he held the door open. "What do you need, Jim?"

"We have the remainder of the targets under constant surveillance, boss. They can't do anything without us knowing about it."

"Okay, don't let them out of your sight," Nowack stated.

"We won't." Jim leaned in toward Nowack. "Any word on our primary target's location?"

"Not yet. Look, I know your guys are getting antsy, but the customer wants them all taken out at the same time. So, keep the guys occupied in the gym, or going over the plans."

Jim stood and stepped toward the door. "I just hope it doesn't take too long."

"It won't," Nowack said as he turned back toward the desk.

Danny was having the time of his life. Dressed in his chef's hat and coat, he walked through the seating area of the restaurant greeting the guests during the evening meal. The comments were all favorable.

He stopped next to the table where the Mayor and her husband were sitting, putting on his best PR smile. Marva hurried to the side of the table.

"Mayor, Tammy, it's good to see you," Marva said.

Tammy Dornier smiled at Marva. "We try to get to every business at least once every quarter." The sixty-year-old Mayor of Leavenworth was the consummate politician, beloved by the citizens.

"Mayor, I want to introduce my new chef, Danny MacDougal. He's also my son-in-law," Marva said proudly.

The Mayor had a huge smile as she stood. "I'm so happy to meet you, Danny. This is my husband, Hank."

Hank Dornier stood up, shaking Danny's hand. "Hank Dornier. Nice to meet you."

"We're so happy for you two. Billie is like our own daughter. We've known her since she was a little girl. Congratulations to both of you," the mayor responded.

"Thank you."

As she sat back down, the mayor turned her head toward Danny. "So, we have you to thank for this great meal?"

"With Marva's help." He held up his left arm with the cast on it. "Still gimped up."

"And the bread," she said as she closed her eyes. "This Focaccia is incredible."

"Thank you," Danny responded.

"So, you guys up here for a while?" the mayor asked.

"We decided to pull the pin and retire up here. Billie misses it too much. Me, I fell in love with it the minute we drove into town," Danny responded with a smile.

"Good, welcome to Leavenworth, Danny."

As Danny started backing away, he nodded toward the mayor and her husband. "Thank you. It was nice to meet you. Please, enjoy your meal."

Marva wrapped both her arms around Danny's right arm as they walked back to the kitchen. "You just won over the mayor. Not an easy feat, Danny," Marva said with raised eyebrows.

Danny started to respond, but was interrupted by his cellphone ringing. He pulled it out of his pocket and answered, "Yeah, Walt, what's up?"

"Lieutenant, Larry and I are getting ready to go in. Just wanted to give you a heads up."

"Okay, Walt. Fazer's on stun, good luck. Kirk out," Danny replied.

"Aye, aye, skipper. "I'll brief you tomorrow morning."

"You got it," Danny responded.

As they entered the kitchen, Danny turned to Marva. "Do you think it would be okay if I went up to the room? I'm beat, and my arm is killing me. Everything is finished."

"Of course, sweetie. See you in the morning," she said as she kissed Danny on the cheek.

Danny walked slowly to the elevator. Stepping inside the car, he fell against the wall. The elevator stopped on the second floor, where a very fit man got on.

He looked at Danny with a smile. "Chef, the steak was amazing. And I don't think I've ever had potato salad that good, either."

Exhausted, Danny forced a smile. "I'm glad you enjoyed it. You up here on vacation?"

"No, just wanted to get away from the city for a while. It sure is beautiful here," the man stated while staring at the elevator floor numbers.

As the elevator stopped on the top floor, Danny and the man got off. "Have a nice stay," Danny said as he walked to the room.

Brad Carver walked down the hall in the opposite direction. He pulled his phone out and texted Garcetti. *Primary down for the night.*

The response came back. *K.*

The clock on the wall of the hotel kitchen displayed 4:35 a.m. as Danny began the day's duties. The industrial Hobart mixer was methodically spinning the dough hook as Danny set out the bread and biscuit trays on the work surface.

The kitchen was filled with the smells of flour, rosemary, onions, and garlic as Danny danced around the work stations to the music coming from his cellphone. With his earbuds in place, he moved the lower half of his body to the music. Everyone at the hotel knew beyond a shadow of a doubt that Danny was in his element and on top of the world.

He pulled the dough out of the mixer, placing it on the work surface. He threw two handfuls of flour on the table, and began kneading the dough. As he slapped the dough onto the table, he spun around, planting his feet hard on the floor. Danny looked up toward the front of the kitchen to see his wife and mother-in-law in the doorway laughing as they watched him.

He pulled off the earbuds, unplugging them from the phone. Placing them in his pocket, he looked at the two women. "What?" he said with a frown.

Billie chuckled as she stepped toward Danny. "Just enjoying my husband," she said as she kissed him on the cheek.

Marva stopped in front of the reefer and pulled out her puff pastry. After setting the dough on the table, she hugged Danny. "Don't let me interrupt your dancing," she said while laughing.

Danny smiled sheepishly as he turned back toward the table. As he was kneading the dough, his cellphone rang. He pulled the towel from his shoulder, wiping his hands before answering. "Hey, Walt, what's up?"

"Lieutenant, I've been trying to get ahold of you for over an hour. You and Billie need to get out of there," a frustrated Walt demanded.

"Sorry, bud, I left my phone in the kitchen last night. What's going on?"

"Larry and I got next to the tower, and the download went off without a hitch."

"Good, so what's the problem?" Danny responded.

"I didn't get a chance yet to look at the data we downloaded; the update is huge. The issue is what Rick found in Wade's room at the tower."

"So, our speculation was right?" Danny said loudly.

"It sure was. Rick said when he put Wade's implant next to the door, it opened right up. He's been staying at the tower; that was verified. Rick also found a thumb drive in his room that showed their plans for us in Seattle—especially you and Billie.

"There's some guy named Auguste Marchand that Wade was communicating with. It shows the three attempts on you guys that failed," Walt stated.

"Three attempts? Are you sure?" Danny asked.

"Yes. They were all Marchand's men. The file indicates that he recently hired a twenty-man team to take us out, Lieutenant, focusing first on you and Mrs. MacDougal."

"How soon can you get that to me, Walt?" Danny asked.

"When the captain saw the data on the thumb drive, he told me, Rick, and Larry to get up to you guys double quick," Walt stated.

"You're on your way here?" Danny said, surprised.

"I'll be pulling into town in about fifteen minutes. Rick and Larry are about ten minutes behind me."

"Okay, I'll finish up, then meet you here in the kitchen," Danny stated.

Danny hung up and turned to Billie. "Honey, Walt's on his way here. They found a credible threat on a thumb drive belonging to Wade. Walt thinks we should get somewhere safe. Could you get my pistol and our radios from the room? I'll finish up here, then meet up with you at the front desk," Danny asked.

"Where's this coming from?" Billie asked.

"Rick found out that Wade was staying in that little apartment under Lambert's office at Ballencourt Towers. While they were searching it, they found a thumb drive with the information on it. Walt will be here in a few minutes, then we can look at it," Danny stated.

"Okay, I'll meet you at the desk," Billie said as she hurried from the kitchen.

Danny turned to Marva. "Marva, we need to keep your guests safe. That's paramount. How many guests are in house?"

"Eleven; not that many. I'll get Gunter and Hans to take the guests down to the gym. They can take Jade, Brenda, the kids, along with Hansel and Gretel with them," Marva stated.

"Where's Karl and Astrid?" Danny asked.

"Karl is at the front desk, and Astrid is up at the house," she responded.

"Okay, I'll brief Karl," Danny said as he turned to leave the kitchen.

Laden down with bags of supplies, Reverend Winters entered the mission through the back door. Still dark outside, he walked slowly to the kitchen in the low light. After placing the bags on the table, he went to the main electrical panel and began turning the lights on inside the mission.

After tuning the radio to his favorite seventies music, he walked into the main hall to start opening the window blinds. As he turned the corner, he saw a man dressed in tactical gear standing by the front door. Winters saw that the man was holding a pistol in his right hand.

Standing in the middle of the hall, he realized he had few options. Winters clenched his fists as he prepared to defend himself any way he could.

Capt. Graves kissed his wife goodbye for the day, then entered the garage. He set his morning coffee in the vehicle's cup holder, then swung his body into the seat of his Ford F-150 pickup truck.

With a croissant in his mouth, Graves backed out of the garage while waving goodbye to his wife. He stopped in the street, putting the truck into first gear. As he stopped at the intersection two blocks from his house, a car slid to a stop in front of him. The man in the car pointed a belt-fed automatic rifle out of the window at Graves' truck.

Graves put the truck in reverse, standing on the throttle as the man riddled the truck with automatic weapons fire. The truck rolled backwards and slowed as it struck a parked car on the street. The car sped off as Graves' truck slowly came to a halt.

Gunter followed one of the hotel guests as he walked down the hall behind the man. He looked down to the man's right side to see the barrel of a gun poking out from under his coat.

Gunter kept his eyes on the barrel as he spoke to him. "Excuse me, sir, you can't be armed inside the hotel." As Gunter got within a few feet of the man, he spun around and struck Gunter in the face with the butt of the weapon.

As Gunter fell backwards onto the floor, the man raised the weapon toward his face. As he prepared to fire, Billie's body slammed him from behind.

Billie rolled to her side on the floor after taking the man down. She quickly got back up, lunging toward him. He spun around, starting to raise the weapon, as Billie hit him hard in the face.

Moving behind him, Billie put her right arm around his neck, lifting the man off the ground with her right hip. He struggled to breathe as Billie's right arm choked off his air. As he was slowly beginning to pass out, his finger pulled the trigger of the weapon.

Automatic weapons fire riddled the floor beneath him. With all the rounds in the magazine being spent, Billie could hear the wheezing as the man passed out. She bumped her hip up, jerking the man's head as it dropped back down. She heard the snapping of his neck as his body went limp.

She quickly bent down to look at her brother. "Gunter, wake up," she said as she gently slapped him on the cheek.

Slowly opening his eyes, Gunter looked at his sister. "What happened?" he asked.

"This guy broke your nose," she said as she nervously smiled with relief toward him. "Are you good to get up?"

Gunter slowly stood with Billie's help. "I'll be fine."

Billie picked up the man's MP5 and reloaded it with a fresh magazine from his belt. She pulled the Glock from his holster and handed it to Gunter. "Here, get down to the front desk and take care of Dad. I'm going down to the kitchen to check on Danny and Mom," she said as she ran toward the stairs.

Hearing the automatic weapon fire coming from inside the hotel, Danny spun around to leave. He saw a man dressed in tactical gear entering the kitchen, carrying an MP5. In one smooth motion, he grabbed the handle of his chef's knife on the table and threw it hard at the man.

The knife entered the man's upper chest and knocked him to the floor on his back. Danny placed his foot on the man's neck, then stomped down hard, crushing his windpipe. He reached down and pulled the knife from the body.

Danny looked up quickly to see Billie entering the kitchen with concern on her face. "You okay, baby?" she asked.

"I'm fine. What happened?" Danny asked as he removed the dead man's weapons.

"One of these guys tried to take out Gunter," she replied.

"Is he okay?" Danny asked.

"He's fine, just a broken nose. Did we get all the guests downstairs?" Billie asked.

"Yeah, they're safe. Hans, Jade, Brenda, the kids, and your mother are with them in the gym," Danny replied as he pulled the MP5 sling over his right shoulder. "Let's get back out front and keep an eye on the entrance of the hotel," Danny said as he quickly left the kitchen.

Arriving on property, Walt drove around to the rear of the hotel as Astrid was running from the house toward him. He exited the car as Astrid was shouting. "Walt, they're shooting at us!" she cried out.

His smile turned to a grimace as he heard her screams. Running toward Walt, automatic weapons fire danced all around her as he lunged forward to cover her. Before he got her on the ground, one of the nine-millimeter rounds struck her in the shoulder, while another hit her in the leg, driving her to the ground.

Walt snatched her up, carrying her behind the Volkswagen. He pulled a handkerchief from his pocket, placing it on the wound on her shoulder.

The assailant began moving quickly to the right to get a clear shot at Walt and Astrid. As he moved into view of the two, a single round entered his head. He fell over on the ground, dead. Walt looked up to see a man holding up his left hand, signaling for Walt and Astrid to move to safety.

Walt nodded to the man, then picked up Astrid, taking her into the hotel through the rear entrance. As he was carrying her to one of the empty rooms, Karl ran to them, armed with his 12-gauge pump shotgun.

"Is she okay, Walt?" he asked in a panic.

"She's fine, Mr. Eck," Walt said as he kicked at the room door to open it. After laying her on the bed, he stood back up to see a man entering the room behind Karl.

Walt leapt at the man before he could fire his weapon. He delivered a roundhouse kick to the man's chest, then swung his hands in small circles in front of him with precision, disarming him, then crashing his right elbow into his face.

As a second man approached from the hall, Karl fired the shotgun at the man's head, killing him instantly. He pointed the Weatherby shotgun at the unconscious man, then jacked another round into the chamber.

Walt reached out, touching Karl on the forearm. "It's okay, Karl. It'll be fine. You need to stay here with Astrid and watch her until we can get an ambulance."

A trembling Karl snapped back as Walt touched his arm. He looked at Walt with fire in his eyes. "These bastards keep shooting my daughters," he shouted, as he kept the shotgun pointed at the man.

"Karl, lock the door after I leave, and keep an eye on Astrid."

"I will," he said as he sat on the bed next to his daughter.

Walt grabbed the man by the collar, dragging him out into the hallway. He removed his weapons, throwing them back into the room for Karl, keeping the MP5 for himself. He removed the man's belt and slings, tying his hands behind him, then lashed his ankles together, securing them to his wrists behind him.

"Keep this door locked, Karl," he said before closing it.

With his Colt Combat Commander at the ready in his right hand, Danny worked his way through the hallways as Billie walked backwards behind him, covering their rear.

When he peeked around the corner, Danny saw a man working his way toward them. He held up his right hand for Billie to be quiet. While holding the Colt, Danny raised his trigger finger, indicating there was one man ahead of them.

Billie got down low to the floor as Danny eased the pistol around the corner. She changed hands, placing the pistol in her weak shooting hand. As the man saw Danny's pistol, he raised his weapon. Billie fired twice, taking him down.

As they moved into the adjoining hall, automatic fire rained all around them. They quickly tucked back into the alcove of one of the rooms.

Pinned down and unable to get away, Danny and Billie held their pistols close to their chests, awaiting the assailant. They heard two shots fired from the other end of the hall and saw the man fall in front of them at their feet.

Brad Carver stepped back around the corner out of sight just as Danny peered around the corner. "Someone took him out," he said as he looked at Billie with surprise.

ith lights flashing and siren blaring, the Chelan County sheriff's cruiser rounded the corner coming into the front of the hotel. As the vehicle stopped next to the building, automatic weapons fire riddled the left side of the patrol car, killing the deputy inside.

Stephan Pappas scanned the tree line trying to find the shooter. As he was looking over the area, he saw a black Ford Crown Victoria pull up in front of the hotel. Stephan increased the power of the rifle scope as he looked at the best possible location the gunfire could have come from.

Rick Barker and Larry Colton started to exit the Ford when the automatic fire commenced. Stephan looked through the scope, locating the muzzle flash. He lined up the target in the scope and pulled the trigger. The shooter's body fell from the tree fifty yards from him.

After the body hit the ground, Rick and Larry ran from the car toward the hotel. Once in the lobby, Rick spoke, breathing hard. "What the hell did we just drive into?"

"And who shot that guy? We seriously need to find out what the hell is going on here!" Larry said, angrily.

Rick spoke with irritation toward Larry. "We need to find out where everyone is first, before we start shooting back!" Rick spoke into the radio.

"Lieutenant, it's Rick and Larry. We're on site. Are you there? Lieutenant, Billie, Walt, anyone out there? Any SPD Officer listening, respond."

Larry held his pistol out in front of him at a forty-five-degree angle as he started moving toward the interior of the hotel. "Well, standing here waiting isn't helping either. C'mon, Rick, let's go find them."

Dent and another of his men, Thomas Pryor, were pushing down from the top floor, hoping to flush the assassins out of the hotel, where they could be dispatched by his men outside. By Dent's own admission, the plan wasn't perfect, but since what they believed were the bulk of the assassins were inside the hotel, it was the plan he went with.

Dent's team strategy was to keep the Seattle group and their family safe while maintaining perimeter integrity. Maintaining anonymity was no longer an option. They had gone way beyond that at this point.

The two men were at opposite ends of the hallway as they moved toward each other, checking rooms. As Pryor tugged at the door handle in front of him, the door burst open, knocking him to the floor.

Dent raised his pistol toward the man exiting the room. As the man pointed his weapon at Pryor, Dent quickly fired four rounds from his HK pistol, slamming him backwards. As he was going down, the man fired a round at Pryor's chest, striking him in the body armor.

Dent hurried to the side of his team member. He looked down and saw the copper jacket of the bullet sticking out of the body armor.

"Come on, get your ass up off the floor, I can't do this on my own," Dent said to Pryor, smirking.

As he stood, Pryor rubbed his chest. "That hurts every time it happens, even after all these years."

They both moved to the opposite end of the hall, and pointed down, indicating they needed to take the stairs. As Dent stepped onto the staircase, automatic weapons fire came up from the lower floor stairwell. Dent fell onto his back and quickly moved his pistol over the stairs, firing blindly toward the shooter.

Pryor bounded down the stairs, entering the third floor. He ran down the hall to assist Dent. From behind the wall at the end of the hall, one of the assassins came around the corner firing a pistol. Pryor raised his weapon as he continued to run, firing at the man, killing him.

As his pistol emptied, he immediately inserted another magazine. He stopped at the door to the stairwell, taking in a deep breath. He raised his right foot, shoving it against the crash bar. As the door flew open, he fired three rounds at the assassin in front of him. The man fell over dead.

Pryor spoke as he leaned to his right. "You okay, Boss?"

From above, the voice responded, "I'm okay."

"Then get up off your ass. I need you down here."

Dent grumbled as he stood. "Smart ass," he responded.

Hans stood fifteen feet back from the front door of the gym as he kept guard over his family and the eleven guests. He held the MP5 at the ready as he watched the entrance.

He heard the door latch click as someone from the other side slowly moved it. He stepped backwards as he looked at his mother, motioning for her to get lower to the floor. He aimed the weapon toward the door as he took the MP5 off safe.

The main door to the gym slammed open as it was kicked from the other side. Still moving forward, the man raised his weapon toward the group. Hans fired and the man fell to the floor dead.

The second man entered the gym firing his weapon. One of the rounds struck Hans in his right quad, forcing him backward. As he was going down, Hans pulled the trigger, holding it to the rear. The remaining twenty-five rounds exited the weapon, striking the assailant multiple times.

Lying on his back, Hans dropped the empty magazine out of the MP5 and reached for a fresh one from inside his front pocket. As he fumbled for a magazine, a third man entered the gym, pointing his pistol at Hans. From behind, Hansel and Gretel lunged at the man, knocking him down and causing him to drop his weapon. Gretel kept her mouth on the man's neck while Hansel locked his mouth on the man's right arm.

Rudy Granger entered the gym, holding his left hand up toward Hans. "Stand down, friendlies entering."

Confused, Hans looked at Rudy. "Who are you?"

"A friend." Rudy looked at the back of the gym to see the hotel guests. "Ma'am, if you'd like to take care of your guests, I'll help him," Rudy said to Marva.

"I'll be okay," Hans responded.

Rudy placed a clean gym towel on Hans' wound, applying pressure. "If you call off your dogs, I'll secure this guy," Rudy stated.

In a forceful voice, Hans gave the order. "Hansel, Gretel, OUT! Watch him!"

The two dogs let go but kept watch over the man as Rudy tied him up. He pulled the man's weapons from him and threw them toward the back of the gym.

With the man tied up, lying on his stomach, Rudy grabbed his belt, dragging him into the hallway. Turning back to Hans, he said, "I'll get someone down here to relieve you as soon as I know it's clear."

Dent and Pryor slowly moved down the main corridor, working their way toward the front desk. As they rounded the corner, the two men held their hands up as they saw Danny and Billie.

Danny lowered his weapon as he saw Dent holster his pistol. "The building is clear from the top floor down to here," Dent stated.

Danny walked toward him. "The rest of the building is clear. We just don't have a lock on the exterior," Danny stated.

"I have two of my people covering the exterior. Hold on." Dent spoke into the mic. "Pappas, Nelson, is it clear?"

Pappas came back first. "The front of the hotel looks to be clear. No activity since the two detectives arrived."

"The back appears to be clear. No activity," Nelson responded.

Dent looked at Danny. "Lieutenant, it looks like it's over. We'll make a sweep just in case."

Danny looked toward Dent. "Man, you guys work close," he said nervously.

"Sorry, more showed up than we expected. They really wanted you bad, Lieutenant," Dent said with his head tilted to the side as his eyes opened wide.

As Danny was getting ready to respond, email and text alert messages began sounding all around the hotel lobby. The Seattle team members, along with Dent, pulled out their cellphones.

Billie's eyes welled up with tears as she read the text. *Capt. Graves shot and in hospital ICU. Reverend Winters killed inside Mission.*

All of the Seattle team received the texts, including Brad Carver, who was standing at the east end of the hotel. Carver immediately began texting his two men in Seattle, checking on their status.

Everyone was gathered in the restaurant as investigators from the Sheriff's Office interviewed all of the people from the hotel. Marva was working the room as she served breakfast to the hotel's eleven guests, along with the team members.

Paramedics had transported Astrid, Hans, and two of the assassins to the Cascade Medical Center. Minor injuries were continuing to be treated by the remaining ambulance crew.

Danny brought a plate to one of the tables in the back of the restaurant. He set the food in front of Dent. Danny turned around and filled a coffee cup from the bar directly behind him.

"Did you have people on Reverend Winters and Capt. Graves?" Danny asked.

"Yes. They were both watching them at distance. The person we had on Winters followed him from his apartment. Once he was safe inside the Mission, he got back into his car. After hearing the shots, he ran inside.

"He said that the assassin was firing at Winters from the front door. Winters was thirty feet away. Based on where the shell casings landed and blood splatters from Winters, it looks like he ran toward the man while being shot at.

"Winters was hit six times but still managed to get to the shooter and break his back before he died. My man got to him, but he was too badly injured. He stayed with him as he passed," Dent stated.

Danny was fighting the urge to get emotional. "And what about Graves?"

"A car drove up to the front of his truck, blocking him. The driver shot up the truck with a belt-fed assault rifle. My man got the assassin two blocks away from the scene. Then he got to Graves and helped him at the scene. It looks like he'll pull through. I'm sorry about your other man," Dent said with a furrowed brow.

"Graves is my boss and friend. Winters was my friend and mentor. I don't have many friends left," Danny said with his head hung low.

As they were talking, Billie came up to the table and sat down. "Well, Mom and Dad schmoozed the guests. They refunded their hotel bills and gave them their meals for free." She turned toward Dent. "We have you and your team to thank for keeping us safe."

"Not at all, Mrs. MacDougal. We were happy to do so."

"Where are you guys staying?" Billie asked.

"I had spoken with your husband, and we were in the process of moving over here when this happened," Dent responded.

"Now that the whole thing is out in the open, get moved in here," Danny responded.

"We can do that. Most of the team, however, will be leaving day after tomorrow. I'll have to leave tonight; I need to coordinate with my guys in Seattle. Two of them will be staying here to keep watch over you guys," Dent stated.

"Tell them they can come over when they're ready," Billie said as she stood.

"I will," he responded.

Danny winked and smiled at his wife as she walked away. He turned back toward Dent. "Well, we've got a lot of cleanup to get to. Thanks again," Danny said as he stood and left the table.

Danny walked into the kitchen and stepped behind the freezer. He placed his right hand against the wall with his head hung down. Tears fell down his cheeks as he grieved over his friend.

Brad Carver opened his hotel room door to see Roger Dent standing in front of him. Dent quickly stepped inside as he fist-bumped Carver

"Hey, Gooch, how'd it go with the local cops?" Carver asked. Dent had earned his nickname years before as a result of his Gucci message bag. The team all gave him jazz for carrying a designer satchel.

"We're good. The whole Protection Detail thing satisfied them. The licenses and identification from the DC contingency satisfied them as well."

"Are your guys ready for this weekend?" Carver asked.

"Yeah, we're good. I'll leave Grant here to watch the MacDougals. With this latest attempt shut down here, they won't bother them for a while," Dent stated.

"I'll leave two people in Seattle to keep watch on things there. We'll only be gone for two days, but a lot can happen in a short time."

"We'll be fine, boss," Dent said while pulling a Coke out of the fridge. He sat at the desk chair. "It sure is nice to just sit back and take orders for once instead of worrying about all the leadership crap," he said with a grin.

"Don't get too comfortable just being a grunt. We're all about to jump into the middle of a meat grinder," Carver stated.

"I know, Brad. Just having a little fun at your expense," Dent responded with a grin.

"I should have never pulled your fat out of the fire in Afghanistan," Carver stated.

"If you hadn't, you wouldn't have someone to blame for your lack of success with women," Dent said with a smile.

"Hey, don't blame me because you're ugly," Carver said as he threw Dent an apple from the fruit bowl.

The two old friends laughed as they unwound from a frenzied morning.

30

Danny and Billie got out of their car in front of the mission. As Danny opened the passenger door for Billie, he stared at the building. Billie squeezed his right hand as they walked toward the door.

Entering the mission, Danny and Billie saw Rhonna Collins running to them. She sobbed as she held on tightly to her friend. Rhonna let go of Danny and hugged Billie tightly.

Danny placed his hand on Rhonna's shoulder. "What can we do, sweetie?"

Rhonna backed away from Billie and ran her hands across her face, wiping tears away. "His old friend and pastor is coming here tomorrow to take care of the mission. We've been shut down ever since he was taken," Rhonna said as she once again choked up.

"Rhonna, we're going to take care of the arrangements. If any of you need anything, please call," Danny said.

"Danny, there's something I think Reverend Winters would have wanted you to have. Wait just a few minutes and I'll get it for you," Rhonna said as she turned, walking toward the office.

Danny saw a stain on the floor. He bent down, looking closely at it. He stood and slowly walked toward the back of the mission. He bent down, placing his open hand on the stain where he believed Winters was first shot.

"What is it, Danny?" Billie asked.

"Well, Dent's man was right. It looks like he was shot here, then ran toward his assailant. This is where he caught up with him," Danny said as he stopped back by Billie.

"Shot that many times, then still managed to kill the shooter," Billie responded as her head moved side to side.

Rhonna came back into the main hall. "Danny, this is the bible you guys gave him. I know he'd want it back with you," she said.

"Thanks, Rhonna," Billie said as she took the bible.

Danny placed his hand on Rhonna's forearm. "We have to get to the hospital. Remember, we're here for you. Please give us a call if you need anything," Danny said with a forced smile.

"I will," she responded as Danny and Billie hugged her before leaving.

Danny and Billie walked down the hall of the hospital toward the ICU. As they stopped in front of Capt. Graves' room, the police officer on duty wrote their names down on his clipboard.

They looked through the window to see Graves' wife, Tracy, talking to her husband. Tracy turned to see Danny and Billie looking through the glass. Graves slowly moved his eyes toward them.

Tracy bent over, kissing her husband on the forehead before coming out of the room. She embraced her friends with an attempted smile. "Thanks for coming, you guys."

"How's he doing?" Danny asked.

"Rick and Larry briefed me once they got back down from the mountain. They said there were almost a hundred bullets in the truck. Their consensus is that because the assault came at him from the front, the bulk of the bullets were stopped by the engine and the front of the truck. If it would have come at him from the side, he—" Tracy began crying.

Billie held onto her tightly. "It's okay, Tracy. It's going to be okay."

"He was shot seven times, Billie. Seven times!" Tracy turned toward Danny. "I never understood how evil the job was. I knew it was dangerous, but I never thought it was this bad. It truly is evil, Danny, isn't it?"

"It is, right down to the core, Tracy." Danny hugged her as he spoke. "I need to see him, would that be okay?"

"Yes, but only one person at a time. He's very weak. Please don't take too long, Danny."

"I won't," he said as he opened the door.

He saw his boss's head bandaged, with stitches on his cheek. His right arm was in a full cast that extended up to his chest and neck. His left leg was in a cast and was elevated.

As Danny stopped next to Graves' bed, he looked up at Danny through tired eyes. "Winters?" he asked softly.

Danny moved his head side to side as he looked at his boss.

Graves' eyes narrowed as he looked at his lieutenant. He whispered toward Danny.

"I'm sorry, boss, what did you say?" Danny said as he leaned in closer.

He whispered toward Danny. "Call Dr. Hale," he said as he winced from the pain in his throat. "Drink?" Graves asked as his eyes saw the glass of water on the tray next to his bed.

Danny picked up the glass, holding the straw out toward Graves' mouth. After taking a small sip, he looked back at Danny. "Call Wanda."

"You mean now?"

"Yes," Graves whispered.

Danny pulled out his cellphone, then punched in the number for Dr. Hale. "Danny, good to hear from you. How's Michael?" the voice on the other end asked.

"I'm in his room as we speak. He's doing okay. He's alive," Danny said as he winked at Graves.

"Give him our best, please," Hale responded.

"Hold on, I think he wants to talk to you," Danny said as Graves whispered toward Danny.

He held the cellphone next to Graves' mouth and ear. He couldn't hear what Graves was saying, but waited for him to quit speaking.

Graves stopped talking, then turned his head away from the phone. Danny pulled the phone up to his mouth. "Were you finished speaking to the captain?"

"Yes. He wants to go forward with Operation Reprisal. Is it feasible with the resources we have on hand?"

"Dr. Hale, we lost our friend and planner night before last. They killed Reverend Winters," Danny said.

"Oh no, Danny, I'm so very, very sorry. Where in the hell were the men we hired?" Hale asked.

"They were in place, but up at the hotel protecting us. There were only two of them down here in the city watching Winters and the Captain," Danny replied.

"How many attackers were there?" Hale asked.

"Seventeen up in Leavenworth, two down in the city," Danny responded.

"So do you think you have the assets to pull off Reprisal?"

"The team was briefed when they got here. They said they could handle it."

"Okay, I'll get in touch with the rest of the DC team, then get back to you asap. Keep your ear to the ground, Danny. The information we got was that twenty men were sent to Seattle, not nineteen."

"I will. Thank you, Doctor. Talk to you soon," Danny said as he hung up. Danny looked at Graves. "We're on, Captain," Danny said with a furrowed brow.

Graves' lips pursed. "Finish it, Danny. Once and for all, finish it," he said in a whisper.

"You can count on it, Captain," Danny said as he turned and left the room.

Danny and Billie sat in Sean's Irish Pub with Walter, looking at the screen of his portable computer. The three people sipped on their sodas as they reviewed the download Walt had made just days before.

Danny's text alert went off as they were reading the file upload. He looked at the screen and saw it was from Dr. Hale. The message read *We're a go*.

"That was from Dr. Hale. She said we're good to go for Reprisal," Danny stated.

Walt took in a deep breath, then slowly let it out. "Lieutenant, I want in on the action. I understand I'm just a computer grunt, but I have to be allowed my pound of flesh," Walt said with determination in his eyes.

"I'll see what I can do, Walt. I also want to be part of it, but with a busted wing, I'm reduced to fighting the battle from the rear. Let me chew on it, Walt," Danny responded.

"I appreciate it, Lieutenant," Walt said as he turned back to the computer screen. "This was what I wanted to show you before we got involved in the shootout at the hotel.

"Maurice Bellows, one of the two names you gave me, is the real estate billionaire in Virginia. He's the number one person in the US who calls the shots. Nothing happens here without his approval. He lives in a huge mansion on the water, just down from Virginia Beach. He would have given the go ahead for the recent attack on us.

"V.H.C., the other person, has an office and house in Brussels, including a villa on Lake Lucerne in Switzerland. Given time, I'll be able to find out his full name, assuming it's a man. The documents just refer to him as V.H.C. It repeatedly states that 'V.H.C. approves or disapproves, or V.H.C. authorizes.' I don't think V.H.C. is the top dog, but it appears he has a lot of juice."

Danny rubbed his right palm on his chin. "Let's have the DC contingency dive into that. They're in a better position to develop that information.

"Anything else in there that's game changing?" Billie asked.

"Yes, ma'am, it reveals all the replacement personnel after you guys decimated their West Coast organization. It doesn't give any new information regarding anything operational, only interim manpower changes, which we already have," Walt concluded.

"It's important that you continue to do downloads every week, Walt. Is that going to be a problem?" Danny asked.

"Every Friday at midnight. Larry said that either he or Rick will accompany me in there for security."

"Good. When will you be going back up to Leavenworth?" Danny asked.

"Saturday morning. I want to be with Astrid every weekend until she's healed," Walt stated.

Billie smiled as she looked at Walt. "She was released from the hospital the same day, Walt."

Walt replied sheepishly, "I know. I'm just concerned."

Danny winked at Billie as they stood to leave. "We'll see you up at the hotel this weekend, Walt," Danny said as he shook his hand.

Danny and Billie hugged Sean and Marylyn before leaving. "Thanks for lunch, you guys," Billie said with a grin.

Sean hugged Billie. "Thanks for coming," he said as he looked at the couple.

"We'll be back soon," Danny said as he draped his coat over his shoulder.

"See you soon," Billie said as she waved at the Coopers and Walt.

After exiting the pub, Danny pulled out his cellphone and punched in a text message to Dent, *Reprisal is a go.*

The responding text came back almost immediately. *Copy, initiating same.*

Garcetti answered his cellphone. "Yes?"

"We just got the go ahead for their operation Reprisal," Carver announced.

"About time. When are you going in?"

"Tomorrow night. Their weekend events are in play for six straight days, beginning tomorrow night," Carver stated.

"Dent and his men are ready?"

"Affirmative, sir. We're leaving four people behind for security. The rest are in the op," Carver stated.

"Do you need anything else?"

"Negative, sir, we're good to go. I'll keep you apprised," Carver stated.

"Carver?" Garcetti asked.

"Yes, sir?"

"What happened with Graves and Winters?"

"Our people were on both of them. With Graves, we were there, but it came pretty fast. With Winters, my man was on him from his apartment down to the mission. He was parked by the back door of the building, and ran inside as he heard the shots. He was with Winters as he died."

"And his assailant?"

"Winters was shot six times with a nine-millimeter. He still managed to break his killer's back. With Graves, my man took out the assailant a block from the site of the shooting. He got to Graves and called 911. Probably saved his life. Sorry, sir, we lost one," Carver stated.

"Understand. It's unfortunate, but it certainly could have been worse. Every one of our team comes home this time, Carver. No more dead friendlies, you got it?"

"Yes, sir."

"Good luck."

"Thank you, sir," Carver stated as the call was terminated.

31

Billie walked out to the chicken coop with a large basket in her right hand. Inside it, was a blue and white hotel towel covering the boxes containing the master file.

Bending down to put the files back in the tray, she was startled by a deep male voice back in the dark corner of the coop. "I'll take those," Allan Nowack stated.

Billie stepped back quickly as she responded. "And who the hell are you?" she said with a scowl on her face.

"I'm the new owner of those files, lady," he said as he raised the Glock P80 toward her.

Billie held the basket out toward him. "Go ahead, take them."

"No games, bitch. Set the basket on the floor, then back away."

Billie set the basket down and stepped back as Nowack picked it up, looking inside. "Well, looks like my job here is done. Too bad I'm in a hurry. I'd sure like to go a few rounds with you," he said as he looked Billie up and down with a lascivious smile.

Unarmed, the only hope Billie had was to try to draw the man in closer to her to mount a defense. Billie grunted as she responded, "Yeah right; with you? You look like you were hit upside the head with an open can of ugly," she said, smiling.

Nowack's smile turned to a frown. "Careful, lady, I just may take it from you anyway."

Billie started laughing. "You don't look like you could even get it up, dirtbag."

Nowack stepped closer toward Billie. "Okay, I just found the time to show you what a real man can do. Spread those legs, bitch," he said as he placed the pistol against Billie's chest.

Billie had successfully goaded the man into moving closer to her. With all the speed she could muster, her right hand struck the left side of the Glock as her left hand hit his wrist hard. The pistol discharged to the left of Billie before flying toward the door.

Nowack hit Billie hard in the face with his left hand. He grabbed a dazed Billie by the hair as he hit her hard in the stomach. He dropped her onto her back on the floor of the coop. Billie struggled to rise as Nowack pinned her down.

As he dropped to his knees between her legs, the door to the coop flew open as Monica Meyer burst through the door. Seeing him hovering over Billie, she quickly leapt toward the big man.

Meyer spun her body around, kicking Nowack in the head. He shook off the attack, standing up rubbing his jaw. "My lucky day. I get two women for the price of one."

He hit Meyer hard in the chest. She took a step backward, then jumped in the air toward him. Her right foot kicked out, striking him in the chest.

Nowack spun around, striking Meyer with a roundhouse kick, lifting her off the floor, throwing her backwards. As he moved toward her, Billie flew from behind through the air, hitting him in the back with both her feet. The full force of Billie's weight drove him to the floor.

Meyer got up, moving toward him. While still on the floor, Nowack swept his right hand around, cleaning Meyer's feet out from under her. Standing quickly, Billie and Meyer faced an angry Nowack.

He cocked his right hand back, preparing to strike, as Billie kicked her right foot out from the side, hitting him on the side of his left leg. Nowack buckled from the pain in his knee. Meyer delivered multiple blows to his face from her fists as Billie hit him with a flurry of blows to the left side of his head.

Nowack went down on his rear end, hitting the floor hard. As he looked at the two women, he pulled a backup revolver from his vest, raising it toward Billie. Two shots from Meyer's pistol struck him in the chest, followed by a third shot to the forehead. Nowack fell backwards to the floor, dead.

Billie turned and looked at Meyer while breathing hard. "Well, I don't know who you are, but I'm sure glad you showed up," Billie said while rubbing her jaw.

"Monica Meyer," she said while shaking Billie's hand. "I'm part of your protection team."

"Thank you," Billie responded.

"I heard the shot. I didn't see him enter the coop, though. He must have been in here a long time waiting for you," Meyer stated while rolling her head around on her neck, trying to relieve the pain.

Billie looked at the dead man. "That was one tough SOB. I had no hope of stopping him." Billie bent down and removed the man's wallet.

"Allan Nowack," she said as she looked at his driver's license. "Virginia license, a few credit cards, that's all." Billie texted Danny, asking him to call the Sheriff's Office. *Dead body in the chicken coop.*

She picked up the basket, then looked at Meyer. "I'll have Danny cook you the best steak you've ever eaten, then buy you as many drinks as you want," Billie said with a big smile.

"Mrs. MacDougal, I'm on duty, but I *will* take that steak," she replied with a smile while rubbing her sore chest.

Brad Carver and Roger Dent stood on the flight deck as they watched the pilot and co-pilot of the C-130 make a long slow turn to the south over central Texas from an altitude of thirty-thousand feet. The night sky stared back at them from the windows of the aircraft.

The pilot turned toward Carver. "Master Chief, you and your team better suit up. We'll begin depressurization in fifteen minutes."

Carver placed his hand on the pilot's shoulder as he spoke loudly. "Thank you, Captain. We'll see you on the ground."

Carver and Dent walked into the cargo bay, signaling the twenty-man team to put on their oxygen masks. After gearing up, they each checked their teammate's equipment.

A (High-Altitude-Low-Opening) HALO jump during the day was dangerous enough, but one conducted at night with night vision gear from thirty-thousand feet was insanity. Each of the team members had made a HALO jump many times while in the military, but still gave it the respect and caution it was due.

The C-130's Loadmaster signaled to Carver that the rear cargo door was being opened now that the pressure had stabilized. With a strap from the cargo bay securing him to the aircraft, the Loadmaster gave the signal for the teams to ready themselves. With the deafening noise from the engines and the wind turbulence filling everyone's ears, the teams waited for the green jump light.

As the light came on, Dent and his nine men left the cargo bay, jumping into the black sky.

Carver's ten men waited for their signal. As the green light came on, the men jumped into the night air.

Carver stepped next to the Loadmaster, waiting for his signal. The Loadmaster placed his right hand on Carver's shoulder and waited. As they came over Carver's target, the Loadmaster slapped him on the shoulder. He leapt into the dark night sky, immediately stabilizing himself from the rushing air over his body.

With his night vision gear in place, he slowly surveyed the night sky. He looked northeast to see the lights of Dallas off in the distance. He dipped his left shoulder slightly, turning himself south slowly, seeing the Lights of Austin directly south of his position.

He looked at the illuminated dial of his altimeter to see he was now twenty-thousand feet AGL. He slowly turned as he scanned the area for the landing pad lights from the ranch.

Seeing the lights from the helicopter landing pad below, he pulled the drogue chute out of its holder on his right side. With no moon in the sky to illuminate his parachute, the chute opened at four-thousand feet above the Johnson ranch. He opened early to mask the noise of the chute unfurling.

Carver circled the ranch house as he slowly descended, looking for anyone below. At three-hundred feet, he turned to land behind the Johnson barn.

Pulling down on both risers of the chute, closing off the vents in the back, the chute was stalled ten feet above the ground. Carver touched down both softly and silently.

He quickly pulled off his chute, gathering it into a bundle, then stomping it into the ground behind the barn. Determining the area was clear, he began a sweep around the house and barn.

The only person in the house appeared to be the Johnson's butler. Carver quickly moved toward the bunkhouse. He looked through the window, seeing two ranch hands playing cards at the main table. He opened the front door and dispatched the two men with his suppressed 1911 .45.

Stepping quickly to the barn, he started to move toward the tack room. He froze as he saw Corpsman Hurd coming from the room carrying a large basket.

As Hurd set the basket down on the seat of the quad runner, Carver heard the cries of a baby coming from the basket. As Hurd started the quad, Carver hit him hard on the side of the head.

Stunned, Hurd fell to the side, off the quad onto the dirt. Carver turned the vehicle off, then placed the end of the suppressor against Hurd's forehead, covering his mouth with his left hand.

"You have one chance to live. Where are you taking the baby?" Carver asked.

"To the grove," Hurd stated through Carver's gloved hand.

"For what purpose?"

"We—" Hurd stopped before answering.

Carver released the safety of the .45.

"Okay, okay, the baby is for the sacrificial ceremony at the grove," Hurd stated quickly.

Carver grabbed Hurd by the collar, lifting him from the ground. As he was moving him to the stalls, one of the quads from security drove toward the open door of the barn.

Hurd broke free from Carver's grasp, running toward the quad. He began screaming toward the two men, "Help, help; Intruders on the property!"

Carver dropped to one knee as the two men began firing toward him. He spun the M-4 around his body, taking aim, dispatching the two men. He spun around quickly to his right, shooting the butler, who was rushing to the barn firing his rifle toward him.

He walked to Hurd, hitting him hard in the face with the butt of his rifle. He sneered at the man as he dragged him toward the tack room by his foot.

After opening the door, he dragged Hurd down the stairs by his leg, allowing his head to hit each step, hard. After removing the cell door key from Hurd, he pulled him into one of the empty cells. Carver stripped Hurd's clothes from his body, leaving him wearing nothing but his underwear. He threw the man's clothes onto the floor outside the cell, then slammed the door. He addressed the girls in the cells. "Who speaks English?"

The one Caucasian girl, along with two Asian girls, raised their hands. Carver began opening the cells. When he got to the Anglo girl, he gently grabbed her by the arm. "What's your name?"

"Patricia," she answered.

"Can you drive, Patricia?"

"Yes, I think so," she answered.

"You're going to have to. There are two vans and one bus by the barn. You can drive one of the vans, I'll drive the bus. We have about twenty miles to drive before we get to where we need to go," Carver stated.

"I can drive," one of the Asian girls stated.

"Good, you can drive the second van. How many other children are on the property?" Carver asked.

"Some more in the bunkhouse," the second Asian girl stated.

One of the girls who couldn't speak English was tugging at Carver's sleeve, speaking Tagalog. "What's she saying?" he asked.

"She wants to know where her baby is," one of the girls said.

"Tell her that her baby is safe upstairs. Now I want all of you to do exactly what I say, nothing more. We'll get you back to your families, but you have to do exactly as I tell you. Do you understand?" Carver demanded.

The three girls nodded in agreement.

"Get everyone together and stay behind me," Carver ordered as he slowly moved up the stairs.

The ten men of team #1 moved quickly around the airfield, locating the security people. As three of the team entered the hangar, two security officers ran toward them with their rifles at the ready. Thomas Pryor and Rudy Granger took them out with their suppressed M-4's.

Grant Westbrook peered up over the windowsill of the warehouse. All he could see inside were twenty children locked in some of the cages. He spoke into the mic, "Are we clear?"

Pryor returned, "The airfield is clear."

"I have approximately twenty juveniles at the warehouse. I need help getting them out," Westbrook stated.

Granger responded, "On my way."

The rest of the team began setting the charges on the eight aircraft parked on the apron.

Sitting in the saddle, one of the security officers watched the perimeter of the grove. He looked through a set of night vision binoculars as his horse stood absolutely rock solid still.

As he moved the glasses through the northern perimeter, he saw a lone person standing fifty yards away looking back at him. As he raised the radio to his mouth, the crossbow bolt entered his chest. The man fell to the side off the horse, hitting the ground with a thud. The horse didn't move as his rider fell over dead.

A second security officer scanning the perimeter looked to see a riderless horse on the edge of the grove. He scanned the ground around the horse to see his coworker lying next to his mount. The man grabbed the reigns and sunk spur to hurry to his partner.

As the horse bolted, a man came out from the trees, pulling the officer from his saddle. Bill Fortier threw the man to the ground, then snapped his neck after he was down.

The two remaining security officers fell over dead as crossbow bolts entered their chests. After confirmation that all the security staff at the grove had been dispatched, Dent told his men to move in closer.

From four angles, the team members took video of the events unfolding at the grove. Members in attendance were all wearing red robes with hoods as they mingled with each other. At the center of the grove, surrounded by trees, a massive fifteen-foot metal statue of Molech stood guard over the ceremony. Seated on top of a box that was the opening for the fire. The raging fire burned at the bottom of the statue, as smoke poured out from the mouth and nostrils of the seated image.

The group all began chanting in unison as they held their hands together. "Molech, Molech, Molech."

Sitting around the grove in various locations, young children were there for the entertainment of the worshipers. The young teenage boys and girls had their hands and feet bound. They wore skimpy white tunics as they trembled with fear.

Watching from fifty yards away, Dent whispered into his mic, "Move in."

The team entered the center of the grove with their weapons in front of them. As they came into view of the attendees, Johnson shouted angrily at the intruders. "What the hell are you doing on my property? Who the hell are you?"

Seeing the team coming into view, Senator Gibbs ducked back behind the audio booth he was standing next to. He got as low as he could to the ground. Gibbs trembled with fear as he watched the grove being taken over by armed men.

Dent's men barked out orders as they detained all of the people. Dent saw people from industry, well known politicians, along with actors and actresses. Every one of the Cabal's governors throughout the country were in attendance, with the exception of Senator Gibbs, who was working his way from the property. Dent's stomach turned as he approached Johnson.

He pointed his pistol at the man. "You're Gordon Johnson?"

"I am. And who the hell are you? Take your masks off so we can see the people who are going to die after we get out of this," Johnson barked at Dent.

Rodney Waterston, Governor of Region Ten pulled a pistol from his belt under his robe. He pointed the weapon toward Dent.

Two rounds from Byron Nelson's sniper rifle hit Waterston in the chest. He fell over dead as the team scanned the remainder of the eighty people at the grove.

"There's two snipers out there, so the next one of you assholes who want to shoot at my men will die before your filthy, perverted, sick body hits the ground."

Dent turned and hit Johnson hard in the face. "And you—you baby raping bastard, you open your mouth one more time and I'll gut you like a fish." Dent pulled his knife out and started cutting the children free.

"All of you assholes find a tree to sit against," he shouted at the worshipers. "Three per tree."

Senator Gibbs removed his robe, slowly crawling away from the grove. His dark clothing hid him from the rest of the group. Once out of sight, he slowly stood and began walking away quickly.

Sitting in his DC office, Garcetti lifted his phone from the table as he heard the text alert go off. *Ranch, grove, and airfield secure. Children safe. In air within the hour.*

He texted Carver back. *Good job. Will meet you in the morning.*

Garcetti stood, putting his suit jacket on. He let out a sigh of relief as he closed and locked his office door.

Dent checked all the people in the grove. Each was tied securely to a tree with parachute cord, their feet bound and mouths gagged. The cord secured each person to the tree from around their waists and their necks.

The children had all been loaded into the vehicle parked at the grove, ready to depart. Dent spun his right hand in the air in a circle as he looked at his men.

He stepped over to Johnson, squatting next to the man. "There's nowhere on this planet you can escape to where I won't be able to find you. If you ever again look at another person who's under the age of thirty, I'll torture you to death over a period of thirty days. Test me! Please test me, you sick bastard!"

Johnson swallowed hard behind the gag in his mouth as he watched Dent leave.

32

itting in front of the radio in the airfield's tower, Carver keyed the mic. "Boxcar, Boxcar, this is Little Brother one. Do you copy?"

He repeated the call. "Do you copy, Boxcar? This is little Brother one."

The radio barked back. "Copy, Little Brother one, this is Boxcar."

"You are cleared for landing. I say again, cleared for landing."

"Copy, Little Brother One, cleared for landing. Boxcar out."

Carver turned the radio off and left the tower. He walked toward the bus and the two vans. Stepping up into the vehicle he looked at the children inside. Each of the girls looked back at him with tears in their eyes.

Eight of the teenage girls were holding onto their babies as they cried while looking back at him. He stepped to the vans and looked inside to see the remainder of the teenage boys and girls he'd pulled from the bunkhouse.

Unwilling to suffer the pain of seeing their faces anymore, he walked to the airport crew. He looked at Westbrook. "He's on his way. Did you take care of the aircraft?"

"Yes, boss. The timers were set for 0500 hundred hours, per your instructions," he replied.

"Very good," Carver responded as he took a long drink from his bottle of water. As he put the bottle back into his vest pocket, he saw the lights from the Hercules approaching the runway.

He looked toward the gate to see Dent entering the airfield in the Johnson ranch diesel pusher motorcoach. "Boy, Gooch sure knows how to make an entrance."

Westbrook chuckled as he shook his head. "Who says we don't have the best job in the world?"

Carver walked to the motorcoach as it stopped in front of the hangar. The door of the bus opened as he looked to see his friend behind the wheel. "Nice ride, Gooch."

"It sure is. Johnson may be a troll, but he sure knows how to spend his money."

"Any casualties?" Carver asked.

"Just one. Waterston, the Governor of Region Ten. He pulled a pistol on us," Dent responded.

"And you got all the kids?"

"Yeah, there were fifteen there."

Carver's upper lip curled as he heard Dent's reply. He turned to see the Hercules landing on the runway, reversing the propellers to slow the aircraft.

Carver shouted to his men, "Let's go!"

The C-130 pulled onto the tarmac in front of the other aircraft, turning 180 degrees. The Loadmaster opened the personnel door on the left side of the aircraft and waved his hand toward the group as the engines howled.

Carver and Dent each picked up one of the little children, carrying them to the plane. All of the team members were carrying the smaller children to the Hercules.

Once at the door, they shouted at the crew over the engine noise as they handed the kids to the men standing in the doorway. "We need blankets and food for them," he shouted.

Carver and Dent ran back to the vehicles to double check for anyone being left behind. Dent entered the motorcoach, walking down the hallway to the rear. When he got to the back, he saw a small foot protruding from under the bed.

He bent down to see a four-year-old little boy. He was trembling as he looked at Dent with absolute terror on his face.

"Come on, buddy, we get to ride on an airplane." He pulled an energy bar from his vest, holding it out toward the little boy. The small hand reached out and gently took the bar from him.

He carefully lifted the boy, cradling him in his arms. As they walked toward the plane, Dent's eyes teared up. He stepped onto the plane, taking a seat next to Carver, as the little boy ate the energy bar while cradled in his arms.

Carver remained silent as he looked at his friend. He pulled the cellphone from his pocket, texting Garcetti. *Departing airfield. Children safe. Cleared and ready for your notifications.*

Once the Hercules leveled out after takeoff, the two ex-Army Medics began caring for the children. Tears slowly disappeared as blankets, boxes of juice, and teddy bears began to be passed out to the younger children.

Carver entered the flight deck, placing his hands on the pilot and co-pilot's shoulders. "Captain, are we still planning for refueling in Tulsa?" he asked.

"Affirmative. The Loadmaster made a fresh pot of coffee and there's enough box lunches to feed an army. Help yourself, Master Chief."

"Thanks. Great job, Captain," Carver responded.

"Three hours ten minutes flight time after we refuel. Get some food and rest up. I'll let you know when we start our final descent," the captain stated.

Carver nodded toward the pilot, then returned to the cargo bay.

Auguste Marchand stepped into his living room as he tied the belt on his bath robe. The grandfather clock in the living room showed 3:30 in the morning. He turned on the floor lamp as he sat down in his recliner.

Startled, he looked at Nicholas Garcetti sitting across from him on the couch. "You!" Marchand said angrily. "What are you doing in my house?" Marchand ordered as his right hand slowly went down between the arm and cushion of the chair.

Garcetti held up the Colt Detective Special. "Looking for this?"

Marchand's lips tightened as he stared back at his revolver. "Trust you to be thorough." Marchand wiped his forehead before responding, "And why are you here?"

"I was out for a morning walk when I saw your house. I thought I'd stop by and say hi," Garcetti said with a smile.

"Nicholas, we both know you're too cautious for that. Can I assume you're here regarding matters in Seattle?"

"You can. Auguste, someone died at the hands of your assassins. Someone who was a civilian. Someone who had nothing to do with your contracts. You tried to kill other people as well. I'm here to even the score," Garcetti said with an emotionless stare.

"So, it was *you* who eliminated my men," he said while glaring at Garcetti.

"Yes, it was. You killed a nice man and his wife, because you *thought* it was him who was protecting the MacDougals."

"Nicholas, can we talk about this? I can make arrangements for your financial future. I can even make sure that your family will never be harmed," Marchand pleaded.

Anger rose in Garcetti's stomach. "*You threaten my family?* The only thing worse than dealing with a frog is dealing with an arrogant one. But then I repeat myself. Save your money. Maybe you can try to bribe God when you see him. Let me know how that works out for you."

Marchand looked around the room as he frantically tried to figure a way out of his situation.

"Don't bother, you just ran out of time," Garcetti said as he stood. With swiftness, he placed the barrel of Marchand's revolver next to the man's right temple, pulling the trigger. He placed the revolver in Marchand's hand.

Garcetti walked to the back door and stepped outside. Still dark, he walked to the end of the alley where his car was parked. After entering the vehicle, he took off his gloves as he pulled away, placing them in his valise on the seat.

Maurice Bellows entered his favorite coffee shop in Virginia Beach. The well-dressed sixty-year-old man was a mousy creature who lacked both guts and a chin. His short hair and clean-shaven face gave him the look of an accountant. Bellows got in the long line of people waiting to be served as he looked at his newspaper. After placing his order, he moved down the counter to the pick-up area.

Getting his coffee, he stepped to the condiment counter, waiting behind a man in front of him. He put two sugars into his coffee cup and waited to get a stir stick. The man in front of him held out the container of sticks. "I'm sorry. Here, please allow me."

Bellows forced a smile at the man, taking one of the stir sticks from among the others sticking up. He turned, walking away from the counter.

After stirring his coffee, Bellows sipped from the cup as he left the shop. Turning right onto the Virginia Beach boardwalk, he took three steps before collapsing onto the ground. People panicked as they saw the man fall down. Some bent down to help him, while others called 911.

As Bellows unsuccessfully tried to take in air, he looked up to see the man from the coffee shop staring back at him, with a scowl on his face. The last image he saw was Walter Killian glaring at him before he died.

———

Danny dabbed at Billie's black eye with a cotton ball. "And you've never seen him before?" he asked.

"No, never. Meyer hasn't seen him before either. We need to get Walt on it, quick," she responded.

"Dr. Hale said there were twenty people sent out here. We could only find nineteen. I'd have bet even money any survivors would have beat feet outta here," Danny mused.

"Not this guy," Billie said while wincing from the pain. "He's not the kind of guy to run away from anything. That was the toughest man I've ever seen, Danny. Meyer and I got lucky," she stated.

Danny threw the cotton ball into the trash can, then kissed his wife. "I hate being laid up. Feeling pretty useless."

"You just get better. I've got big plans for you when you heal up," she said while winking at him.

Danny kissed his wife. "You can count on it." His voice turned to business as he stood. "I need to get with Walt before I leave, babe. We need to close this out," Danny stated.

"He got back last night. I think he's up at the house," Billie announced.

"Let me guess, he's consoling Astrid," Danny said with a smile.

"Boy, if anyone ever made a case to be Astrid's protector, it was him. According to Mom, Dad, and Astrid, he should be knighted."

"Well, I'm happy for them. They make a cute couple," Danny said.

"Now you *really do* sound like Marylyn," Billie said. "I'll tell Walt you want to see him in the kitchen," she stated.

Danny winked at his wife as he poured himself a cup of coffee.

As Carver and Dent looked out of the terminal windows of the Reagan National Airport toward the C-130, Nicholas Garcetti stepped up behind them. "You looked good down there, boss. Obviously, you're not camera shy," Carver said with a grin.

"Comes from being in DC for so long. Sling it wide and deep," he replied.

"Do you think they bought it?" Dent asked.

"They don't have a choice. After the alternative media gets done showing this all over the web, they'll be forced to report it. The days of selective reporting are over. Hell, half of the people in the videos at the ranch are in the media and entertainment industry. The house of cards *will* come down."

"Boy, I sure hope you're right, sir. Looking into Johnson's eyes, I got the distinct feeling he knew he was going to get away with it," Dent stated.

"I wouldn't worry too much about that pencil neck. He'll get his," Garcetti responded. "Look down there," Garcetti said as he pointed to the children being taken off the plane. "That's what's important. You guys, along with your men, gave those kids a second chance. That's where your focus should be, not worrying about the filth who abused them. I'm proud of the work you guys did."

All of the team had changed into civilian street clothes on the plane before arriving in DC. Their equipment and clothing had been transferred to a van driven by Garcetti as they exited the aircraft on the taxiway, then rode back to the terminal.

Not trusting the mainstream media, alternative media sources were given the story by Garcetti and were the first on the scene. Copies of the videos taken at the ranch were given to reporters by Garcetti as well. He told the reporters that he and his department were investigating the entire incident.

Garcetti knew by giving the press the videos he compromised any hope of prosecution. The goal with the operation was not to prosecute, but to destroy. Before the year was out, every one of the people at the grove would be taken out by the cabal. The Globalists didn't suffer fools, and would 'clean up' the mess they created.

Carver and Dent looked down on the ramp as the children were being loaded onto buses. The young girl, Patricia, looked up to the window and waved at the two men before getting onto the bus.

"Well, Gooch, we did our good deed for the month," Carver said as they turned around to leave.

Dent slapped his friend on the back. "Okay, it's beer-thirty, my treat. It's been a long couple of days."

"No, my treat," Garcetti stated as he stepped between the two men. "A two-inch thick ribeye steak, and scotch, no beer." The three men laughed as they walked to the main entrance of the airport.

Nicholas Garcetti entered his outer office carrying a cup of coffee and his messenger bag over his shoulder. Seeing his administrative assistant, he stopped at her desk to pick up the mail, "Good morning, Sheila."

Sheila Monroe looked at her boss. "Good morning, Mr. Garcetti. Are you okay? You look a little under the weather?"

"I'm fine, just a little too much celebrating last night with some friends."

"Speaking of friends, your friend Fred Harris from the Academy is coming by in a few minutes. Says he has something important to tell you."

Garcetti smiled broadly. "I'll be darned, haven't seen Fred in two years. Send him in when he gets here, please."

"I will, sir."

He entered his office and placed the cup of coffee on the desk, then slung the messenger bag over the back of his chair. He flipped through his mail as he sipped at the coffee. The intercom sounded. "Mr. Garcetti, Mr. Harris is here to see you."

"Send him in please."

He set the mail down on the desk and turned to greet his friend. As the door opened, his smile turned to a frown.

"Good to see you, Nick," Danny MacDougal said with a smile. "It's been a while, hasn't it?" he said as he entered the office. "Wow, Deputy Director for the Office of Intelligence and Analysis for Homeland Security. Perfect place to hide, Nick," Danny said with a smile.

As Garcetti closed the door, Danny sat in the chair in front of the desk. "So, Fred Harris, huh?" Garcetti said with a frown.

"You'd be surprised what our new IT guy can dig up. He's so good, he could tell us what kind of toilet paper you used this morning."

"Sounds like he's being put to good use. So why are you here, Danny?"

He reached into his right coat pocket, holding out a Glock 23.

Garcetti's body tensed as the pistol was held out toward him.

"Thought I'd return this. You were good enough to return my knife to me; just returning the favor. It's unloaded, by the way. If you ever want to get the bullets back, just stop by the PD—I'd be happy to give them to you," Danny said as he stared at Garcetti.

He took the pistol from Danny, setting it on the desk. "One bullet at a time, I have no doubt. You'll forgive me if I'm not more welcoming, Lieutenant. The last time we talked, you said you'd cut me up into little pieces if I ever got around you or your wife again."

"Well, Nick, I'm getting to like the taste of crow lately. Been eating a lot of it over these last few months. By the way, I need to thank you for saving my wife's life. I was preparing for the worst. Thank you.

"Also, I misjudged you. I assessed you at the same level as that idiot, Franks. He said hi by the way."

"I heard you paid him a visit," Garcetti said.

"Yeah, I did. I also visited one of you guys' henchmen, Terry Post. Post gave up Franks, along with you, for all the sudden suicides happening around the country earlier this year," Danny stated.

"Yeah, I did that, no argument. Is that why you're here, Danny?"

"No. What you did was for King and Country. Franks is a different story, however. He knew what was going on with the file. He said he read it cover to cover. He also said you were too much of a boy scout to look at it. I don't hold you responsible, you were just doing your job."

"But in the end, it didn't matter, did it?" Garcetti stated.

"No, it didn't. But I did get some needed information from them," Danny said with a sneer.

"And what are you going to do with that information, Danny?"

"Get as close to the top of this trash heap as I can."

"Danny, there's no head to cut off. This is a multi-headed hydra. Cutting off a head doesn't matter. It just grows another one," Garcetti stated.

"Then why are *you* doing it?" Danny asked curiously.

"They used me, MacDougal. They used me to cover for their sick twisted purposes. When I joined the FBI, no one was prouder than me. I was a super patriot. Now, almost twenty years down the road, I see it all meant nothing. There are only the users, and the used. I was used, and I didn't like it."

"Well, my motivation is a little different," Danny replied. "The Federal Government came to my town and pissed all over it. Six months ago, I was happily ignorant of this whole New World Order BS. Now, I can't get the stench out of my nostrils.

"Raping children, starting wars for profit, killing off people because you think it's too crowded on the planet, that's the kind of stuff that drives me crazy. That's why I'm doing this, and that's why I'm taking out the next rung on the ladder," Danny said with a scowl.

"And who might that be?" Garcetti said with his head tilted down with a frown.

"I guess you'll just have to read about it in the paper," Danny replied.

"Lt. MacDougal, I could have you arrested for what you just said."

"Yeah, but you won't, 'cause you hate them just as much as I do. The only reason you'd want to take me out of the game is because you want to have all the fun for yourself and don't want me pissing on it," Danny replied.

"You're out of your league, MacDougal. These guys will sift you like wheat," Garcetti warned.

"We may not have the numbers you have, but we have the technology, the equipment, the talent, and now, thanks to asset forfeiture, we have the money.

"Nick, we don't need to have a three-letter acronym behind our names to be effective. I'm here for three reasons; to thank you for saving the life of my wife, to apologize for my past conduct, and to return that," Danny said while pointing at the pistol.

"I'm not stupid, Danny. You're going after Cornell at CIA. If you do this, the whole world will fall down on your head."

"Do I look like I care?" Danny asked.

"Except that you have a wife now. And from the looks of things, she happens to be happy with you, although for the life of me I don't know why. Go off and be happy," Garcetti pleaded.

Danny leaned toward Garcetti with fire in his eyes. "We tried that! We left the PD, went to work in a hotel in Leavenworth, Washington, *and those bastards found us anyway!*

"The only way to end this is to take as many of these pricks out before they get to us. I've lost friends, dear friends, to include one just recently. No, Mr. Garcetti, the minute I raise the white flag, they'll step on the gas and kill us all, including your dumb ass.

"You saw what they were going to do to Billie. The word depraved doesn't even begin to describe the evil going on here. I'm performing a public service, Garcetti; stopping these degenerates before they can hurt anymore kids." Danny stood with a clenched fist, hitting the top of the desk. "I'm done playing nice!"

Garcetti held up his right hand. "I get it. I'm on your side, MacDougal, but we have to do this smart. Otherwise, they'll have the skin on our backs mounted on the walls of their offices.

"There's something you need to know. We coordinated with your security guys for the operation in Texas," Garcetti stated.

"Don't you think we knew that? Do you think we're so stupid as to miss what you were doing? We're not a bunch of hicks, Garcetti. We're smart enough to figure out who's staying in our hotel," Danny replied with a frown.

"Okay, point taken." Garcetti stood, handing Danny a business card. "Keep that in your wallet. It'll come in handy in the very near future." Garcetti put the Glock into his desk drawer and looked at Danny. "Let's get out of here. There's a great deal of information we need to discuss. Lunch is on me."

Danny was shaking his head as he followed Garcetti out the door. "You're mental, Nick, a full-blown deep dive nut job."

"Now you're sounding like my mother-in-law," Garcetti replied with a smile as they left the office.

33

Tracy Graves sat in the chair next to her husband's hospital bed, reading a book. With the exception of going home to shower and change clothes, she had been by his side since he got out of the operating room.

Graves slowly opened his eyes, looking at his wife. As she looked back at him, he winked at her with a smile. Tracy held a glass of water toward him, placing the straw into his mouth.

He stopped drinking, turning his gaze toward the television. Tracy turned the volume up as she looked at *Breaking News* on CNN.

The reporter was standing on the highway in front of the gated entrance to a ranch in central Texas. The female reporter was in front of the yellow police caution tape, as she reported on the 'Early Morning Mayhem in Texas.'

Central Texas has erupted in chaos since early this morning, as police and fire officials are investigating a massive case of child sex trafficking and child sacrifice, occurring just five miles from this location on the Bar Ten Ranch, belonging to Gordon Johnson, Texas software billionaire.

Helicopter coverage of the ranch and grove came onto the screen. From three hundred feet above the ground, police were seen placing handcuffed attendees into sheriff's office buses.

The reporter continued as helicopter coverage of the airfield came onto the screen. Eight smoldering hulks of aircraft were seen on the screen next to the airfield's hangar.

At five a.m. this morning, the eight aircraft you see on the screen caught fire, completely destroying them. This reporter received information from an anonymous source on the ground that holding cells used to contain the children were discovered at both the airfield and the Johnson ranch. Other sources told this reporter that a raid of the property at all three locations last night rescued approximately sixty children and arrested over eighty people at the ranch and airfield.

Graves whispered toward his wife with tears falling down his cheeks. "Call Danny and give him my congratulations."

Tracy leaned over and kissed her husband on the lips. "I'm so very, very proud of you, honey. You and the team of people here in Seattle are my champions."

Peter Cornell stopped at the finish line of the track behind the Georgetown gym. He bent over with his hands on his knees as he fought to catch his breath after his daily run. Standing, he slowly walked to his small Igloo cooler next to the back door of the gym. He pulled out a bottle of ice-cold water, drinking intensely. After putting the cap back on, he sat on the bench, leaning back against the building.

The cold morning air was biting at his body as his spandex running clothes did little to stave off the chill. He slowly picked the bottle up from the bench as his hand began to tremble. He panicked as he started to lose feeling in his arms and legs. The bottle fell from his hand, rolling off the bench onto the ground.

Danny MacDougal stepped over to him and picked up the bottle, setting it back on the bench. "Right about now, your whole body is beginning to go numb," he said as he sat on the bench. "In about two minutes, your heart will slowly, and painfully, start slowing down, until it finally stops beating. That assumes, of course, that you have a heart. One could argue that, given all the people you've ordered to be killed. Oh, but I'm sorry, you and your peers like to refer to it as eliminated, or sanctioned."

Cornell was barely able to open his mouth as he tried to speak. The only thing coming from between his lips was spittle, oozing down his chin. "You see, your brain is fully functional, but it can't order your body to do anything.

"The drug that was placed in your water was something the CIA developed, with the help of the pharmaceutical industry. Odorless, colorless, and undetectable, it's pretty nasty stuff. Ironic, really, that it should be used on one of the assholes who championed its development.

"When you arrive in hell mere moments from now, say hello to Auguste Marchand. He arrived there yesterday." Danny stood as he prepared to leave. "Oh, I'm sorry, how rude of me; Danny MacDougal. Pleased to meet you," he said as Cornell's head fell back against the building's wall.

Danny picked up the bottle and walked away. As he passed through the opening in the perimeter fence, he opened it, turned it upside-down, pouring the remaining water out onto the grass. He tossed the empty bottle into the trash can on the street next to the gym.

Danny pulled his rental car into one of the stalls at the Dulles International Airport Executive Terminal. He reached across opening the driver's door with his right hand. He slowly got out of the driver's seat and stood, stretching his body.

An attendant approached, handing him a cellphone. "A call for you, sir."

Danny put the phone next to his ear. "Yes?"

"Mr. Brown, this is Daniel Landon from Landon Automotive. Was the car and special options satisfactory for you, sir?"

"Yes, Mr. Landon, I found everything to be quite in order," Danny replied.

"I've charged your corporate card for the rental, sir. Will that be satisfactory?"

"It will. Thank you."

"Thank you for choosing Landon Automotive, Mr. Brown. We look forward to serving you again in the future."

"Thank you," Danny said as he hung the phone up, handing it back to the attendant.

Danny pulled his satchel from the rear seat of the car and walked to the shuttle bus.

Walt sat at the foot of the bed, working on the computer as he watched over Astrid. He turned his head as Marva opened the door, smiling at him.

He quietly got up, going out into the hall. After he closed the door, he smiled at Marva and Karl. "What's up?"

"We just wanted to see if you were hungry. You've been here all day. Can we bring you something?" Karl asked.

"No thanks, I'm fine. But I did want to talk to you guys if I could?" Walt asked nervously.

"Sure, Walt, what do you need?" Karl asked.

"I wanted to see if, you know, I mean if it's okay, I'd like, uh, Astrid is—"

Karl and Marva smiled at him. Karl grabbed Walt's forearm. "Son, we'd be thrilled to have you as our son-in-law. We're happy to give you our blessing," Karl stated.

Walt took in a deep breath, letting it out. "Whew, I've never been so nervous," he said as he smiled at the couple. Marva tearfully hugged Walt.

A tired and hungry Danny MacDougal came out of the concourse of the SeaTac airport. He saw his wife standing on the other side of the security barrier, smiling at him.

As he reached Billie, she gave him a huge hug, accompanied by a long kiss. "I missed you, baby," she stated.

"I missed you too, sweetie," Danny said as he put his arm around Billie's waist. "Boy, it's good to be home," Danny said with a sigh.

"Well, you couldn't have arrived at a better time," Billie said.

"Oh?" Danny said as his head moved back. "What's going on?"

Billie smiled at him as she bumped her hip against his. "How good are you at baking wedding cakes?" she asked.

Danny stopped walking immediately. "He finally asked, huh?" he stated with a beaming smile.

"Yeah, he asked Dad for his permission this morning," Billie said with a huge smile.

"Well, let's get back up to Leavenworth. This calls for the opening of a nice bottle of cabernet," Danny replied.

"And some of your hors d'oeuvres," Billie said while slapping his rear end.

"Don't push it, Mrs. MacDougal," he replied.

She hit him in the shoulder as she stepped away from him. "Catch me, and you can have me, Lieutenant."

Danny started to run but was held back by the cumbersome cast on his left arm. He stopped by the news stand to catch his breath and saw a copy of the <u>Seattle Post Intelligencer</u> front page's lead story. He paid for the newspaper, then stepped against the wall.

Concerned, Billie looked at him. "What's the matter, Danny?"

He didn't answer. He just turned the front page toward her so she could read it.

The story jumped out at her. *An American Airlines flight from Dallas to Washington DC went down in rural Tennessee this morning in what some witnesses on the ground said was from a large explosion in the air. Among the 114 who perished was Senator Harold Gibbs, US Senator from Virginia, along with one of his senior staff members, Jeri Patronne.*

Danny looked at Billie as they exited the terminal into the parking garage. "Looks like it was time to pay the piper," Danny said with a sneer.

Billie didn't respond. She only held on to her husband's right arm.

Nicholas Garcetti leaned back in his chair as his cellphone rang. "Mr. Carver, thanks for calling. Were you discovered?" Garcetti asked.

"No, he didn't know I was there. I don't think he would have appreciated it if he had found out," Carver stated.

"I couldn't risk it. I know he wanted to do it on his own, but packing around that cast on his arm while doing a job was a recipe for disaster," Garcetti stated.

"Don't tell me you're actually going to let him continue with this?" Carver asked.

"Yes, I am. He's a highly motivated individual and a bulldog when he gets ahold of something. Besides, he's going to do it with or without our help. Might as well be with," Garcetti stated.

Carver raised his eyebrows. "Okay, we'll make the best of it. By the way, we depleted a lot of the capital for Reprisal. If anything comes up now, we'll be operating in the red," Carver stated.

"Not to worry. MacDougal's IT man seized Johnson's accounts. His empire just got a whole lot smaller."

Carver smiled as he responded. "Well, with all the top bad guys gone, we should be fine for a while. But just in case, we need to keep frosty."

"I agree. Have your team stand down for a few days and relax. Keep who you need to watch over Seattle and Leavenworth. Take some much-needed rest. Also, find out how many of the crew want to stay on board. We need to keep as many in place as possible. Let them know the pay stays the same. Also, make sure every one of them gets a two-thousand-dollar bonus. They earned it."

"I will, sir. Thank you, they'll appreciate it. I'll be in touch," Carver said as he hung up.

The Eck family sat around a large table in the restaurant with smiles on their faces, especially Astrid. In spite of the need to walk with crutches, she had spent the last two hours showing everyone her engagement ring.

Karl and Marva Eck sat at the head of the table. With a big smile, Karl raised his wine glass. "I'd like to propose a toast to my youngest daughter, Astrid, and her fiancé, Walter Killian. You'll never know how happy you've made this family." Karl raised his glass. "Salute," he said loudly.

Danny leaned over toward Walter. "Okay, Walt, now that I'm going to be your brother-in-law, can you please start calling me Danny?" he said.

Walt smiled. "Of course, Lieutenant."

Danny laughed, shaking his head as he took a sip of his wine.

Marva clinked her wine glass with a fork. "Can I have your attention for just another minute, please? We just received our first booking since the incident here. There are five families coming next week. And since the repairs will be done by then, we're back in business," Marva said with relief in her voice.

Everyone was having fun around the table as they ate, drank, and hugged each other. Karl and Marva were in their element, surrounded by family.

Danny was watching the festivities with a blank stare. Billie squeezed his hand under the table. "Are you okay, baby?"

Danny turned and looked at his wife with pursed lips. "I'm okay, honey, just thinking about Reverend Winters," he said with sad eyes.

Billie held tightly to Danny's right arm. "I miss him too, baby. We'll be going down for the services next week."

"It sure would have been special if he could have married Walt and Astrid," Danny said as he stared out into the dining room.

Billie didn't respond. She just looked at the happy couple while holding onto her husband.

TWO MONTHS LATER

Danny sat in a small coffee house on the outskirts of Lucerne, Switzerland. The café overlooked Lake Lucerne and was one of the favorite places of many of the locals. Known for its decadent pastries, flavorful coffees, and incredible sandwiches, the café was busy, no matter the time of day.

The winter season had officially begun in Switzerland, as attested to by the Christmas decorations showing up in the local shops and snow skis strapped to virtually anything that moved.

Danny had gone to great lengths to look like one of the locals. He intensely hated bringing attention to himself. He was enjoying a coffee and an apple strudel at one of the tables by the front window. He avoided eye contact with everyone, as he searched the map of Lucerne on his phone.

Finally free from the cast on his left arm, he was now fully mobile and in a better mood, at least according to his wife.

He received an email alert on his phone and opened it immediately. It was from Billie, asking how he was doing, and when he thought he'd be coming home.

All is good. Hoping to get home late next week or maybe early the week after. Miss you, he responded.

Miss you too. See you soon, Billie responded.

He sipped at his coffee as he stared out the window of the café. The steep mountains surrounding Lucerne were covered in trees and almost vertical as they descended into the lake. The scenery was spectacular, rivalling his new home of Leavenworth, although he wouldn't trade *his* home for anything.

Danny looked toward the counter as he took another bite of his strudel. These past weeks of patience had paid off. He was looking at the man he'd spent the past three weeks studying and waiting for, Victor Hugo Claes, or V.H.C as he was known in the pages of the Master File.

Claes was always surrounded by security in Brussels and at his home on Lake Lucerne. His occasional trips into town without his security team was a luxury he enjoyed. Besides, he was often quoted as saying, *It was always safe in Lucerne.*

Danny stepped to the counter with his coffee cup for a refill. As he passed by Claes, he gently rubbed the collar of his coat, transferring a small tracking device to Claes' collar. He went back to his seat, typing an email to Billie. *Just might be home earlier.*

The End

Acknowledgements

Once again, I happily find myself thanking an incredible editor, Michael Garrett. I can't begin to thank you enough, Mike. You're the best.

To the many unnamed and underappreciated men and women who have kept guard over this incredible nation. You have been in the shadows, selflessly keeping watch over us for 245 years. May God bless and keep you.

To my amazing wife Claire. Your encouragement, patience, and love keep me moving forward and on track. I couldn't do this without you.

Last, divine intervention, as always, plays the ultimate role in any venture we undertake. God's perfect grace is present in everything we do.